# ALLURING DARKNESS

# Alluring Darkness

### Nelly Alikyan

ALLURING DARKNESS



Published by Innocent Sinner Publishing LLC

Find me:

https://nellyalikyan.com

Copyediting: Katie Wismer [https://www.katiewismer.com]

Cover Design : Maria Spada [https://www.mariaspada.com]

ISBN: 978-1-956847-01-7

First Edition: November 2021

10 9 8 7 6 5 4 3 2 1

*To Me.*
*Thanks for making this happen.*

**Whittle Magic Series**

Alluring Darkness

Beholding Darkness

Claiming Darkness

Desiring Darkness

**Catchers Series**

With the Flames Catching Midnight

With the Rains Catching Dawn

With the Ice Catching Twilight

With the Storms Catching Dusk

With the Winds Catching Sunlight

With the Ashes Catching Daybreak

# ALSO BY N. ALIKYAN

Buttercup Baby

Promise of A Lifetime

*V*era kept her gaze facing forward and forced her eyes to remain dry. She would not cry over something so pathetic.

The job she'd just lost was quite pathetic, but more so than anything else was that she hadn't been able to hold a job down for over a year now. Losing her father had affected her more than she cared to admit.

On top of all that, Vera knew she didn't want to do any of the jobs she continued to get. She wanted, more than anything, to begin a freelance baking business for herself. To be able to bake and bake and make money from it. Nothing sounded better. But nothing sounded more expensive either. What with starting, building clientele, and everything that went into running a small business. That brought tears back to Vera's eyes.

No, she wouldn't cry.

She would hold herself up and do what she always did—look for another job.

Resolved with her decision, Vera was determined to make it home as soon as she could and begin the search for this new job.

Plus, she was about a week away from getting kicked out of her apartment, so there was no choice but to make something work, it was all she had left.

Vera was walking down Main Street on the way back to her place when the tugging feeling deep in her core began. It was the same uncomfortableness she always felt around this part of town, but apparently no one else had the same sensation. When Vera had asked others if they felt it too, they had looked at her oddly. So no, they didn't feel anything. Vera was alone in that too.

The tugging, which felt like a string was attached to the inside of her lower belly and was pulling upwards, began when she walked toward the end of Main Street. It had started not long after her father passed away, but it always seemed to ebb away, so Vera never put too much thought into it.

But the tugging wasn't going away. It was getting stronger.

"Great," Vera thought aloud as she placed her hand to her stomach as if it were merely a cramp. "Just what I needed today."

She moved her gaze to the shop fronts as she continued walking and realized why the tugging hadn't gone away; she'd never walked in this direction. Normally she took the alleyway between the cafe and the boutique to walk back to her place, but it seemed today, Vera had chosen a different path.

The tugging feeling tightened and now was beginning to feel a bit more like a cramp, but she'd never felt a cramp like this before.

Trying to ignore it and hoping it would go away soon, Vera neared the next alleyway she knew would lead back to her place. She needed to find a job and an apartment to keep.

Passing the eyewear store, Vera came closer to the corner that lead to the alley she needed, Vera felt the tugging shoot straight through her and bent forward, no longer able to hold herself up. She grasped her knees and held tight as she tried to breathe the pain away.

She looked up to see herself mirrored in the dusty shop window. Her brown spiral curls were seated by her shoulders, just as they always were, the fronts held back by a clip. Though a couple of curls fell forward, Vera saw past the hair to the deep brown eyes staring back at her. Her face was scrunched, and Vera knew she did not want anyone to find her in this position. She wouldn't be able to hide the humiliation.

Allowing her gaze to move a bit higher, Vera noticed she'd stopped in front of an old antique shop she'd never seen before.

Slowly picking herself back to a standing position, she glanced around and breathed a sigh of relief that no one had been around to see her. She looked back to the shop and felt the tugging in her core was now pulling her forward as if begging to enter the store.

"So this is what the tugging is about," Vera whispered to herself but didn't know what to think about the whole thing.

Testing her walking, she found that her body was adjusting to the sensation in her abs, so she stepped into the antique shop.

Impossibly, the tugging seemed to grow stronger, but the pain wasn't there. Instead, it felt like a persistent child trying to pull their mom to the toy they wanted.

Vera strolled into the cluster of the store, finding stacks of old chests, toys, and rocking chairs. Blankets and clothes and mirrors. The store was piled so high and so tight that the walking paths were hardly big enough for one person.

As she followed the tugging, Vera scanned the piles, finding old storybooks, typewriters, and albums. She took in everything around her, but didn't stop for any of it.

Given she wasn't paying attention to the path before her, Vera didn't notice until it was too late that she had bumped into a man. Holding out her arms to steady him, she noticed the man's arms tightened around a storybook he held close to his chest as if he were afraid she would try to steal it from him.

Vera looked up to find an attractive man looking down at her, though fear laced his gaze as he pulled the book closer to his chest. He was bald with a light goatee and glasses. Dorky, but cute.

"I'm sorry," Vera said softly. "I wasn't paying attention."

She ignored the persistent tugging as she watched him. He nodded quickly to her apology and walked past her to the counter. Vera furrowed her brows and again whispered to herself, "Odd. But then again, what part of any of this," she pointed to her stomach, "isn't odd?"

Turning again, she followed the sensation around the store. Passing a pile of books on an old chestnut dresser, Vera felt the tugging hit a crescendo. She braced herself on the dresser and looked down to her stomach. "Okay. I get it."

The feeling eased ever so slightly. Enough for Vera to turn her attention to the pile of books, unsure if that's what was so important.

She grabbed the book on the top of the pile and held it, feeling the tugging pull, as if saying this wasn't it. She placed the book to the side and tried the next one. Again, this wasn't it.

Vera tried book after book until her hands fell onto the second to last in the pile, and the tugging eased completely. That feeling was more odd than not, given Vera had gotten used to the tugging, and she now felt a soreness in her abs as if she'd been doing crunches the past half hour.

Ignoring that, Vera paid attention to the book in her hands. Somehow, this book had caused a tugging sensation to bring her to it.

It looked like an old Wiccan book the witches always had in movies. Bracing it on one arm, Vera flipped through it and glanced at the tons of spells and descriptions and drawings. It was a cool book, but Vera had no idea what this had to do with her.

Coming to the end, Vera was ready to close it when she noticed the edge of a picture. Holding the end of the book open, Vera paused short as paralysis took hold of her body.

Taped to the end of this book was a picture of her mother and father standing in front of an old Victorian house, and in her mother's arms was a baby Vera. It was the exact same picture she had framed in her room.

Vera lightly touched the picture, wondering about her mother and missing her father dearly.

Her mother had left her as a baby, and the part of Vera that should resent her for it couldn't. Her father had never allowed that. He had always made sure her mother was loved in their household.

And her father, her best friend, had passed away over a year ago, and she still felt the pain every single day.

As her eyes began to water, Vera touched her tongue to the base of her mouth to stop the freefall and glanced at the other picture taped right beside her family one. It was another picture of her mother, but this time, she was holding a little girl on either knee. Girls that looked a bit like her mother, a bit like Vera herself.

Gasping, Vera brought the book closer to her face, but couldn't believe what she was seeing. Sisters. She had sisters.

She let go of the breath she'd been holding and slammed the book shut. Holding it to her chest as tightly as the man before had been holding his storybook, Vera walked up to the counter and bought it.

She was now determined to get home, but for an entirely different purpose: she had sisters to find.

*Two Weeks Later*

"I just think you would be less emotionally charged if you let some of that feeling out," Maya stated as she followed her sister through the house.

Camilla tried ignoring her sister, but that didn't seem to be working. "Warren and I have only been together a month. I don't know how I feel about him yet."

Maya's brows quirked.

"I just don't think I love him yet," Camilla defended herself.

"You don't have to love him to fuck him, dear sister." Maya pet her little sister on the top of the head as if talking to a child.

Camilla rolled her eyes and walked away, leaving the kitchen and heading to the foyer for the staircase. She could at least try to hide from her sister in her room. "Maybe you don't, but I do. I mean, remember Liam? I was *in love* with him."

Maya scoffed. "Yes, I remember that tool. I'm just saying, if you see Warren and your bits tell you to jump him, you should consider it."

Camilla stopped at the base of the stairs and turned to her sister, narrowing her eyes. "Well, Maya, unlike some people, I don't jump every person my *bits* find attractive."

Maya raised both brows and grinned. "Little Sister, how often do your bits talk to you? Mine haven't spoken in so long I'm starting to believe they're broken. I'm jealous."

Camilla threw up her arms, giving up on the conversation, and turned back to the stairs. But of course, Maya wasn't ready to drop this. Apparently, she had found Camilla minding her business in the kitchen and decided annoying her was on the agenda for the day. Joy, what siblings were for.

As Maya tugged on Camilla's arm to grab her attention, the doorbell rang, saving Camilla. Smiling broadly at the door, Camilla walked past Maya's grimacing face and opened it.

Standing on the other side was a girl maybe a couple of years older than Maya, if Camilla had to guess. And a few inches taller too. Her dark brown curls stopped just past her shoulders, and the darker caramel of her skin shimmered in the sun that beamed down at them regardless of the chilly air.

She held a large book against her chest and looked to Camilla then to Maya, who had followed Camilla to the door and now stood behind her.

Camilla smiled warmly, knowing there would be no welcome upon Maya's appearance. "Can I help you?"

"Hi," the girl said hesitantly, then pulled herself up straight and looked Camilla in the eyes. "My name is Vera, and I think I'm your sister."

Camilla felt her brows scrunch together and Maya stiffen behind her.

"Excuse me?" Maya almost snarled at the girl.

The girl—Vera—raised a picture up for them to look at. A picture of their mother in front of this house, but with a man by her side and a baby in her arms. A baby Camilla knew wasn't Maya or herself, but definitely saw the resemblances in their baby selves.

Camilla looked at Vera, both intrigued and confused, and stepped to the side, pulling Maya back with her. "Come in."

<hr>

The girl, Vera, walked in and followed Camilla into the kitchen. Maya was slow to follow them as she kept her eyes on the back of the girl's body. Camilla was far too trusting, but the girl looked harmless enough. Though Maya knew one thing for certain—looks could be deceiving.

Following them through the house, Maya took a seat at the table in the kitchen, keeping her back to the wall. Vera took the head, and Camilla walked up and sat opposite Maya after placing the kettle down for some tea.

Maya allowed her cold gaze to sweep the newcomer, watching her fidgeting at her seat, and waited for Camilla to sit, then looked at Vera expectantly.

Camilla pulled her chair closer to their guest and placed a hand to her arm, a show of comfort against Maya's harsh stares.

Maya rolled her eyes at her sister and looked at the girl that claimed to be their sister. Feeling Camilla's gaze on her, Maya swept her eyes over and read the threat in Camilla's hazel eyes, *behave.*

Maya smirked to herself. What fun would that be?

Camilla turned to Vera and sweetly prodded for the explanation.

Vera gave a small smile and began from the beginning, explaining the tugging feeling she got every time she was on Main Street in her town and how that feeling had grown when she stepped into the antique shop and evaporated altogether when she picked up the book.

"It looks like a Wiccan book," Vera stated quite obviously. "But that wasn't what kinda freaked me out. I flipped through it while I was in the store and came upon these pictures."

She flipped the book to the end and allowed Maya and Camilla to observe at the two pictures taped to the inside of the back cover. There, still taped to the book, was the picture of Vera and her parents that Vera had shown them. She'd likely had a copy of the same one.

But more important to Maya was the picture taped beside that one, the one she had in the rear of her dresser mirror in her bedroom—a picture of Maya, Camilla, and their mother at their annual Halloween dinner. She was about six in the picture, Camilla only two.

The kettle chose that moment to whistle, pulling the two Whittle sisters out of their shocked states. Jumping out of her chair, Camilla threw the book closed and rose to grab the kettle, her phone on the table chiming with a message as she walked away. Maya watched her little sister closely. She looked freaked and a bit pale.

Camilla poured the water into three cups, likely too in her head to recognize that she'd gotten a message. Maya picked up her little sister's phone. "Warren says he's at the quad at school if you wanna hang out."

Camilla turned in her spot by the counter to look at Maya and let out a breath. She left the tea on the counter and walked back to the table, looking down at the book Vera had flipped back to the front cover.

Maya couldn't help her intrigue at the design on the front of the book and felt her hand reaching out to touch it at the same moment Vera and Camilla did.

And like in slow motion, Maya felt the two fingers touching the book begin to heat, then pulse, and as she saw a spark light those fingers, her body flew across the room. She hit the wall behind her, which was only about two feet, given she was already in front of it.

Collecting her thoughts enough to focus and lift herself off the ground, Maya's gaze swept the room for Camilla. She was at the other end of the kitchen, where she'd fallen into the sink after hitting a couple of cabinets.

Vera too, was picking herself up off the ground from the end of the kitchen where she'd hit the window, cracking it lightly.

All three looked to each other in turn, then to the book that still sat on the table. Maya turned her attention back to this new 'sister' of theirs. Looks could be deceiving, and she didn't know what game this girl was playing with them.

Before she could do anything, a man landed in the opposite end of the kitchen. One moment nothing, then out of thin air, there he stood.

"Oh dear," he stated in a beautiful British accent as he took in the sight of the girls' mangled appearances.

Maya was the first to react, pulling out of her shock and wobbling up to the table, though keeping her eyes glued to the man. She couldn't trust Vera either, but this man had literally appeared out of thin air. Vera and Camilla slowly followed suit.

"Who are you?" Vera voiced from behind Maya.

"*What* are you?" Maya corrected, a light growl forming around her words.

The man smiled. He stood maybe a few inches taller than the five-eight Vera likely was, and his dark brown hair seemed perfectly held back. His three-piece suit was impeccable and his tie in perfect place. He looked properly posh.

"Ah, Maya, blunt as ever." He smiled. "I am Harry, a friend of your mother's. Of your entire family, actually."

"Oh? Some friend. Do you normally give friends heart attacks by popping up out of thin air?" Maya shot back.

The man gave a small, knowing smile. "Of course not. They've always known I could do this."

Camilla took in a large breath of air before Maya could say anything else and released it as she shook her head. "This isn't happening. No. Nope." She began to freak out as she took them all in, then landed her gaze to Maya's. "I'm gonna go see Warren."

Maya nodded, and just like that, Camilla sped out of the house, as fast as she could in the limping wobble the fall had caused.

The inkling of her heart that cared for her sister worried for how Camilla was feeling, but she knew there was nothing she could do about that at the moment. Having Warren clear her mind would do better than anything Maya tried.

Maya looked at the strangers in her house and smiled. "She'll be fine." Her pride dictated that she not wobble to the counter, but she couldn't help the light limp as she made her way to the now slightly cooled teas, placed them on a tray, and turned, holding the tray up. "Tea anyone?"

Camilla cleared her head of the obvious daydream she had been experiencing at home. The entire walk—wobble, walk, same thing—to campus, she thought back to it. It was a daydream, it had to be. Otherwise, Camilla would have to believe that books could throw people across rooms and men could pop into her house from thin air.

A definite daydream.

Sometime during the walk, her gait turned normal, the slight ache disappearing, though she was sure she'd have a bruise or two.

Camilla stopped at the edge of the quad on campus, the different pathways all intersecting and leaving spots of grass for the students to hang out. And on the grass, every so often, sat round, iron tables for the students to do their work outside.

Her gaze stopped on Warren at one of those tables. It was the only one that sat underneath a large tree with hanging leaves—his favorite.

His black locks tussled in the light breeze and fell over those hazel eyes of his as he read his book. Another Dante, Camilla was sure of it.

She contemplated standing there and watching him, his lean body hunching over the book as he took in every word. The light bite that scraped his lips every time he got more invested in the book. The slow taps his fingers made on his bicep as he read. It was done unconsciously, and Camilla loved it.

She pushed herself to move and stopped at the bench behind him, leaning over his hunched form to wrap her arms around his neck and give his cheek a small kiss. "Hey, pretty boy."

The slow tilt of his head and the wide grin turned her heart to liquid. "Pretty?"

Camilla shrugged and took a seat on one of the benches at the table. She smiled with a light blush as she watched him take her in. "Pretty. And kinda hot, but shh, don't tell my boyfriend I said that."

Warren bit his lip lightly, the grin taking over as he leaned into her. "Your secret is safe with me."

As Camilla giggled—yes, giggled—at his remark, he leaned in to give her a light but knowing kiss. "I'm glad you decided to join me."

Camilla smiled back as he leaned away and looked at her. "Me too. I needed this."

He gave a wink that sent her heart on a marathon and turned back to his book as Camilla pulled her own out, a reading for her psychology class, and began.

Or tried to.

Without the immediate distraction of Warren's lips, Camilla found it difficult not to go back to what had happened at the house.

She had another sister.

And a random family friend that showed up out of thin air.

And a book that was trying to kill them.

Camilla stared at the open book before her and tried to focus. She read the paragraph. Then reread it. And read it a third time. She had no idea what it said. Her mind wouldn't leave the feeling of getting thrown across the room out of her head.

She hadn't realized she was fidgeting in her seat until Warren grabbed her forearm on the table and let his thumb rub soothing circles on it. The expression on his face would surely send Camilla's heart on another marathon.

"You okay?"

She looked into the depths of those hazel, almost green, eyes and let everything that had happened earlier fall from her thoughts. Warren had a way of making her forget what she was thinking about. "Yeah. Just got a lot on my mind."

"You wanna talk about it?"

And sound like she needed a trip to the insane asylum? No thanks.

Camilla shook her head. "No. I just wanna study."

He barked a laugh, though he made a sad excuse at trying to cover it. "Well, there *is* a first time for everything."

She rolled her eyes, a grin eating her face, and grabbed the hand that still rubbed her arm, bringing it up to her lips. She gave him a small kiss and let his hand fall back to her arm as a thought that wasn't hers invaded her mind.

*She's so cute. I wonder what's bothering her.*

Camilla pulled her arm out from under him, unaware of what just happened. She stared at the spot their skin had just touched and listened to her mind—no extra thoughts.

Camilla looked to the furrow forming between his eyebrows then back to his hand.

"Babe?" He sounded like he was ready to lock her up.

Camilla breathed out, knowing she was being crazy, and went to grab his hand again.

*Okay, something is definitely wrong.*

Something *was* definitely wrong, but those hadn't been her thoughts. Pulling her hand back against her chest, she looked up to him. She could only imagine how crazy she looked.

Turning to the book that sat before her, she dropped her head into her hands and closed her eyes. The daydream was coming back. Because that was the only explanation.

This was a daydream.

"Babe." Warren's voice broke through her thoughts. "Everything okay?"

When Camilla didn't respond, Warren moved to straddle her bench. His hand reached out to grasp one of hers and pull it away from her face.

Nothing was happening. Her thoughts were all her own.

Camilla breathed a sigh of relief and looked up to those perfect eyes and smiled, her free hand falling over the one that held her.

*What should I do? Fuck, I hope she's okay.*

Camilla dropped his hand and pushed to the end of the bench, almost falling off. She pushed away from the table as Warren went to stand. Before he could make a move, Camilla took a few steps away from him. "I have to go home."

She turned and ran.

V era had taken the seat at the head of the table once more when Maya walked up with the tray of teas. She watched Maya circle the table and end up back in her seat, though Vera wasn't sure if that was because she actually wanted that seat or because it would keep her back safe from the two strangers in the room.

Harry, the so-called family friend, had moved to sit beside Vera, taking Camilla's forgotten chair. They sat in silence and enjoyed their cups of tea with the biscuits that Maya had added to the tray.

Maya watched both her and Harry with both suspicion and amusement. The first made sense to Vera—she was her sister but still a stranger. The latter though, that worried her a bit. What was so amusing about the predicament they were in?

Harry, for his part, looked amazingly comfortable sitting in the silence with the two of them. Gorgeously comfortable. What right did he have to be that attractive? But the comfortability confused Vera more than anything, but then again, he had popped into the kitchen from thin air, so why wouldn't he be comfortable now?

Vera wished she could hold herself as well as her companions did. Instead, her mind felt like a battlefield as she tried to fight off breaking the silence. She was sure she looked absolutely awkward on the outside.

Likely the reasoning behind Maya's amusement.

They were on their second cups and had barely spoken a word in the hour they'd sat together. The silence was quite literally killing Vera from the inside out as she controlled her need to fill it.

She breathed a sigh of relief when Camilla broke the silence, slamming the front door behind her as she ran into the kitchen. Coming to an abrupt halt at the kitchen table, she bent over and breathed in large gulps of air.

Vera's hands tightened around her cup as Camilla lifted her gaze and met Vera's. She no longer looked friendly.

"What did you do to me?" The accusation in her tone dripped acid in the air.

"I don't know what you're talking about," Vera stammered out.

"Cam, what's wrong?" Maya's amusement dropped as she watched her sister lift to her full height.

Vera tried to stop herself from fidgeting as she felt Maya's attention on her before it moved back to Camilla. The last thing Vera needed was to be on the receiving side of Maya's wrath. The girl scared her already.

Camilla didn't respond to anyone as she walked up to Maya

and took her hand. Not a second later, she dropped it and pushed herself away, shaking her head. "Yup, I'm definitely losing my mind."

Vera didn't know what to think about the moment, and more importantly, how it could be her fault.

They watched as Camilla turned away from them and walked straight up to the wall, lightly banging her head against it.

"Camilla," Maya said slowly. "What happened?"

Vera sat up taller at Maya's tone. That was the tone of a woman not used to being ignored. The tone of a woman who likely had to watch her sister all the time, be the parent.

Camilla stopped banging her head and instead allowed it to lie against the wall for a moment. The three remained in the silence as they waited for her.

It took another few seconds before Camilla picked her head up again and faced them. "I can read minds."

Vera felt her shoulders drop.

"Excuse me?" Maya asked, leaning forward to make sure she had heard correctly. Vera couldn't help but follow suit.

"I can read minds!" Camilla repeated with a vigor that didn't allow room for question.

Camilla dropped to the opposite end of the table, and slumped into the chair. "I was with Warren, and I touched his hand, and suddenly I had these thoughts that weren't mine in my head. When I pulled away, they vanished. Every time I touched him, I read his mind. And just now, My, I read your mind."

The determination in her voice pulled Vera to believe her, even if it sounded unbelievable. Even with a book that called to her, then threw her across the room and popped a stranger into her life, Vera found *reading minds* unbelievable. Or she wanted to. This was too much for her logic to take.

"Are you sure?" Vera couldn't help but question it.

Camilla threw her a dark glare, but didn't answer.

Maya reached her hand out to her little sister. "Okay, try it again."

Camilla moved her gaze, which softened completely, to Maya, then took her hand. She pulled away immediately and narrowed her eyes at her sister. "Stop that!"

Maya laughed. "So she *can* read minds."

"What did you hear?" Harry spoke up for the first time since Camilla's departure over an hour ago.

A blush took over Camilla's body, but she didn't answer. Instead, Maya did. "I asked if her bits talked to her when she was around Warren."

Vera's brows lifted and the tinge of a smile quirked her lips as she looked between the two sisters. Her two sisters. They had about a quarter century of sisterhood that Vera knew she could not just fall into, and for that, she resented both of her parents.

Had Vera not been separated from them before Maya was born, which she guessed was a bit over twenty years ago, she would have the relationship of sisters that teased each other incessantly but cared for each other deeply. She wouldn't be alone when she lost her father; she'd have two built in best friends. Vera hadn't processed how much she'd actually missed out on when she'd found out she had sisters, but the more she saw them together—and totaling it had been like half an hour's worth so far—the more the ache in her chest grew.

Pushing those thoughts aside given there was nothing she could do about them now, Vera turned her gaze to Harry, who remained calm after the revelation.

Actually, now he looked amused.

Camilla turned to Vera. "Your book did something to me. This morning I was normal!"

"No," Harry interrupted before Vera could voice her equal confusion. "It did something to all of you."

The unified exclamation from three sisters met the man's remark. "Excuse me?"

"The book unlocked your powers," he said, apparently pleased with himself for the revelation.

Again, Vera said alongside her new sisters, "Excuse me?"

3

Harry took his time looking over the three faces staring back at him. They looked so much like the friend he had left behind twenty-three years prior, and now would unfortunately never see again. He felt the ache of missing Loretta, but pushed it aside as he looked over each of Loretta's daughters.

Maya and Camilla had taken after their mother where their hair was concerned. And while the dark waves effortlessly fell down to Camilla's shoulders, Maya's fell to her waist. Harry never found out if they were Bishop's daughters too. He saw bits and pieces of him in them, but he wasn't convinced that it wasn't just a projection.

Harry smiled at the girls as he sat up in his chair. "You three are witches."

The scoff erupted from Maya first, closely followed by her sisters. They laughed at the ludicrousness of hearing about the magical world for the first time. Harry remembered the feeling all too well.

"I know. It is quite extravagant." He pretended he didn't know they were laughing because they didn't believe him.

"Fantastic is how I'd describe it, but to each their own," Maya said as she leaned back into her chair, crossing her arms before her. Of course Maya would be the one to come out with the snarky comments. Harry had heard that about the middle Whittle.

He looked the others over, then turned his gaze back to Maya's raised features, her chocolate brown eyes challenging him to continue.

Harry bit the inside of his cheek, unaware as to where Maya got the bravado from. Loretta was something, but definitely not like her middle child.

Vera and Camilla looked wary of hearing anything else from him, but they fixed their gazes, ready nonetheless.

Good. They were all open to the idea.

Given the book had thrown them across the room only an hour ago, he wasn't sure how they wouldn't be.

"Your mother, Loretta, was a witch. A very powerful witch heading one of the most powerful covens of all time in Europe when she picked up and moved out here. That's why you three do not know the coven. Your coven."

Vera and Camilla's hesitance at receiving the news held, but Maya looked in thought, intrigued at the prospect. Harry saw it in her eyes—she wanted to believe him.

"Power can be both a great thing and a terrible one," he continued. "Your mother was able to help hundreds, but she was also hunted for her powers. Plenty of witches are, but especially those from the Whittle coven. But she was also hunted for that book." Harry pointed at the book still sitting in the middle of the table. "Each coven has their own, each family their own within the coven. The more powerful your coven and family, the more your book is sought out, because you see, it contains some unique spells. Loretta knew any child of hers would never be safe, so the day she had each of you, she placed a spell on you that would lock your powers until the time was right. Magic has a funny way of figuring when that would be."

"So she made sure we couldn't be witches," Maya clarified though she looked annoyed.

Harry shook his head aggressively. "It was her way of making sure nothing would come after you as you were growing up. She was excited about showing each of you the ropes of the coven."

The girls were processing the information well. The secret their parents had kept from them their entire lives seemingly settled into them.

And they all kept their gazes on him, ready to hear more. Either they were beginning to believe him, or they were giving him the benefit of the doubt because of the supernatural things they'd experienced already.

"You three were safe, your powers locked. No creature, no matter what they were, would be able to detect you. You were just any other human to the creatures of this world, and life continued."

"Why weren't you ever around? If Mom thought of you as a friend, wouldn't we have seen you?" Maya interrupted.

Harry's smile held no joy. "Your mother told me to remain with the coven in Europe. Said there was no need for me here, so I did as she asked, but kept an ear out for the moment I was needed here."

Harry could see the gears moving in their minds—should they believe what the strange man said?

He continued, "Covens don't cross territories. Once Loretta decided to leave the European territory for the North American one, she became the only member of the Whittle coven, North America. The European one couldn't help her. They've got plenty of problems of their own." Harry didn't stop to think about that as he continued, "You were safe. Until your mother decided it was time to cloak the book. The moment she did that was the moment she knew *she* was no longer safe. She placed those photos in there because she knew she would not make it long enough to tell you what you were and to unlock your powers for you, so she made sure one of her daughters would be able to bring all three together. As I said before, magic has a funny way of deciding when the time is right."

Harry's gaze dropped to the book on the table. He remembered receiving the letter Loretta had sent him with the details before vanishing altogether. Not two days later, he found out she had passed.

"The photos were there to tell the daughter who found the book that it was a family book. Your mother believed that whomever found it would then find her sisters, and together, they would unlock their powers." The silence held for a few minutes after Harry's final words.

"What kind of creatures would come after us?" Vera broke it.

"Demons mostly," Harry answered right away, glad to be receiving questions. "They're a witch's natural enemy. Just about everything you've heard about them is true. They're quite loathsome creatures."

"So they're evil?" Camilla asked, worry lining her eyes.

Harry felt a twinkle in his eyes. It seemed the girls were coming around to the idea of the supernatural world. Rather quickly too.

"Well, no." Harry struggled to come up with a proper way to explain it. "There are two types of demons. Creature demons and animal demons, that's how they're classified in their species. The animal demons are the one's humans picture, the grotesque monsters. Those? Yes, I'd say those are evil."

"And the creature demons?" Maya's voice held the slightest bit of fascination, like she was memorizing information for a thesis paper. Harry pushed the thought aside, happy for them to learn everything.

"Creature demons are more like witches. They look like us,

and their powers work like ours. Inherently, they're not evil, the same way witches are not good. Every creature is more like humans, a mix of good and evil within each of us. The difference with demons compared to just about every other one of the species is they don't easily care for others the way most creatures would."

"Meaning?" Camilla asked.

"Meaning were a stranger to get hurt, you and I would worry for them and want to make sure they're all right. Demons don't have that feeling. They couldn't care less if the stranger lived or died. Similarly, even if we do not care for someone or something, we would have trouble hurting it. Creature demons do not work that way. If they do not care for the whomever or whatever is in their way, they have no problem with hurting it, killing it."

"So," Maya elongated the word, then asked, "You're saying they could care?"

Harry nodded vigorously. "Yes. Of course. They care. They even fall in love, just as any creature does. It's just not innate with them. It takes a lot more than it would any of us."

Harry watched the intrigue, and possible delight, light Maya's gaze as she processed the information. She seemed to have no more questions as she thought over what she'd learned about demons, so Harry turned to the sisters on either side of the table. They, too, looked to be processing, so Harry allowed them to sit in silence for a few minutes.

"You still haven't told us what you are," Vera said.

Harry looked at her and gave a warm smile. "I am a warlock."

"A male witch?" Maya was seemingly unimpressed. "That's it?"

Harry couldn't hold back the chuckle that bubbled at her reaction. Vera and Camilla seemed just as unimpressed. "Well, yes, technically that is it. But it is quite different from what you're thinking. Warlocks are some of the rarest species in the supernatural world. We can live for centuries, although we can choose to continue aging if we start families."

"Why was Mom adamant about you staying with the coven?" Camilla asked.

"We are a kind of guardian to witches. We all have the same powers of healing and porting—the popping into thin air trick —and act as a mentor to our witches. Well, we're supposed to act as mentors, but I definitely would not be considered so. I never paid enough attention to know how to handle situations like the other warlocks did, but I was your mother's 'mentor,' and her mother's, and her mother's before that. But because we're so rare, Loretta wanted me to stay with the coven rather than come out here."

"Even though you're useless?" Maya spoke, receiving a smack on the arm from her little sister.

Harry chuckled. "Even though I'm useless."

"How old are you?" Vera blurted.

Harry looked over to her and noticed the slight tinge of pink light her brown skin. "I stopped aging at thirty-three, but I am a hundred and thirty-four years old."

Impressed expressions met his, but none commented on his age. Instead, Vera asked, her tone octaves softer, "Do you know why Mom left me?"

Harry felt his composure drop. "I'm afraid not. That is a mystery even to me."

"Do you know why the book threw us across the room? If it's our family book, why try to kill us?" Camilla asked.

Harry allowed his gaze to rest on Vera another moment before turning to Camilla's hazel eyes. "It was not trying to kill you. It was merely unlocking your powers. What happened was just a burst of power. You three were unprepared, you couldn't control it, so you flew. Nothing to be worried about."

Not two seconds after his words, the kettle sitting on the

stove top flew across the room and banged onto the table, spilling water as it rattled to a stop.

The room sat frozen, staring down at it.

Harry looked up to Maya, then Vera. "Which one of you did that?"

Maya held up both hands and shook her head. "Not me."

Harry moved his gaze to Vera and stopped, quirking a brow.

"I—" Vera stared at the kettle, bewildered, then looked to Harry. "I don't know. I was just thinking that this conversation calls for another cup of tea, and the whole kettle flew at us."

Harry gave her an encouraging smile. "A telekinetic. Brilliant." He turned to Camilla. "And a mind reader." And finally to Maya. "Now you. Your sisters' powers came naturally. Soon we'll see what you have."

Maya gave a single nod, but the excitement was radiating off of her. Completely unlike her sisters.

"Wait," Camilla cut in. "You said earlier that Mom knew she was no longer safe. Does that mean her death wasn't an accident?"

Harry grew somber. "I'm afraid not." He looked at each of the girls in turn before settling his gaze once more on Camilla. "Demons have been after her for quite some time. I just can't be sure which one got her."

Harry felt the quiet turn from the intrigue they should be feeling at finding out they were witches to the possibilities surrounding their mother's death. He clapped his hands together to break it. "Alas, we can discuss that at another time. Right now, you three have some decisions to make. Your primary powers have begun to come in, but we can put a stop to it before you gain any more."

"We can say no?" Camilla sounded bewildered at the prospect.

Harry stood from his seat. "You can. And I will cloak your

powers once more and you will go back to being normal humans."

Maya lightly slammed her hands onto the table. "Well, I'm all in."

"What? Maya, don't you want to even think about this? You don't even know what your power is yet. What if you don't want it?" Camilla sounded bewildered.

Maya gave her sister a mischievous smile. "I want it."

Harry looked to Vera, who remained quiet. He empathized with her; it couldn't be easy being the odd sister out.

He looked back to the others. "Think on it." Then he ported out of the room.

4

________

Camilla still found it difficult to wrap her mind around Harry's vanishing into thin air. Porting, he called it.

He'd been gone a few minutes, leaving the girls in silence as they each thought through what had been revealed. If Camilla hadn't experienced the mind reading herself and seen the kettle fly across the room, she was sure she would believe Harry a hallucination altogether.

But, it seemed to be true. She was a witch.

Camilla had known Vera all of two hours, and she was already picking up that her new sister—that was gonna take some getting used to—didn't like to sit in silence.

Vera broke the air with a small shrug and a push of her chair. "I should get going. I've taken up plenty of your time already."

"Where are you staying?" Camilla asked, still unaware of any facts surrounding this new sister.

"At a hotel about fifteen minutes from here," she answered.

"But where do you live?" Maya asked, completely beyond being pleasant. At least Vera was getting the sibling thing from Maya right away.

"Um, I was living a couple towns east."

"Was?" Maya questioned.

Boundaries. Maya did not have them.

Vera looked unsure of how to respond.

"Don't feel pressured to answer, Vera. You can ignore Maya's rude questions," Camilla tried comforting.

"How is that rude? She's our sister, isn't she? I'd like to know a simple fact about her," Maya fought back.

"It's fine," Vera interrupted before Camilla started a fight. "I just got kicked out of my apartment. I figured it was fine because it would give me the excuse to move out here and find you guys. I've just started looking into apartments around town."

"Why would you do that?" Maya remarked.

Vera looked unsure, and Camilla was ready to smack her sister for being so crass.

"To get to know you guys," Vera answered apprehensively.

Maya rolled her eyes, seemingly at the both of them. "Move in here."

Camilla froze. Maya wasn't being rude. She was being a sister, exactly what Camilla should have been.

She mentally smacked herself for not thinking to offer Vera lodgings with them. How did Maya turn into the more generous of them? Then again, Maya had been the responsible one in the household for forever.

"What?" Vera sounded perplexed.

"You don't have anywhere else to stay, and why would you? You're our sister. If I was unsure of it before, Harry has confirmed that much. It's as much your house as it is ours. There's a spare upstairs. It's yours," Maya said nonchalantly.

Camilla looked her now middle sister over. She'd always been authoritative. Sometimes even their mother listened to whatever Maya said just because Maya tended to see outside of emotion. Camilla and their mother were not like that.

Vera turned raised brows over to Camilla, assessing what she thought. Camilla understood. It was likely more shocking, considering the warm welcome Maya had given Vera earlier.

Camilla glanced at Maya, who looked bored with the conversation, ready to leave once the matter was settled. Back to Vera, Camilla nodded her affirmation. "I agree. You're our sister. Move in."

It took a moment for the smile to grace Vera's lips, but when it did, it matched the twinkle in her brown eyes. Maya's brown eyes.

The doorbell rang just as Vera spoke, "I should go get my things then."

Maya rose from her seat and walked to the door, Camilla following behind to walk Vera out.

Maya opened the door, and Camilla was shocked to see Warren standing on the other side, her bag in hand.

"Warren," Maya teased out the name. "Have the bits called out to you from so far away?"

Warren's furrowed brows caused a deeper tinge to coat Camilla's light caramel skin. She pushed her sister out of the way with a, "Go away, Maya!" and stopped at the door, Vera beside her, as she took in Warren's appearance.

Maya's laughter carried as she bounded up the stairs and away from them.

Camilla followed Warren's gaze to her new sister. Vera's smile was hesitant as she looked between the two of them before stopping on her. "Um," Vera pointed out with her thumb, "I'm gonna go."

Camilla smiled and nodded to her sister as she watched Vera pass Warren and begin her walk down the block.

"Who was that?" Warren's question brought Camilla back.

"Long story. I'll tell you later."

"Okay," Warren said slowly, then held up Camilla's bag. "You left your things when you ran away from me."

Camilla felt the light tinge that had tinted her skin before deepen, an embarrassed smile gracing her lips. "Yeah, sorry about that. I don't know what happened."

"Are you okay now?"

Lords, Camilla felt her heart melt at the true concern in his eyes.

"Perfectly." She smiled up at him. Grabbing her bag and throwing it inside, she stepped out of the house and closed the door behind her. "In fact, I think we should head to Steve's. He's having a party, right?"

Warren's brows rose. "He is. Are you sure you want to though?"

Camilla smiled up at those shining eyes. "Absolutely."

V era has just stepped into her hotel room, and let herself relax against the door. She leaned against it for support as her thoughts raced back to the events earlier.

She'd met her sisters.

She'd been thrown across a kitchen by a book.

She'd watched a man pop up out of thin air.

And found out he was a warlock.

And she was a witch.

And magic was real.

It was a lot to take in. Even with the small walk she'd taken to get to the hotel, Vera was still unable to grasp it, but she was happy. Truly happy for the first time in over a year.

And cooler than anything she'd learned was the fact that she could make things move with her mind.

Still leaning against the door, Vera decided to attempt this new power. She'd only used it once so far, and that was definitely involuntary. Looking around the room, her gaze settled on the journal she'd left on the bedside table the night before.

Thinking about wanting it the same way she had the kettle, Vera tried to slowly levitate the journal toward herself. And it was working too. She had control.

Until she realized she had control and allowed her mind to slip. Without the control, all the magic knew was that she wanted the journal so it went flying toward her at top speed.

Ducking out of the way before it could smash into her, the journal hit the door and fell onto her crouched form. She let it fall off of her as she walked into the room, picking up her duffle bag.

She'd moved with barely any luggage. The small bits of memorabilia all sitting in the one by the desk. Another holding some clothes. And this duffle, which held the items she would require on a day to day basis.

Placing it on the bed, Vera looked around the room for the few items she'd taken out last night when renting this room.

She had powers; there was no need to move. Plus, she needed to learn to control these powers.

Slow and controlled, she used her mind to pick up the hairbrush that sat on the desk and brought it toward the duffle. It was slow going, but it was working. And it wasn't trying to kill her.

After some time of controlled concentration, she got the brush to fall into the duffle. A smile lit her face, wide and beaming.

Vera continued the same trick with the rest of her items—her toiletries bag, her charger, her favorite recipe book, and her headphones. Each item moved infinitesimally faster than the one before it as she began to understand her control. Finally, with only the journal left, Vera fell onto the bed and looked at the book on the floor. A memory flashed into her mind of the last two weeks since she'd found her family book, all her efforts written out in that little journal.

*After the antique shop, Vera had gone back to the apartment she was close to being evicted from and over to the laptop sitting on the small round table. She'd opened it and looked for a Lore Whittle with two daughters. Nothing.*

*At least she'd always assumed Whittle, that was her name, but it didn't mean it would be her mother's.*

*She'd been frustrated. She'd done it before, but she'd never looked up a woman and her other kids. She'd always just tried Lore Whittle. That's what Pops always called her. Lore.*

*Frustrated, she'd gone to the small bits of memorabilia she had from her father and begun to rummage, as if she hadn't already done so time and again. She hadn't found anything telling that first day. Or that first week. But a few days ago, out of her apartment and staying in a hotel, she'd found it. Engraved into the fabric of some lace were the names Bishop and Loretta. Bishop for her father. And Loretta must have been the long version of Lore.*

*She'd looked up Loretta Whittle and, with some snooping, found her that night. Well, found her stone. Vera had assumed she'd been dead, but she'd always assumed it had happened a long time ago, not long after she'd left Vera. Seemed she'd been wrong.*

*Finding her sisters, girls named Maya and Camilla, wasn't so difficult after that. And another shock, they were younger than her. Vera had assumed that picture had been taken before Vera had come around, but it seemed not. They were four and eight years younger than her.*

*She'd felt her heart jump for joy at that moment, especially finding that they lived so close to her. Her entire life, she'd lived this close to family and she'd never known. Lords, she wanted to yell and scream at her father for never telling her. But she couldn't. He was gone. But they were still here.*

*And they all shared the same last name!*

*Maya and Camilla Whittle, living in an old Victorian house two towns west of her. She'd smiled to herself and hopped on the bus to make her way over as soon as possible.*

Vera came out of her memory, her gaze once more focusing on the journal on the ground. She tried her power again and watched as the journal rose from the ground and starting hovering over to her before landing in her waiting hands.

She beamed as she looked at it, both from the joy of this new magic she had and the outcome of finding her sisters. "This is awesome!"

T he party was well kicked off by the time Camilla and Warren showed up. It was just as Camilla expected, drunk kids everywhere just having fun. Exactly what she had hoped to see.

Camilla walked hand in hand with Warren as they passed the crowded room in the front and made their way through the house. She couldn't help but look at some of the kids she went to school with and wonder what they were thinking. She gave a small smile as she and Warren stopped behind a crowd in the hall. She had been able to control her new power so she wasn't constantly in Warren's head by locking down her mind. It was very draining. But she loosened her grip on that control to see what would happen.

*Fuck, man. Get out of the way. We shouldn't even be here. I'd rather take Cam back to my place.*

Camilla felt the blush take a hold of her features as she smiled at Warren's thoughts. She pulled her hand away before she heard any more, unwilling to strain her mind any longer with the block.

Warren turned a worried glance over to her as she wrapped her hands around his clothing-covered biceps, holding on tight. He smiled at the attention she gave him. Take her back to his place indeed, Camilla thought.

As Warren turned back to the crowd and pushed his way through it, Camilla kept her tight grip and followed. Making it into the kitchen, she saw huddles of friends and smiled. This was entirely human.

But she was about to change that. It was time to test her powers.

Warren stopped before one of his flatmates, Matty, and began talking, Camilla remaining by his side and answering the few questions Matty threw her way. She was waiting for someone to get close enough to touch just as Alyssa, a girl from their literature class, stumbled up to them.

Perfect timing.

Alyssa threw her arm around Camilla. "Hey, Cam!"

Camilla smiled and wrapped a free hand around Alyssa's shoulder. "Hi, Alyssa."

*Ooo who's that hunk talking to Warren? Damn, he's fi...I should get another drink.*

Camilla bit the inside of her cheek to stop from smiling as she felt her power working.

Alyssa pulled away and strolled off to the drinks on the counter, but Camilla didn't care. Her power had worked on someone she wasn't close to. Brilliant.

But then a kid bumped into her, and nothing invaded her thoughts. She scrunched her nose. Why wasn't it working?

Camilla threw her hand out to the guy who had bumped into her and placed it on his arm.

*I wonder what size skirts horses would wear.*

She immediately pulled her hand away from the bizarre thoughts. Okay, maybe her power only worked if she initiated it.

Warren hadn't been paying attention to her interactions given they were bumped into every so often in the middle of a party all the time. He was engrossed in a talk about who made the best nachos with Matty, another one of his flatmates, Dane, and their friend.

Camilla pulled her free hand to meet the one still wrapped around his bicep and cuddled in.

He leaned down to her, half his attention still on the boys. "You okay? We can leave."

Camilla allowed a hand to fall to meet his fingers.

*Please say you wanna leave. Let me take you back to my place.*

Camilla smiled as she pulled her hand back up and leaned up to give him a quick kiss. "Great. We don't have to go anywhere."

His jaw tightened, but he gave a nod and turned back to his friends.

Camilla spent the rest of the night waiting for people to pass by her so she could reach out and read their minds.

*This bitch needs to stop talking to me.*

*I think I need to make out with Lucy tonight. Or Greg. Or Lucy and Greg!*

*I should call Professor Lingley and see if she wants to fuck tonight.*

As Camilla watched the party pass her by, she looked down to her hand and whispered so lightly no one would hear her, "This is awesome."

---

Maya had the house to herself.

Vera was likely still at the hotel, or she'd decided to move in the next day, Maya didn't particularly care.

Camilla was enjoying the night of being human. And hopefully getting the fucking she deserved.

Maya had the house to herself, and she was determined to figure out what her power was. She had stomped around the foyer for about ten minutes before coming to the resolve that she would figure out what her power was on her own. No need to wait for it to happen.

She turned to the living room and paused as she stared at the room. Taking in a deep breath, she concentrated on the apple sitting in the fruit bowl Camilla insisted they have on the coffee table.

Remembering what Vera had said about wanting something to happen and it just did. Maya thought about wanting the apple to come to her. Nothing.

She tried again with no improvements, so she moved on. It made sense that she would have a different power from her sister. Camilla and Vera's powers were entirely different.

She stared at the apple and wanted for it to cut in half. Nothing.

She picked the apple up and threw it into the air, attempting to freeze it midair. Nothing.

She tried with her hands rather than her mind. Nope.

As the apple toppled to the ground a fourth time, Maya looked around the room. Her gaze landed on a small vase she had found at the local vintage market in the corner of the room.

Maybe her power was about fixing things.

She strolled right up to the vase, picked it up, and let it fall out of her hands, shattering to a dozen pieces as it hit the ground.

Maya looked at the pieces and urged them to mesh back together. Nothing.

Nothing, nothing, nothing.

Huffing out a breath, she left the broken shards on the ground and walked to the kitchen. She turned the faucet on and stared at the falling water, but couldn't figure out what she was meant to do with it. And nothing was happening, so she blew out a breath and turned it off, turning to lean on the counter as she looked around the room. "This is ridiculous."

Maybe it required her to be around other people like Camilla's.

Walking back to the foyer, Maya picked up her favorite black leather jacket and walked out of the house.

She walked the few blocks to the Mom and Pop shops lining the long street in silence and attempted more uses of her power along the way. It wasn't very surprising when nothing happened.

Stopping at the corner of the block and looking out to the people walking in the night, Maya's attention zoned in on a couple seated at one of the tiny tables in front of the gelato shop. They were deep in conversation as they ate some of Mario's gelatos. Maya loved Mario's gelato.

She focused her attention on the couple and tried to get them to pause in their places. No.

She tried to get them to move however she pleased. To alter the emotions they felt for the person in front of them. To generally change their attitude.

Nothing.

She turned her attention to the children playing by the fountain across the street from her. She tried to get one of them to move the way Vera made objects move. She tried to make them expand or shrink. She even tried to make one disappear.

Nada.

Maya folded her arms before her chest and closed her eyes, leaning against the brick wall behind her. She lightly banged her head back and breathed in and out.

After a few moments, she opened her eyes and settled her gaze on a group walking her direction.

"Okay, Maya," she spoke to herself, "last option, maybe you need to touch them."

She pushed off the brick and strolled toward the group, 'bumping' into one of them and making sure her touch remained on the girl long enough to see if anything happened.

Mind reading. Emotion changing. Disappearance.

When nothing happened, Maya pulled away and apologized,

turning to walk back home. She had exhausted her options for the night. It seemed she would have to wait it out after all. Or at least wait until the next day before she thought to try again.

Both Vera and Camilla's powers had come naturally. Maya was sure hers would too.

Back in her room, she slumped onto her bed and stared up at the ceiling. "This is so *not* awesome."

5

Harry ported back into the kitchen the day after the girls found out about being witches to find that the two girls with powers were off testing them. Maya, however, was stuck at home still trying to figure hers out.

"Don't rush it, Maya. It'll happen." Harry tried to soothe the girl, but she just looked at him like he'd be her first prey.

"I'm not rushing. I'm simply looking through the book."

"For a way to speed up getting your powers?"

Harry laughed when she didn't respond, but stopped, unable to hide the smile as she narrowed her gaze at him.

He moved to sit beside her at the counter and looked down at the book. "How about this? How about we get you trained up on other magic while we wait for your power? While your power is your primary weapon, not everyone's is very weaponry. You still need magic."

Maya didn't seem like she needed convincing. "Deal."

This time, Harry narrowed his gaze at her. "Is that what you were doing? Trying to learn some other magic?"

Maya didn't react. "You said it yourself, it's important to know other magic as well."

"You just wanted to make it sound like my idea?"

Maya smirked as she picked up the book and made her way to the stairs. "Then I could bitch at you, and you can't throw it in my face that I asked for it because I did no. Such. Thing."

Harry laughed as he followed her to the attic. He began pulling the necessities—candles and salt—to teach her the basics first, and turned to find her sitting cross legged in the middle of the rug, book by her side. Ready.

"Well, Mr. Mentor Man, what're we learning?"

---

Camilla followed Vera into the attic. Maya was sitting with her legs spread on the orthodox rug that covered the back end of the room. She had the family's spell book, the one that had thrown them across the kitchen, on the ground before her and was hunched over it. Her elbows on the ground, she held her head in her hands while she read.

Yoga and studies. Productive.

"Maya," Vera said. "What're you doing?"

Maya didn't move a muscle, merely allowing her eyes to swing from the book to the two of them by the door. "Teaching a frog to swim."

Camilla saw the light blush erupt across Vera's face at Maya's comment. She still hadn't gotten used to Maya's ways. It would happen soon enough. Hopefully.

Camilla rolled her eyes. "Maya, you know what she meant. You're supposed to be getting ready." Camilla strolled up to her sister, picked the book up from the ground and away from Maya, and turned to place it on the pedestal. "Not rereading this book. You've read it a handful of times already, and this thing is like a thousand pages. It's not going to make your powers pop up any sooner."

Maya slowly and gracefully lifted herself to stand. "I know. But it's also important to know those spells and test out those potions. I'm studying, seeing as I don't have powers to train up on, as you so love to remind me."

Camilla watched Maya walk over to the door, putting her boots on. It'd been six days since they found out that they were witches and she and Vera had received their powers. Six days of them knowing about the magical world and Maya not being able to do much about it.

Camilla knew it frustrated her, no matter how much she tried to hide it. She was sure anyone would be able to see it, but Camilla *understood*. She'd grown up with Maya, always known that Maya liked the occult. Finding out she was a witch with a power on the way would have been a dream to her. It truly must be killing her to have to wait it out.

"And I am ready," Maya finished speaking and turned away from them, heading downstairs.

Camilla nodded for Vera to follow as they trailed out of the room.

"You know," Vera called out to Maya as they stepped out of the house and onto the porch. "Having powers isn't all you're imagining it to be. It's not always fun. Actually, it's becoming a hassle."

"Tell me about it," Camilla remarked from Maya's side.

Vera took Maya's other side and they started their walk to the cemetery. It was time to visit their mother, Vera's first time.

"Yesterday, everyone decided to pile out of class at the same time and I got stuck in the middle. I read five different people's thoughts all at once. More like I got a headache. I couldn't figure one thought out from another," Camilla continued.

"Last night I went to bed, but forgot to grab my water from the dresser and move it to my nightstand, so when I thought 'I want some water,' and it happened to be on the other side of the room, the entire thing came barreling at me. It soaked the entire bed. I had to sleep in the living room," Vera one upped.

"I lose control every time Warren and I are making out, and I get his very *private* thoughts on what he'd like to do to me. Yes, Maya, I'm sure that wouldn't sound bad to you, but it's distracting."

"I accidentally summoned a cupcake away from a child the other day."

"I found out my professor is having an affair with three students."

"I almost summoned a cane away from an elderly gentleman."

"I..."

"Enough!" Maya interrupted Camilla's next horror.

Camilla stopped short at the sudden outburst and saw Vera do the same. They cleared out of their shock and caught up with Maya who had not stopped to wait for them.

"I am so tired of hearing you two complaining. Yes, there are some negatives, but that's fucking life. Everything comes with positives and negatives. At least you two get the positives!"

A light frown marred Camilla's face. Maya was right, of course.

With her final words out, Maya stormed off ahead of them. Camilla looked to Vera, who seemed worried that she'd royally pissed Maya off and shook her head. "She'll forget about it in two minutes. Maya doesn't hold grudges."

Camilla wrapped her hand into the crook of Vera's elbow and walked off after their sister.

---

It had been some time since she or Camilla had visited their mother's grave site, and Vera had never been, so Maya was glad to finally be stepping into the cemetery again. She knew they would be talking to the air, but she still enjoyed getting the chance to 'talk' to her mother, especially with the recent news of the supernatural ancestors—Loretta Whittle had a lot of explaining to do.

The calm rushed over her as they walked past the headstones on the way to their mother. Camilla laughed from behind her, and Maya paused to allow her sisters to catch up.

"How can we not be supernatural? We're all so at ease at the cemetery. Hello! That's like Supernatural 101."

Maya's lips quirked upward and she saw Vera's bright smile. Camilla's comments were something.

A black bird was perched on her stone. It was usually there when Maya came around. And usually gone by the time she made it to the headstone, like it was giving her privacy.

The three made it to their mother's grave, stopping a few feet from the headstone, and Maya watched Vera step up to it. It was her first time at the sight of a woman she never knew. Maya couldn't imagine what she was feeling, but she remained back with Camilla and allowed Vera the time.

A quiet broke out that Maya wasn't used to when she came to the cemetery. She was used to talking her mind off, filling the grounds with her voice. It was a quiet that Maya would have expected Vera to break. But it stuck around.

It was a while before Vera stepped back in line with her sisters. Camilla took her turn, stepping up and placing the bouquet of flowers she'd stopped to buy at the local shop in front of the stone.

"Hi, Mom." Camilla smiled as she stood back up, looking down at the stone. "It's been a couple of weeks, but we came, and we brought your first daughter with us."

Camilla stepped back, knocking her arm against Vera's with a warm gaze. Maya smiled softly as she looked at them, then turned to the stone. "Mom. You ever plan on letting me know Camilla wasn't my annoyance to bear alone?"

Scoffs and sputters came from her sisters at the same moment Camilla's arm reached across Vera and smacked her.

Maya turned to her little sister and gave her a wink.

As the silence took hold, Maya looked down at the stone. Her mother had been young when she had them, around Maya's age currently, so it'd been an easy friendship with her. Losing her was more than losing a parent to her and Camilla; they lost the one person they went to with all their dumb complaints or embarrassing secrets.

"Mom," Vera broke the silence, then scoffed. "Mom? That sounds so weird. I've never really had a mom. Dad made sure to talk about you, but I didn't have you, and now you're gone, and I didn't get to meet you."

Maya watched Vera hug herself, the pain of losing a woman she never knew deep in her chocolate eyes. "I should hate you," Vera continued. "But I can't. Dad always made sure you were treasured in our house, and I don't know why." She took a breath, then shook her head a couple small times. "I don't know what to say."

Maya thought about Vera's father, who could or could not be their father too, Harry wasn't too sure. But he did tell them about Bishop leaving the family he was warlocking for to be with Loretta.

Maya watched Camilla's hand wrap around their eldest sister. Camilla's control on her power had come relatively fast—both of theirs had as much as they liked to complain about the mishaps that came along with it—so Maya had no doubt her sister kept Vera's thoughts out of her head.

After a beat of silence, Camilla looked back down to the stone. "Mom, what happened? Why did we grow up without our sister? Why did you lock our powers? Why are you gone?"

Her voice was hardly audible by the time she finished. Maya stared at the stone and felt the ache of missing her mother, her most prominent question who their mother had been running from. If that person killed Loretta and Maya got around them, she'd skin them alive.

Just as Maya noticed Vera's hand reach up to hold Camilla's, she felt a sense of deja vu. Of getting thrown into the air. But in the middle of a cemetery where the only stops were stones, this time, it would hurt more.

It definitely hurt more.

Picking herself up from the stone she hit and feeling the blood trickle down her scalp, she looked out for Camilla. When she noticed that her little sister was completely unhurt, her gaze moved to Vera, who looked to be in pain, but okay nonetheless. More important at that moment was what the hell had hit them.

Nothing. There was nothing there.

"Maybe another power thing from Mom." Vera sounded hopeful as they limped closer to one another.

Maya's body worked off the adrenaline, not feeling the pain of hitting a headstone, as her gaze landed on it. Standing behind her sisters was a slobbering monster, definitely the animal demons that Harry had mentioned.

Maya shook her head as her sisters slowly turned their heads to the beast. Its brown skin looked more like goo than skin, and it slobbered like a dog at a feast. Its eye sockets were orange, which somehow was worse than if they had been the endless depths of black or even red.

It just stared at their motionless stances.

The mistake was when Camilla took a step back; the monster didn't seem to like that.

As another blast that would have surely thrown them through the air again came their way, the three ducked to the ground.

"Where's Mr. Mentor Man when you need him!" Maya exclaimed as Camilla let a few choice words out and Vera screamed for Harry.

And Harry showed up.

Just like that.

The shock on Vera's face meant she hadn't expected it either.

"Hello, ladies. Glad to see you're calling m…"

"Not now, Harry," Maya interrupted as the three girls dropped to the ground once more, dragging Harry with them, then picked themselves back up as Vera used her power to throw the beast back.

"What the *hell* is that?" Camilla exclaimed.

Harry seemed entirely unperturbed. "Oh dear. Well, it seems the demons are aware the book has been relocated. Or that you three have gotten your powers. Well, at least most of you."

Maya rolled her eyes but didn't say anything as Vera threw the demon back once more.

"Okay, Harry. Glad to know you're unconcerned with the beast, but what're we doing here?" Camilla rushed the words out.

"I could take you away right now," Harry began. "I'll take you home, wipe your memories, and lock your powers back up. The demons will lose trace, and everything will go back to normal. "

Harry ducked out of the way alongside them as another blast came from the beast. "Or you could accept your ancestors. I could give you a spell to use, and you could destroy the demon. But if you accept this now, you accept being witches. This isn't a game that you can pick up whenever you wish."

"You guys know I'm in." Maya didn't hesitate.

"I want to know my family. I'm in," Vera said as she threw the beast back once more. She looked tired, like she wasn't used to the control of exerting so much power at once.

Camilla's hesitation was evident as she looked at them. It was a consideration for her. She could go back to being human. But this was a family matter, and Maya knew that mattered more to Camilla than a normal human life.

"Okay, fine, yes, I'm in!"

Harry smiled at the outcome, Maya having to smack him

on the arm to snap him out of it, and quickly give them the spell to cast. Maya felt the words naturally flowing out of her mouth when they recited it as if they were meant to be spoken by her.

And like a firework show, the demon combusted right before them.

"Whoa." Maya felt the word leave.

"Yes, don't get too excited. They don't all vanquish like that," Harry remarked as he walked up to Maya, reaching his hand up to her temple.

He didn't touch her, but Maya felt a warmth around her cut, then nothing. The feeling then rushed her body before going away. The ache of hitting stones was gone. He had said his power was healing.

"Can you not vanquish demons yourself?" Vera asked.

"Of course I can. But what good would that do the three of you? You need the experience." He turned back to the others and moved to heal their bodies as well before sticking out a hand. "Now, shall I take you home?"

With a look to her sisters to confirm, a smile tugged at Maya's lips as she told Harry they'd meet him there. They had adrenaline to walk off.

He seemed pleased with the answer and ported out of the cemetery. They were lucky no humans often walked this part of town.

With Harry gone, the girls joined arm in arm and began their trek back home, taking the longer path that moved along the forests. It was a walk of ecstatic giggles and exaggerated emotions.

"We're pretty badass," Camilla praised.

Maya smiled, shaking her head. They'd hardly done anything, but she could already imagine what would come for them.

They were about halfway home, along the path that Maya

loved but most stayed away from, when the sounds of crunching came from behind.

They turned just in time to see another animal coming at them. It looked like a combination of a cheetah, a seal, and a jellyfish. Disturbing.

And it was running fast.

Gripping tight, the sisters didn't hesitate to recite the spell Harry had just told them. And nothing happened.

They tried again, and still nothing.

Maya was sure they were saying it correctly, which just meant that this one would need a different spell. Perfect.

Before they could try anything else, the demon jumped at them, and they all threw themselves out of the way, landing on opposite ends of the clearing the path had led them to.

The beast turned, unperturbed, in Vera's direction and lunged before she could get her arm up to swing him through the air. It threw her to the right, landing right beside Camilla as she hit the tree.

"Vera!" Maya screamed as the demon turned for Camilla. And Maya felt her heart drop.

Camilla sat by Vera's side, pulling Vera's head up to make sure she was okay. Of course she was checking on others rather than protecting herself.

Maya called out to Harry the same way Vera had earlier and heard him pop up behind her at the same moment the beast jumped for her sisters. Her skin grew cold, then blazed hot, and Maya threw her arms out, screaming for the beast to stop.

The beast didn't stop, but her magic finally showed up, and a bolt of fire shot out of her hands. It was alight and burning as the flames continued to flow from her hands to the beast, stop-ping only when it had been reduced to ashes.

With the ash and light smoke blowing around her, Maya looked down to her hands, breathing hard. The flames were gone, leaving behind pristine hands. Hands that had been holding fire, controlling fire, only a few seconds prior.

She looked up to see her sisters standing by the tree, Harry supporting them as he healed Vera. Then all at once, all three sets of eyes were on her. No, not her. Her hands. And at once, they all moved to look her in the eyes.

6

---

*D*emons were doing well in finding them. Harry was sure it was just a coincidence of the day. It'd been six days, and this was their first attack, but he didn't want to take any more chances, so he ported them home, right into the kitchen.

It was a big space, with the island surrounded by counters on one half of the room and a casual dining table on the other. The formal dining room was hardly ever used, this one much more preferable for daily use.

Harry helped Vera to a chair at the table as Camilla took a seat and Maya walked off for the kettle. Vera kept her attention on her middle sister as Harry crouched before her, declaring he wanted to make sure she had no other injuries.

Maya filled the kettle and set it on the stove when Harry took the seat beside Vera and everyone's attentions settled on the middle Whittle's back. She just stood there before the flames that licked the kettle.

Neither Camilla nor Maya had been seriously hurt. For that, Vera was grateful. She'd just met them, but she already felt a tightness growing inside her when she thought of anything happening to them, when she had noticed the small cut on Maya's temple earlier.

They were all fine, just a bit mussed.

Vera watched Maya's back in the silence. Her favorite leather jacket had dirt stains, but it looked perfectly fine, basically indestructible. The black of her jeans held remnants of dirt as well, though her knee high boots had taken a larger portion of it, and Vera was sure when Maya turned, her black shirt would bear the same brunt.

Black. Maya wore a lot of black.

The silence was becoming almost unbearable for Vera when the kettle finally began to whistle. She watched Maya busy herself with pulling out four cups and settling them on the tray with the kettle and the tea bags, sugar, and honey.

Vera noticed the deep rise and fall of Maya's shoulders before she lifted the tray and turned to them. She placed the tray in the middle of the table, made herself a cup, then took a seat at the head closest to the exit of the room.

The silence rang in Vera's ears, and she wanted desperately to break it, but she didn't know how.

She followed her sister's ministrations and made herself a cup too. Staying busy might block out the silence that rang around her. She stared at her cup when she heard an annoyed Maya. "What?"

Vera's gaze shot up to find Maya's bored expression watching Camilla and Harry. Apparently, they hadn't bothered with the teas, instead keeping their stares trained on Maya.

"I just figured you'd be more excited about finally getting your powers." Camilla's words were nonchalant, but there was a ring of worry behind them.

"Adrenaline withdrawals," Maya simply stated. "It'll kick in soon."

Camilla blew out a breath that meant she wasn't happy with

that answer, but didn't respond. Instead, she began to fiddle with the kettle as she prepared her cup.

It took another second before Harry followed her. Still, Vera noticed, Harry kept a watchful eye.

"What?" Maya sounded past annoyed.

Harry took a sip of his bland tea, then turned to her. "Your power. It has not been seen in a witch in centuries."

"A unique power!" Vera tried to clear the air. "Maybe that's why it took so long to come in."

"Not exactly," Harry said. "Fire control is a very rare power... among demons. Among witches, it is almost non-existent. I've only heard of two other witches who held the power, and I don't even know their names. Just that there were two others that had held it at one point."

Vera noticed Camilla still from her periphery.

"It's a demon power? How would a witch get that?"

Harry shook his head. "Not a demon power. Powers are not classified as demon or witch; they're classified as dark or light. It tends to be that witches receive the light powers and demons the dark, but they are not mutually exclusive. A witch can have dark," he waved Maya over as an example, "and a demon light. But it is rarer than you can imagine."

"And fire control is a dark power?" Maya didn't seem worried about the information, just curious.

Vera felt nervous for her. And she could tell that Camilla did as well.

Harry nodded to Maya. "Not just any dark power. Fire control is a high-level dark power. Only a few demons can claim it."

Vera's interest was suddenly on high alert. "Level? There are levels to it?"

"Yes, yes." Harry turned to her, his perfect hair falling to his eye before he pushed it aside. "There are low, medium, and high level powers for both light and dark. There's no real rule to classifying them, but it is basically looked at as how much destruction the power can cause. Basically, how much control does the power give you? As you can imagine, fire gives you plenty of control."

"What are we?" Camilla asked.

"Mind reading is a low-level light power. Telekinesis, a medium-level light power. But fire control." He whistled, then continued on in that beautiful accent. "Fire control is a high-level dark power."

"Are higher levels rarer?" Vera asked.

"No. There are plenty of low and medium level powers that are rare as well. You three will continue to gain powers, these just happen to be your primaries, but those new ones may be rare ones."

"Will this be dangerous to Maya?" Camilla turned the conversation back to their middle sister.

"*To* Maya? No."

Vera felt a breath of relief at the same moment she saw Camilla breathe out.

"It is her power," Harry continued. "It would do her no harm at all. Once she trains it, she will have full control. *For* her though? That will be an entirely different conversation."

Vera stiffened in her seat at the same moment as her sisters.

"Meaning?" Maya asked.

"Meaning, when demons find out that you have it, they'll want it for themselves. More demons will come after you specifically to gain control of your power. And those demons with the same power may want to take yours to make themselves more powerful. All in all," Harry moved his gaze to each of them before landing on Maya, "demons are going to become zealous for that magic."

Vera let out a snort she couldn't hold back. "So now demons will be after us for the book, just because we're witches, *and* for

Maya's power. How are we supposed to keep Maya safe from that?"

"You can steal powers?" Maya asked at the same time.

Harry answered Maya first. "You can. I don't know how it's done, as it is a demonic pasttime and I never particularly paid attention in warlock training." He turned to Vera. "And in terms of keeping Maya safe, she could always give the power up. When she gains her other powers, it won't be very noticeable…"

"Absolutely not!" Maya cut him off. "This is an amazing power. Better than anything I could have asked for. Why would I give that up?"

"To be safe." Camilla's tone conveyed reason that Vera knew all too well Maya would not see.

"We're witches. A part of a powerful coven. With a powerful book of spells. We're not going to be safe no matter what," Maya argued.

She wasn't wrong.

Harry rebutted, "You could always keep the power a secret. Not use it."

"No." Maya gave no reasoning.

"Maya, be reasonable," Camilla argued.

Vera watched the two of them, understanding both sides of the argument.

"It's a desired power for a reason," Maya told her sister. "It's a power to learn and use. Under the protection of this house, I won't be detected as I practice. You guys are so focused on the negatives. This can keep us safer. Yes, demons will want it, but guess what? They'll want your powers too. This power will scare others from coming for us."

Camilla stared dumbfounded at her sister.

Vera didn't want to anger her, but she couldn't help but say, "That's true." The protection cast around their house made it so that no magical creature could pop in if they haven't been allowed in before. It kept the book safe—along with the extra protection on the attic so no one could just pop in and grab the book—and had been keeping them safe in the process. The only problem then was not knowing what magical creatures Loretta had allowed into the house before she'd died, but hopefully they would be okay from anyone popping up with ill intent.

Just as expected, Camilla threw her a dirty look. Better Camilla than Maya though. Especially when Maya was right.

"But it is a high-level demon power. Yes, it's technically a dark power, but only demons have it. I'm just nervous about what that could mean," Vera argued.

Maya huffed out. "Well, it's a good thing it's my power then. I'm keeping it *and* using it."

With those final words, Maya walked out of the room.

Vera looked to Camilla, who just looked worried now, and Harry, who looked to be in thought.

"I hate to do this." Harry looked at the two of them. "But I agree with your sister. This could bring some positives as well."

Camilla slumped back into her chair and folded her arms. "I know."

---

Maya left the kitchen for the bathroom, getting cleaned up then changing into leggings and an oversized sweater, before heading out to the backyard. She sat cross legged in the middle of the grass, the crisp fall breeze soothing her skin.

A bucket of water sat beside her. Just in case. She was determined to learn to control her power. But a precaution wouldn't hurt.

She raised her arms out in front of her and closed her eyes, full of thoughts of wanting the flames to blaze across her arms. Thoughts that were quickly washed out with the doubts of her entire family, the concerns and urges for her to give up her power. She shook her head and focused on her hands.

After a few moments of not feeling anything, Maya opened her eyes to find clean hands staring back at her where there should be flames.

She narrowed her eyes at those hands and once more closed her eyes. Again, her thoughts went directly to her family's hesitations around her power. This time, the doubts felt deeper.

Again, she felt nothing and opened her eyes to find clean hands.

Frustrated, Maya dropped her hands and looked out to the setting sun. She thought about how it was flaming up in the sky, yet was the source of peace when looked upon.

Peacefulness. That's what she needed.

She needed to get the doubts and concerns out of her head.

Taking a deep breath and letting it all go, completely clearing her head, Maya raised her hands out once more and closed her eyes. She thought of the sun setting and how light and warm it felt to watch it happening. How calming it was to anyone paying attention to it. She thought about calming her thoughts and focused on lighting her hands like the sunset lit the sky.

She felt nothing for a couple of seconds, then a warmth radiated from the tips of her fingers. She hadn't had enough time to think about the feeling earlier, given she was so focused on saving her sisters, but she could do so then. There was a warmth that embedded under her skin. She only felt it at her fingertips, but it was like a rush of flames licking her insides. It was intoxicating.

Slowly, making sure to keep her head clear and focused, Maya opened her eyes. She focused her gaze on the bits of fire coming from her fingertips, and couldn't help the smile that began to grow. This wasn't as dramatic as the flame-engulfed arms she'd had an hour prior, but it was progress. And it was a power. *Her* power.

The fire remained, trained at only the tips of her fingers, for a couple of minutes, then snuffed out completely. Her smile was wide as the sun by then.

It was time to try again.

Maya stared down at her hands. "Now *this* is awesome."

---

Vera had seen Maya walk out to the back yard and stood by the window at the kitchen for a while, watching her. The smile that had eaten Maya's features when she'd gotten the first bits of flames to appear had warmed Vera's heart.

It was a dangerous power, but it was Maya's. It fit her well. And most importantly, it made her happy.

She watched another few minutes after the first lighting before heading out of the kitchen and to the back of the house. In her tour when she'd first moved in, she'd seen the piano room and couldn't stay away from it any longer. The room held a grand piano and nothing else. It was beautiful.

Vera took a seat at the piano bench and looked down at the keys. She let her fingers dance over them, not yet touching. It had been three years since she'd played. Her father had said she had gotten her musical abilities from her mother.

Vera felt an ease take over her body she hadn't felt in too long as her fingers fell onto the keys and danced as if this were a ball and they were the prized show.

When the song came to an end, Vera listened to the silence in the room and basked in it.

"That was lovely."

She jumped, turning to find Harry standing by the door.

"Thank you," she breathed out, turning back to the piano.

He moved into the room, standing beside the length of the piano. "Will you play another?"

Vera met his gaze and felt the blush take over at his attention. Playing in front of others had never been a problem, but staring at them while she did was too much for her. She closed her eyes and allowed her fingers to move.

She hadn't realized she'd moved from one song to another until she opened her eyes and noticed the room had darkened. The sun was almost gone.

"You're better than your mother was," Harry said, bringing her attention back to him.

"Am I?" Vera asked, playing with a couple keys as she awaited his answer.

Harry nodded. "Loretta was brilliant, but you're effortless. It's graceful and beautiful and hypnotizing. She would be proud."

Vera smiled at him. "She would be."

7

$\mathcal{C}$amilla hadn't realized how badly she needed time away from this new supernatural that was her new witch life until she saw Warren's smile. Now, holding his hand and walking the path along the lake felt like Christmas to Camilla—a gift of normalcy. Sad, considering it had only been a week since they'd found out about being witches.

They'd spent the day on a simple date, and Camilla was basking in every moment. From going to the movies and watching a comedy to picking up some ice cream and sitting across from each other at one of those tiny tables, half smearing the ice cream on one another's faces. They'd washed the stickiness from their skin and headed for a walk by the lake that sat in the middle of the expanse of the park. Warren had stopped their walk to drop to the grass, dragging her down with him and lying back, cuddling Camilla into him as they laughed, making a game of coming up with backstories to the shapes they saw in the clouds.

They'd stayed down for at least an hour before Camilla's stomach began to rumble. Warren had rolled over her, dropping his mouth to her stomach as he threatened it to be quiet.

Camilla hadn't been able to stop the giggles—and the fluttering of a million and one butterflies in her stomach—as she'd stared down at him. She'd pushed him off, and they'd gotten up and continued their walk through the park. Camilla had the widest grin she could imagine as she leaned into Warren's arm on their stroll.

"Loretta! Loretta!"

Camilla's smile dropped at the sound of her mother's name. It was still hard when someone with her mother's name was around. Hearing it caused an ache to break through her chest. That ache jumped when a hand landed on her arm and turned her around. "Loretta, dear, I finished…"

The woman cut herself off when Camilla turned and she noticed it was not Loretta standing before her. The blush began to bloom across the woman's cheeks as she put her hand to her chest. "Oh dear, I'm sorry, from behind you looked just like someone else."

Camilla looked the woman over. She hadn't just heard her mother's name, her mother was the one being called. Camilla didn't know how to feel about that.

The woman had to be in her sixties, but she was vibrant and full of energy. Her skin wrinkled, and her face showed the evidence of a million smiles. She stood at Camilla's average height, and her thin black hair reached the bottom of her back as it flowed in the chill. Damn, to be that old and have all that color.

Camilla brought herself back to the moment, feeling the warm smile blossom on her face at the woman's remark. "It's okay. Loretta was my mother."

The woman mirrored her warm smile. "Oh. Well, yes, I see that. You look just like her."

Camilla hadn't realized how much she wanted to hear those words until they were in the air. "What was it you wanted to say? When you thought I was my mother?"

"I was going to tell her…" She paused to think about it. "Huh, I can't seem to remember." She flushed as she scratched her head like that would remind her. She looked at Camilla. "You know, I cannot seem to recall."

Camilla felt her eyebrows draw together as she looked the woman over. "You do know Loretta isn't here anymore, right? She passed away almost two years ago."

The woman baffled at hearing that, staring between Camilla and her hands as she shook her head like something was blocking her. Camilla watched, a strange feeling arising within her.

"You sure you don't remember what it was you wanted to say?" Warren asked sweetly.

Camilla felt her body jump at the sound, having forgotten he was there, even though one of her arms still remained wrapped around his.

"You were telling Loretta that you finished something," he prodded her.

Camilla felt her eyebrows draw deeper. Warren sounded eager to hear what this woman had to say, but she couldn't concentrate on that. There was a strange feeling in her, like she should know what this woman wanted to say.

"I remember." She seemed eager. "I was going to say…" She stopped again and furrowed her brows. "I cannot recall."

It seemed odd. The woman looked like she'd recalled, but seemed unable to voice it. Odd. As odd as finding out about the magical world. Camilla looked her over and tried a calmer, sweeter tone. "I'm Camilla. I didn't catch your name?"

She beamed. "Oh deary, I'm Lana. Camilla, yes. I remember Loretta speaking of you. Her nurturing one."

Camilla's heart warmed at the sound. Her mother speaking of them and calling her 'her nurturing one' melted her.

But it did not distract Camilla from the situation. Lana had something to say, and Camilla wanted to know what it was. She rested a comforting hand on Lana's arm and allowed the woman's thoughts to invade hers.

*You wanted to tell Loretta that the piece she wanted placed in her headstone was done. Why can you not get the words out? The piece is placed. The job is done. Why won't it come out? Odd.*

Camilla slowly pulled her hand away and gave what she hoped to be a reassuring smile. "It's okay. Memories, they come and go all the time."

Lana smiled and apologized for the mistake and her inability to voice her thoughts. She grabbed Camilla's hand and looked her over like she was truly seeing her old friend. With a final tight squeeze of the hand, she walked off. Camilla watched her go and thought back to what she'd just read. Odd indeed.

Warren pulled on the hand he still held in his, bringing her back to the moment, a smile brightening his features. "The nurturing one?" He leaned in and kissed her. "It definitely suits you."

---

Vera was sitting at the kitchen table with two large photo albums sitting before her. Maya sat at her right and Harry her left as they slowly flipped through an album of Vera growing up and compared it to an album of Maya and Camilla growing up.

Camilla walked in glowing. She'd been out with Warren all day, somehow deciding that going to the movies at noon sounded fun. She leaned over the table and took a look at the photos before them, and Vera watched the glow evaporate, her smile fading completely.

"What?" Maya asked as she glanced up from the album to catch Camilla's somber expression.

Camilla was looking at a picture of their mother. What was the problem with that?

"I was having such a lovely day, I forgot!" Camilla breathed out and dropped into the chair across from them.

"What?" Vera probed.

Camilla recited her afternoon walk in the park and her bump in with the woman, Lana. "It was odd," Camilla continued. "When I read her mind, it was all there. What she wanted to say was there, but she couldn't verbalize. She was aware of it, but couldn't get around it. It was like her brain cut her off and was like 'nope, no can do.'"

Vera frowned and noticed Harry's contemplation.

"What do you think, Mr. Mentor Man?" Maya asked.

Vera bit the inside of her cheek to stop from smiling at Maya's remark. Harry had told them he would be their friend, *not* their mentor. He'd informed them that he didn't know enough to be their mentor, but Maya still found every chance she could to call him it. She was many things—intimidating being at the top of the list—but she somehow was the best at making them feel like family. She didn't try to be nice just because they were still basically strangers. Maya treated both her and Harry like they were part of the family. And that meant teasing and snarky comments.

"She could be under a spell." Harry ignored Maya and focused this attention on Camilla. "It could be whatever it was your mother had asked of her was too important for Lana to accidentally tell anyone. A spell would detect whether or not it was truly Loretta she was talking to so no demons tried to transfigure to gain the information. Lana not even being able to remember every time she tried to speak would likely have been for her own protection."

Vera thought about it. If that were the case, which she had to admit seemed viable, then whatever was hidden was important. Really important if it made it so that she wouldn't be able to remember every time she tried to speak it. That would never give her the opportunity to tell another. And if their mother had thought it through completely—which Vera was sure she had—she would have made sure Lana wasn't able to write it either.

"Well," Maya said, "guess that means we're headed back to see Mom."

"You want to see what it is?" Vera was surprised by the shock in her voice. Of course Maya wanted to see what it was. Vera did too, but Maya was far more likely to throw herself into danger for curiosity's sake.

Maya nodded. "Whatever this thing is she's hiding could be the reason she died. I'm gonna find out what it is."

And for once, the curiosity seemed to take all of them because it was the first time they'd all agreed with no discussion.

Instead of walking, they had Harry port them; the curiosity was too much to casually walk to the other side of town when they could just pop into the middle of it.

Vera stood before her mother's headstone for the second time in as many days. "Right," Vera shook her hands out, "what are we looking for?"

"I don't know. Lana's thoughts weren't specific," Camilla answered.

"Okay," Vera replied slowly, then locked her attention to the headstone. "It's a headstone, so unless there's something on it that we're just not seeing, there must be a latch. Something that opens up for a spot to hide whatever she wanted hidden."

"Do you always think aloud?" Maya asked, genuine curiosity in her gaze.

Vera felt the rush of blood erupt across her face. "Not always."

Maya quirked her eyebrows. She didn't believe the half-hearted answer.

Vera sighed. "I also talk to myself a lot. Sometimes I'll ask a question, people will answer me, and I'll be standing there like 'who was talking to you?' It's kind of a problem."

Maya shrugged. "It's cute. Dorky, but cute."

Vera felt the tightening around her heart at Maya's kind words. She wasn't kind often. She wasn't mean either, just not kind. But when she was, it held a harder punch.

Joining sisters who already knew and loved each other was hard. Especially for someone who was so used to going about things on her own, not having someone around to truly allow into her heart and care for. And on top of it all, Vera felt the irritating nag that she never wanted to 'intrude' or try too hard at the whole 'sister' thing.

"Thanks," Vera squeaked out as Maya crouched in front of the headstone, beginning to feel it up.

Maya fiddled with the entirety of the stone, trying to find a piece that would open a latch. Harry followed in Maya's lead and crouched on the backside of the headstone, beginning to fiddle with it. Camilla, on the other hand, seemed to be paying attention to their surroundings, as if whatever Lana had been thinking of was around the headstone rather than attached to it.

Vera turned her attention back to Maya and Harry and watched just as a black bird cawed in the air. Maya's hands moved across the words, the action freezing her in her spot.

The words.

Vera tilted her head slightly as her eyes narrowed to the inscriptions on the stone. Each inscription looked different from the ones around it, each letter even more so. "If all the characters look different, no one would think to question one letter big enough to hold a latch."

"What was that?" Harry looked up to her, his hand still fiddling with the top of the stone.

Vera moved Maya out of the way and crouched in front of the stone. She ran her fingers over the inscriptions. "The latch is between the characters. Using the letters as a place for your fingers to dig in and open."

Thinking aloud also helped her focus.

"If only one character was misshapen, it would draw attention. Be questioned. But have them all misshapen, and no one would bother to pay attention to it."

As she finished her sentence, Vera stuck her fingers into the 'v' to "beloved" and pulled to the side, and just like that, the 'v' shifted open like a safe deposit box. Then paused.

Vera smiled as she looked down at it, feeling the stares of the others around her. "And she definitely would not have allowed just anyone to open the latch."

"You're thinking blood from your line?" Harry asked.

Vera shrugged in response as she brought her finger to the small letter that would open the latch. "I'm assuming."

A small drop of blood oozed from her finger, and soaked into the stone. She brought her finger up to her mouth to suck dry as she watched the latch fully open.

Sitting inside was a long, dark marble piece. She didn't know what it was. It was a long line of black marble that almost sparked under the sun. The bottom—or was it the top?—looked to be missing something, and the side as well.

Vera pulled it out and made sure there was nothing else in the latch before closing it back up, standing carefully with the piece in hand.

Camilla and Maya looked at it, dumbfounded.

"What is it?" Maya asked.

Vera shook her head, at a loss.

"That," Harry spoke up with a shake, "is a piece of the Hell's Gate key."

His face had gone completely somber, whitening as he looked around the cemetery apprehensively, then he went to grab for them. "We can talk about this at home," he said with a final check that no one else had seen the piece.

Harry landed them in the living room of the Whittle house, Vera moving immediately for the couch to the left, Camilla to the one opposite, and Maya moved to sit on the ground between the couches before the fireplace. Vera would have thought Maya's attraction to the fire came from her newfound power had she not been at the house almost a week before Maya got said power. She'd witnessed her sister before the fire every night. It was likely in her blood, the attraction to the flames.

Harry remained standing, pacing back and forth, before stopping and turning completely to the three of them. "Humans know Hell as one thing," he began to explain. "In reality, it is simply where demons are from. Nothing like the ravenous things humans come up with, even with the animal demons. It's just the demons' origin. *Hell's Gate* is like a prison in Hell where the worst of the worst are taken. These are creatures that even demons find too troubling to have roaming around."

"Demon prison?" Maya repeated, both intrigue and apprehension ringing her tone.

"Not only demons." He began pacing again, seemingly not able to focus on any one point as he spoke. "But witches and faeries and centaurs. The worst of any and all creatures. They're held prisoner, and the only way out is if someone topside has the key to let you out. There is only one key."

"And this is part of it?" Vera indicated the marble still in her hands.

Harry stopped and gave her a nod, the intensity of his gaze catching her breath. "And because these creatures are some of the worst beings in existence, the key was broken up in order to be sure no one could break anyone out. As I'm sure you are beginning to understand, in the magical world, three is an important number, so the key was broken up into three pieces."

Three. A piece for the bottom, and the actual key part were the two missing pieces Vera had noticed before.

"That," Harry indicated to the piece in her hand, "is one of the three."

It was an interesting system of going about things. For a world where the creatures held such powers, there was a place they would be sent if they went too far. It felt good to know that at least existed, though Vera couldn't be sure what constituted evil enough to get thrown there if it would have to be something even the demons weren't okay with.

"How did our mother get it?" Vera asked.

Harry breathed out and moved to take his seat beside Vera. "When broken, each piece was given to a different creature. As all magical creatures are kept in Hell's Gate, no one creature was trusted to keep all three. One was given to the demons, as it is a demon's domain, and they are one of the two most powerful magical beings. Another to the witches," he pointed once more to the marble in Vera's hands, "as the other most powerful magical beings. And as the natural enemy to demons, they would be the least likely to come together to use it."

"And the final?" Vera asked, her breath hitching at the end.

"The final piece was given to a creature that had no connections to Hell's Gate. No being from this line has ever been or will ever be held there."

"Humans," Vera thought aloud.

"Yes. With no connections to the magical world, they would have the least motivation for abusing their piece. It was given to a holy family to keep safe, so I can only assume a priest may have the piece now."

Harry took the piece from Vera and looked it over. Vera watched him a moment, noticing the small furrow between his eyebrows as he looked it over. His hazel eyes were endearing—Vera could look into them for hours—as he contemplated what to do with this piece. Vera shook herself out of her thoughts and turned her gaze to her sisters. Camilla looked to be in thought, and Maya seemed to be inspecting everyone's reactions in the room. Vera stiffened under her sister's scrutiny.

Luckily, Maya's gaze did not remain on her for long before turning to Camilla. Vera looked to Camilla, who was being awfully quiet, as if in her head about something entirely other.

Maya seemed to be scrutinizing her younger sister, and Vera wondered if Maya could guess what was going on in Camilla's head just by looking her over.

She was brought out of her thoughts when Harry spoke. "It seems your family got the witches' piece. Meaning for generations, your family has been responsible for keeping this safe and away from others. Demons, especially. It seems your mother chose to bear that responsibility in death so you girls would not have to."

Vera looked at Harry's handsome features as he finished speaking and breathed out. Loretta Whittle had done so much for them, and after learning from Harry that her father was also a warlock, Vera couldn't help but wonder if he'd helped. In her heart, she knew he had. He'd never stopped loving Loretta, that was evident to the day he died.

Taking in Harry's features one final moment, Vera closed her eyes and breathed out again.

8

———————

Camilla was sure she had seen that marble piece before. Or something like it. The piece she was thinking about wasn't long at all, but an intricately woven design. It could be the bottom of a key, she thought. But it was definitely a part of this collection. That marble was entirely other, too magical for Camilla to think otherwise.

And Camilla was sure she had seen that piece in Warren's room.

They'd given Harry the piece to keep hidden. Maya had argued that they take it back to the cemetery, what better place to hide it than a latch that no one knew of?

Unfortunately, she lost three to one.

And part of Camilla knew that was a bad idea. Maya was normally right about practical matters like this, but she felt safer knowing Harry had it hidden. She'd have felt just as safe having Maya hide it with as far as she'd come with her supernatural education in only a week's time. Harry had spent plenty of time with her training up on the spells and potions of the book—she and Vera had some catching up to do.

Camilla hadn't been able to sleep thinking about the marble

piece she was sure was in Warren's room, so bright and early the next morning, she got up and went to school, heading for Warren's rooms.

He lived in an apartment just off of the campus with five flatmates, but given they all had their own rooms, Camilla wasn't worried about running into anyone else, especially this early in the morning.

Unfortunately, Camilla would not be so lucky, for Warren's roommate, Knox, opened the door on his way out just as she was stopping before it. And the noise behind him informed her that all flatmates were awake and not in their rooms.

Knox smiled in her direction as he walked past her, leaving the door open for her to step in. Shutting it behind her, Camilla walked in to find all the guys scattered throughout the room, some lying on the couches, some in the adjoining open kitchen.

Warren looked up to her with a grin from the couches and immediately walked over.

"Wow," she commented as he took her head in his hands and kissed her good morning. "I did not expect all of you up this early."

"The fire alarms went off at five in the morning. Whole evacuation in the freezing cold and everything. We couldn't get back to sleep," Lynus, another flatmate, grumbled from his spot on the couch.

Warren's hands skimmed down her arms. "Not that I'm complaining, but was there a reason for the early visit?" He knew she liked to sleep in. Maya was the early riser in her family.

There was a hint of concern in his tone, and it warmed Camilla's heart to hear it. "Um, yeah," she said, taking his hand and heading for his room.

One of the guys whistled. "Damn, Camilla. This early?"

"Don't be too loud in there!" Matty called in after them. Camilla was sure she heard the grin as she closed the door behind her. The others began to laugh as Warren rolled his eyes, though the smile was still evident on his face.

Camilla's gaze shot directly to the painting on the opposite wall—exactly why she'd come over. A painting that she had knocked over a few weeks ago while Warren was in the shower. A painting that should have a piece of something, possibly the Hell's Gate key, attached to the back.

Camilla turned to Warren's waiting gaze and racked her brain for a way to preoccupy him. "Um, I was wondering if I could get your purple sweater?"

Warren's face scrunched up. "My purple sweater?"

"Yeah. I really like it, and I wanted to wear it today."

Warren looked her over, then gave a small laugh. "Sure. It's at the bottom of my closet though. I haven't worn it in a few months."

Bingo. He'd shown her pictures of it, but she'd never seen it in person. But she had told him that she wanted it, so this should seem all too normal of a request. "I've got all the time in the world," she drew out nonchalantly as she danced her way deeper into the room.

Warren laughed and gave her a wink, moving to his closet.

Camilla hoped the boys' exaggerated volume on the other side of the door would be enough to hide any of Camilla's snooping. Making sure Warren wasn't paying attention, Camilla turned to the painting and slowly lifted the bottom off the wall. She dipped her head to look under it and saw that it was still there, taped to the middle. A small thing, likely the size of her palm.

Camilla looked over to Warren to make sure he still had his back to her and lifted her hand to the piece, slowly pulling it free from the painting. As she lightly pressed the painting back down, she noticed Warren turning from her periphery.

Quickly throwing the piece into the bag at her hip, she turned to him with a large grin. "You found it!"

"I found it!" He exaggerated as he opened the head of the sweater and pulled it over her head. "You know, I think you should keep it. It looks real good on you."

Camilla smiled as she looked down at the half put-on sweater. It was a royal purple with a small inscription on the left breast that read *Warren for your heart,* a Christmas girl from Matty that Warren wore as a joke more than anything. "It does, doesn't it?" she remarked, modeling it.

Warren laughed and took her head in his hands, eyes glittering as he leaned down to kiss her.

Camilla stuck around another ten minutes but found an excuse to leave as soon as she could, stating Maya had texted her to get back home. She'd felt the antsy need to look at the piece in her bag the entire time, so before heading home, she took a moment to hide behind a tree and examine it. She was sure it looked just like the one they'd found in her mother's headstone, albeit a different shape.

Now, engulfed in Warren's purple sweater, Camilla walked into her house, finding the others in the kitchen.

"You were up early this morning. That's unlike you," Maya remarked.

"That's because I didn't sleep," Camilla said as she placed the piece on the table.

All three eyes moved to it as one, deep furrows blooming on their faces.

"Where did you get that?" Harry asked, his breath hitching deeper now than it had the night before when they had found the first piece.

"Warren's room."

"Excuse me?" Maya bit out.

"A few weeks ago I knocked down a painting in there, and when I was putting it back up, I noticed something taped to the back. I didn't really think about it after, but then I saw that piece from Mom's headstone last night, and it all came back."

"I thought the human piece was with a holy family?" Maya said.

"Well, no." Harry broke out of his thoughts. "I said I *presumed* it would still be with a holy family. In fact, it may not even be in Warren's family. He is renting the room, no?"

Camilla nodded.

"It may have been kept there for safekeeping. If a creature went to the responsible family, they would not be able to find it because it was a part of a college apartment decoration."

"But how would you make sure it was kept safe?" Vera questioned.

Harry didn't seem to know the answer to her question. "Those boys aren't home at all times. It is likely whoever hid the piece goes back to check on it from time to time."

"And if something were to happen to it? Say, it were taken?" Vera asked, looking over to Camilla accusatorially.

Camilla blanched, expecting the criticism from Maya, but not Vera. Though she knew she should begin to, given they were growing closer and sisters bickered and disagreed all the time. It was time to think of Vera as such and not just another blood relative. Plus, she knew it was stupid to bring the Hell's Gate key one step closer to getting put together, but she couldn't help but need it away from Warren's room. Like if they had it, a demon wouldn't be likely to go in there and find it.

Harry was at a standstill. "I haven't a clue."

Maya took the piece from the table and examined it in her hands. It was pure black marble like the original one they'd found, and like the original, there was a shimmer to it.

"Do you see the fire?" Maya asked.

"Fire?" Camilla's brows furrowed.

Maya nodded, her eyes transfixed with the piece. "Like white flames escaping through the black."

Camilla shook her head. "I see a shimmer. I wouldn't call it fire."

"It is likely your fire power calling to the Hell's Gate magic. Hell's Gate uses plenty of fire, as you can imagine," Harry lazily threw in as he fixed his gaze on the piece.

"Having both pieces..." Vera began.

"Is not good," Harry finished. "This makes it easier for anyone that would want it. Now instead of looking for two individual pieces, they could look for a pair. The most important thing we can do now is make sure that both are hidden. Apart from one another. No one of us should know where both pieces are. Now, I have the first piece hidden." He turned to Maya. "Maya, I think you should hide this second one."

Maya gave him a blank look. "Why me?"

"You've studied the book the most, and I've been training you, unlike your sisters. I trust you've seen spells you could use. Plus, it is noted that you are the coldest sister. You'd be the least susceptible to manipulation. Out of all four of us, not just between your sisters. But again, no one of us should know where both pieces are. I cannot hide it."

"Well, he's not wrong," Vera affirmed.

Maya looked at Camilla.

"I agree," Camilla voiced. "Hide it."

Maya looked to each of them, finding affirmations within each of their eyes, and nodded.

## 9

Hunter wasn't in a very good mood at the moment. Quite honestly, he was in a particularly foul mood. And having his father leisurely lounging on an armchair wasn't making it any better.

Augustine Delvaux was smiling up at his son, amused by Hunter's current demeanor. "Calm down, son."

Hunter rolled his eyes at his father, pacing in front of the fireplace, attempting to calm himself. "What was the piece doing behind a painting to begin with?"

"I had it placed there," Augustine nonchalantly responded.

Hunter froze abruptly in his pace and turned to watch his father. The man's black eyes—the only similarity Hunter had with his father—shined. "You what?"

"When I heard of that girl, Camilla, I figured she could be part of the Whittle coven. You know how I've always suspected them to have the witch's piece. It seemed I was right. If she has taken it, then the witches have two out of the three pieces. And I don't see that coven using it for themselves."

Hunter attempted to suppress his irritation. "And had someone else taken it?"

Augustine shrugged, his short black locks, so similar to those of Hunter's brother and sister, and so unlike his slicked back golden brown, bounced lightly. "I had a spell placed on the binding, letting me know when it was taken. I then sent your brother to check on it and got a breakdown of everyone that was in the room at the moment. The witch has it."

"And what makes you think the witches have the other piece now? What if she took it as a precaution?"

Augustine finally seemed to be considering the situation. "Could be. But I doubt it. The binding had been disturbed before when Camilla was over, and the piece was left alone. I'm presuming she didn't know what it was before, which also tells me they likely just found their piece."

Hunter stood rigid as he considered his father. Augustine stood from his chair and walked up to his son—Hunter shared his father's height as well, barely taller than the man at almost four inches past six feet—and clapped a hand to his son's shoulder. "We almost have them all, son."

Hunter thought of his father's ludicrous plan, which had somehow worked wonderfully if he was correct about the Whittle's holding two out of the three pieces. They still had no concrete proof that the witches had a second piece. But, working on the theory that they did, that only left Hunter the challenge of finding the human piece.

Well, not a challenge at all. He already had his predictions on where the final piece was. The witches' piece was the only one they were truly having problems with. If this Camilla girl had the witches' piece as well, he would be closer to having the whole key.

At the back of his mind, he wondered how it was possible that all three pieces ended up in the same country, better yet the same town. Finding the key was just becoming all the easier for him.

Hunter finally relaxed his posture, turning to look at the

flames raging in the fireplace and allowing his father's hand to remain on his shoulder. "Well, I guess it is time to get the human piece then."

Augustine laughed. "Indeed it is."

Hunter found out about the missing piece early in the morning, and by late afternoon, he'd shadowed to the church at the end of town with Loki, his father's most trusted guard.

Researching the human family that had been given the final piece of the key and finding that they had somehow ended up back in the same town as the Delvaux's, Hunter couldn't find better luck.

Hunter looked to the silent man and gave a singular nod, then allowed the shadows to engulf his form and transport him into the church. Surprisingly, they found no safety measures to keep demons out. Luck truly was on his side.

Hunter and Loki immediately spread out, taking opposite ends of the church as they searched with their eyes only. No need in touching anything less it were necessary.

The human piece was the one that went on top, the true *key* of the entire object. The witches' had been given the middle part because they were the intersection species between demons and humans. Like demons in their magical abilities, like humans in their empathy. Pathetic.

Hunter stood in the middle aisle, slowly eyeing all aspects of the interior, his gaze falling on the cross that sat in the center of the wall to the front of the church—where all churchgoers' eyes would fall.

In plain sight would be the best disguise.

The cross sat about triple the size of a human and was bejeweled with different forms of marble.

Plain sight indeed.

Hunter carefully racked his gaze down the cross until he landed on a piece, right at the end of the left side of the enormous cross. At the end, yet still trapped from all sides. Brilliantly hidden, but the fire in him noticed the white flames dancing within the solitary piece.

Hunter smirked to himself as he shadowed himself into mid-air and ripped the piece from the cross. Shadowing back down, Hunter found Loki waiting for him.

Apparently the safety precautions he had been expecting when they shadowed into the building finally alerted. He tried to shadow out of the church but had no luck. This would require them to walk out. Not the best precaution. Humans should have tried better than that.

As the two demons took their first steps off of the dais, a priest walked out with a beautifully golden staff in hand. He seemed unafraid of the demons as he walked toward them, knocking the staff against the ground and reciting something Hunter was sure he didn't like the sound of.

As the ground began to quiver, he took no further chances in waiting and playing with the man. He attempted to shadow once more, finding their little precaution didn't inhibit the shadowing ability, it just didn't allow them to shadow *out* of the church. A mistake. A pathetic mistake at that.

Hunter felt the laugh trickle out of him as he landed before the priest, grabbing the human by the neck and lifting him off his feet. Hunter shook his head with delight. "Oh, you guys make it too easy."

He knew Loki had walked up behind him, awaiting his instruction. Hunter looked to the staff the man still gripped, though he was unable to do anything with it, then to Loki. He handed the piece to his companion. "Take this and leave. I'll see you at the manor."

Loki gave a singular nod and walked out of the church.

Hunter watched the church doors close behind his companion just as the priest's oxygen gave out, and Hunter released his grip, allowing the man to fall to the ground and choke out for air.

Hunter enjoyed the moment, taking a slow stroll around the human before ripping the staff from the man's hands and kicking him so he was lying straight on his back. The priest's fear met Hunter's gaze just as the demon lifted the staff, top first, and pushed it into the human's chest, killing him instantly.

Hunter ripped the staff out just as the church doors opened.

<hr>

Maya hadn't spent too much time with her new sister, and she knew she had to make up for that. Camilla having an exam to study for and kicking everyone out of the house made that one-on-one sister time all the more possible as Maya and Vera decided to go out for a stroll.

They had been walking for some time, somehow making it to the other end of town, right where the holy grounds stood, a side of town Maya had never been a fan of. They'd talked about their teenage years and laughed about one ridiculous story after another. Maya had listened to Vera speak of Bishop and felt a small ache at the loss of never having a father. She could only imagine what missing a mother, a mother she knew of her entire life, felt like for Vera.

They were just passing the church when Vera's arm struck out, grabbing Maya's forearm and stopping them in their tracks. "Do you feel that?"

Maya looked to her older sister, then glanced around them, finding nothing amiss. "What?"

"I don't know," she said slowly, then turned to the entrance of the church. "It just feels like something is happening in the church. Like *something* is in there."

Maya looked to the church doors, which seemed undisturbed and perfectly fine to her, then back to Vera. Harry had said they would have other powers, maybe whatever Vera felt was an indication to that. "Let's check it out. This could be another power of yours speaking to you."

Vera looked her sister in the eyes, and Maya could see that she was thankful Maya was going along with this. They walked to the double doors together and heard something on the other end. Maybe Vera had been right, or maybe it was a church and there just happened to be people within.

They each pulled a door open and were struck with shock as they witnessed a staff being pulled out of the priest's chest. The man with the staff shot his gaze up to meet theirs, and something in Maya told her instinctively that he was a demon.

A creature demon.

And Maya's bits had never been so loud as they were at that moment.

His black eyes gleamed and his smirk grew as he witnessed their shocked expressions, and Maya had to push her thighs together as her bits began to sing a symphony for the man before her.

His golden hair was slicked back, and he was dressed impeccably. Not like Harry, this man seemed to dress up the casual look with a simple black sweater and trousers that covered slight boots. But equally impeccable.

Maya bit the inside of her cheek to bring herself back to the moment.

From her periphery, she saw Vera's hand shoot out, ready to throw the demon across the church. It seemed the man was ready for it, and he moved out of the way, almost like Harry's porting, but like the shadows were taking him instead.

He landed five feet before them.

"Well, well, well, witches, are we?" His tone teased the air, and Maya bit her nails into her palms as she squeezed her legs tighter together. She'd never been so affected by a *voice*. She'd never been so affected, period.

Though her body screamed for her to take him right in the

middle of the church, Maya pushed the ridiculous thoughts aside and allowed the same adrenaline feeling that had set the demon on fire when she'd received her powers to kick in.

The gleam in his eyes as he held the bloodied staff didn't look too good for them no matter how much her bits enjoyed it. And that realization cleared her mind up just as his gaze settled on her. It twinkled as he took her in, and Maya felt the uncomfortable feeling of dread rush her body. She hated being afraid.

Within their second's long stare, Maya's heart rate picked up but whether from fear or lust, she couldn't tell. All she knew was that her eyes likely twinkled back to him, and she *did not* like that.

Maya noticed Vera trying to throw him back once more, catching his attention. Afraid of what he might do, she shot her hand out, the fire bolting straight toward the demon.

Well, she'd aimed for the demon, but her power wasn't completely controlled yet. Especially not when her body was acting inappropriately.

The bolt of fire quivered past him.

Although it missed him, the fire caught his attention, and he glued his gaze to hers. No longer was there the cruel glint that he'd aimed at Vera just a half second prior, rather, intrigue blazed in his eyes.

Maya's attention was caught in the demon's, so she barely noticed when Vera called out for Harry, and he ported behind them, catching their arms and quickly porting them out.

Maya noticed a gleam return to the demon's eyes right before they left. A gleam that promised they'd meet again.

And Maya couldn't help the rush of excitement that spread throughout her. Her nails dug deeper into her palms—she would not allow *any* excitement for the demon.

## 10

Camilla was sitting in the formal dining room with Warren as they studied for their literature exam. Warren was surprisingly well versed in all of Dante's works, so having him by her side was making the entire studying process all the easier.

"You're like my sister. I bet you and Maya could spend hours debating Dante's works."

Warren looked up from his book and smiled at her. "I'll take you up on that. I need a way to bond with your sisters."

"You want to bond with my sisters?" Camilla couldn't suppress her shock.

"They're important to you, and you're important to me, I want them to like me. Oh, I'll need some pointers on Harry too. He seems like an important person to your family, considering he's always here, whoever he is."

Camilla felt her grin break out. "He's a close family friend, and he's always here because he lives here. Vera took our Mom's room when she moved here so Harry could take the spare."

Camilla watched Warren as he considered what she'd said. There was no jealousy, Harry was far too old for her, but there certainly was curiosity. Before he could get a word out, Camilla heard movement in the other room, and moments later, the family they had just been discussing hurriedly came into the room looking slightly panicked. They made an abrupt stop when they noticed Warren sitting beside her.

"Warren! Hey!" Maya called out just too enthusiastically.

"Hey." Warren stood and looked at Vera, sticking out his hand. "Hi, we haven't officially met. I'm Warren."

Vera shook herself out of her thoughts and shot out her hand, taking his in a strong grip. "Hi. Yes, I know. I've heard a lot about you. I'm Vera, the new sister." She laughed that small, embarrassed laugh that Camilla was coming to associate with her eldest sister.

Warren reached his hand out to Harry. "And the close family friend."

Harry smiled politely. "Harry. Pleased to meet you."

Camilla studied her sisters, noticing that they were both acting off, a little too normal. And Harry looked in a desperate need to spew out question after question.

Camilla stood, figuring this would be important and definitely not something Warren should hear, and turned to him. "Hey, I actually totally forgot we have this cousin thing we have to get ready for. Can I see you tomorrow? We can finish studying before the exam."

Warren looked to Camilla, then her family with suspicion rising in his eyes, before turning back to her and giving her a small smile. "Sure thing."

He packed his things and gave Camilla a chaste kiss before walking out of the dining room. Camilla waited until she heard him at the foyer, the door closing behind him, before turning to her family. "What the hell is going on?"

Maya went to take a seat at the formal dining table. Considering they never used this room except for special events, Camilla enjoyed using it to study in. Her family settled in.

"Today we found out that not all demons look like monsters from scary stories," Maya sang to her, a wicked gleam in her eyes that didn't entirely hide her worry. When Maya sang to her it meant one of two things: she was thoroughly enjoying herself, or she was properly concerned and didn't want to show it. Having grown up with her, Camilla recognized this as the latter.

Camilla stared at her sister for a few moments before accepting she had no idea what Maya was talking about. "What?"

"Creature demons," Vera answered, then continued to recount the entire story of the run in with this particular demon. Harry seemed to be learning of the encounter for the first time as well, and the two of them sat there as Vera explained what this demon looked like. "He looked so normal. So much like any one of us. He was tall and had the perfect light caramel skin and the slicked back hair, well dressed. Then he looked up at us and he had black eyes, like completely black, but they glinted in the cruelest way as he watched us watch *him* pull the staff out of the priest's chest. But still, he looked normal."

"He looked human? Attractive?" Camilla tried to wrap her head around the story. The details indicated a man they would normally find attractive, but that couldn't be possible.

"*Yes!*" Maya enthusiastically emphasized as Vera responded with a more hesitant "Yup."

Camilla was having a difficult time accepting this. "Really?"

"Camilla, when I tell you my bits chose a rather inappropriate moment to start speaking again, I am not teasing." Maya looked her sister in the eye.

Now Camilla was convinced it couldn't be a demon. "A demon though? Are you sure he was a demon?"

"He was a demon. I don't know how to explain it, but when we stood before him, you could just tell. It was like my instincts were telling me," Maya responded.

Vera nodded her agreement. "That *and* I think I've realized a new power, a sensing power, I guess. I hadn't realized it with the other demons we had seen, but I get this feeling every time we're around one. It's kind of like my body is telling me there's an enemy around. I sensed him when we were walking past the church, even though Maya didn't."

"Another rare power." Harry looked to Vera over slowly. "It's a low-level light power, but a very rare one. Useful, though, as you can imagine."

Camilla watched the interaction, thought about the benefits of this new power, but still, she could not get past the attractive part for some reason. "Maybe he was using a transfiguration power to make himself look good? Like a distraction."

Harry smiled weakly at her. "Demons can be attractive, Camilla. I told you before, they are just like any other creature."

"I know." Camilla felt the acceptance settle as she slumped back. "But it's so much easier to think of them as these monsters from the stories that we defeat."

"I think we need to focus on the bigger problem here." Vera changed the topic. "He killed the priest, which makes me believe they got the last piece of the key. Which also makes me question whether Warren had the human piece or demon one."

Camilla's head snapped over at the comment. "Excuse me?"

"I think Harry's original assumption was correct. The human piece was with a holy family, and this demon killed them to get to it. Which leads me to believe that the piece from Warren's room was the demon piece," Vera explained, then quickly added, "I think our original theory about the piece was right though. Demons probably hid it there and go to check on it every now and then, rather than the humans we assumed before."

"And you're presuming they had a check in and found it missing?" Harry asked the eldest Whittle.

Vera shrugged. "It would explain why they went for the final piece. They figure having one piece, whether it's the demon piece or human, is better than anyone else having all three."

"And let's face it," Maya threw in, "the human piece would have been the easiest to retrieve."

"I would presume they now think two of the three pieces are together, or they hope so, but that just means they will be putting in the effort to find the last one. And if after today that demon believes it's with us, they'll likely be after us," Vera continued.

Camilla stared at her sister. She really did think aloud.

"With the final piece in their hands, they'll have everything required to put the key back together," she finished her thoughts.

Camilla couldn't help the urgency in her tone. "We need to take their piece. Vera or I can hide that final one. They'll all be under witches' hands, but they'd be safe."

Maya shook her head. "What we need is to find out who that demon was. All creature demons can't be terrible. Maybe he was just angry that his piece was stolen, and he went for the human one just so he could have one."

There goes Maya, devil's advocate.

Harry cut Camilla off from arguing. "That's true. He could just be angry about getting his piece stolen. Albeit not an excuse for killing a man, but still."

"You didn't recognize him, Mr. Mentor Man?" Maya's lips quirked up.

Camilla bit the inside of her cheek to keep from smiling at Harry's irritation.

"Afraid not, but there are plenty of them. Even if he were a part of a major family, which I would assume, given he likely had the demon piece, I don't know what most of them look like."

"Okay." Vera slowly nodded her head. "So what's the plan? How do we find out who he is?"

"We need to attract him out," Harry thought.

"So use Maya," Vera simply stated.

Everyone's brows quirked at that remark.

"Maya's power. He seemed intrigued, as we'd assumed, when she used it. If he sees her by herself, he'd be more likely to approach."

Harry nodded. "We could give him more too. Let him believe he may be getting another piece of the key." Camilla noticed Maya about to argue at the same moment her mouth opened. Harry cut them off. "We won't actually do it."

Vera nodded as she thought aloud. "Maya could walk through town holding 'the piece' wrapped in fabric so he doesn't actually realize it's not the piece. Let it be seen that she has it tightly in her hold. I'd assume that demon would have stuck around town in search of the other two pieces. Then she could walk into the woods and wait for him to come after her. I think if we can make it look like she is alone, he'll definitely go for it. Get the witches' power and the piece. Think about it, even if he doesn't fall for the piece, he could still want her power."

Maya narrowed her gaze at them, but didn't argue the plan.

Camilla turned to her sister. "What do you think?"

Maya stared at the group another moment before turning to look at her. "I think he's smart. There was a glint of calculation in his gaze." She took a moment's thought. "But I also think he's greedy. It's likely he'll come if he gets the piece and an unmastered witch with a power he could thrive with."

Camilla couldn't help but believe Maya and turned back to the others. "How do we help?"

"We'll be there too, hidden behind the trees, ready to help. We just have to make sure he doesn't know we're there."

"He comes, we find out who he is and if we can trust having him keep the piece, then port out," Maya concluded. "And if we decide we don't want him anywhere near the pieces?"

"We'll come to that when the decision comes," Harry

answered. "But likely, if we got him once, we could get him again, and that time, we'll be ready to stop him."

Maya quirked her brow. Camilla knew from the expression alone that Maya thought the second part too simple, but hopefully they didn't have to get there.

Harry looked to Maya and gave a final decision. "You need to train your powers more if you're going to be 'alone' with this demon."

It was decided then: Maya would meet with the demon.

---

Maya didn't love the plan, but she couldn't argue with its merit. And more than anything, she couldn't argue with that piece of her heart that asked whether this demon may have had something to do with her mother's death.

That demon wore the cruel smirk Vera had mentioned, but more prominent was the spark in his eyes. Maya knew he would meet her in the woods; he would not allow another to get to her. And she hated herself for the thrill that shot threw her every time she thought about it.

She had to think about this rationally. He'd killed a priest and smiled about it. Somehow, that didn't bother her body. What *did* get her to concentrate though was the fact that he may be a lead closer to finding out what happened to her mother.

Maya spent a couple of days training her powers, each time thinking about that demon in the church and allowing his distracting visions to help in perfecting her power until it came as naturally to her as walking. She could not afford to be distracted by her desire for him in such a dangerous situation.

With her power trained, she just had to put her bits in check —no more thinking about dropping to her knees before the man with the wicked smirk and gleaming black eyes.

11

———

Maya walked away from the patio table of the cafe in the middle of town, leaving Harry, Camilla, and Vera behind. They were meant to wait about fifteen minutes, then port out to the area of the woods they had chosen to rendezvous, a precaution lest anyone were watching.

Maya was alone, at least to anyone's watchful eyes.

She carried a wrapped piece of fabric long enough to be the witch's piece in her hands, gripping it with both hands. The more she told herself it was the real piece, the more real the grip would seem. Though thinking about it, why would she be stupid enough to walk around town holding it? Hopefully the demon would just think her brainless.

Maya estimated it would take her about half an hour to walk to the area in the woods—not too close to civilization where they'd be heard if something happened, but not too far out that she'd get ambushed before she stopped in front of her family—giving her family enough time to get there and situate themselves perfectly hidden.

Maya stepped into the woods about twenty minutes after leaving the cafe, the crunch beneath her feet as she walked through the dried leaves causing her heart to race. And as much as Maya wished to say it was because she was nervous, she knew it was a lie. She *was* nervous, but that had nothing to do with the shot of anticipation that sent her heart racing and her legs squeezing together.

She would see *that* demon soon.

She knew it would be him.

And she hated herself for being excited about that. Hated her body for buzzing at the thought of him. Hated herself for not being able to control it, to push it down.

But she couldn't help it. She wanted him. Her *body* wanted him. But that would not be happening, and luckily for her, Camilla's power only worked on thoughts when she touched, so Maya made sure to conceal any dirty fantasies surrounding the demon when her sister was around. This was her secret to bare alone.

And how she knew it would be *him* to show up, that glint in his eyes said it all. He wanted the piece, but he also wanted to find out more about her—a witch with a rare high-level dark power.

She'd been able to stave off thoughts of him with the possibility that he could have had a part in her mother's death. But that was merely a possibility. And possibilities were having no say in her very real thoughts at the moment.

The wind rustled around Maya as she finally stepped into the small clearing in the woods, and stopped in the middle of it. She didn't turn her head, but she was sure her family was around. They wouldn't leave her vulnerable to him. Camilla especially.

Glued to her spot, Maya closed her eyes and breathed in the autumn air, the fabric still gripped between both hands. She took those moments of solitude to appreciate the season and control her body.

She had just gotten herself under control when a rock lightly grazed her foot, a signal from Vera that a demon was around. Maya didn't sense anything, which meant Vera was using that demon-sensing power of hers.

She squeezed her hands tighter, hating that her body jumped at the mild mention that she may be around the demon again. This was absolutely ridiculous. She'd seen the man once for all of two minutes. Her body was in a desperate need for attention, and her bits had found the most inopportune time to remind her.

The rock hit her other leg at the same moment she felt her body react to the change in scent in the clearing, a strong mix of sandalwood, bergamot, and musk. He was here.

Her eyes remained closed as she forced her body to relax. And finally, oh so slowly, she opened her eyes. He was behind her, but she would play the role—she wasn't worried.

She slowly tilted her head to the side, her periphery picking him up. He was just as relaxed as she was forcing herself to be, except she was sure he wasn't faking it.

Maya had no plans of moving. She would not be afraid to have her back to him, though she felt her heart rate pick up, both from lust and the danger she knew she was likely in, being so nonchalant around a demon who had pierced a staff through a priest's heart.

Eventually, the demon moved, walking around Maya and coming to stop before her, a mere five feet away. Pressed trousers covering boots, and the fitted dress shirt beautifully accentuated his features. He was dressed in all black, like she was, but somehow that made the black of his eyes pop. Or maybe it was the gleam of wickedness that lived beneath those depths.

Maya looked him in the eyes, then allowed her gaze to slowly move over him, from the tips of his toes to the very top of his brown, silken head before meeting his eyes once more.

She squeezed her legs together in what she hoped was an imperceptible movement.

The gleam in his eyes moved to cover the rest of his features as he watched her. "Like what you see?"

"Depends," Maya answered, the drag of her tone belying confidence. "What is it I see?"

He laughed, and Maya felt liquid pool around her center at the sound. Heavenly. Quite the irony of her life. "Even a new witch like yourself should be able to figure out I'm a demon."

"Oh, I figured that out. I just haven't figured out what kind." Her tone mimicked true intrigue. "What monster do you most resemble?"

He smirked at her. "The most frightening monster of all." And the smile that accompanied it was frightening. "Humans."

Maya contemplated the answer. He was right. He looked human just as she looked human. And Maya also realized how accurate it sounded, that the most frightening creature out there happened to be the least powerful one, because she agreed with him, humans were the most frightening.

Maya looked him over. "What's your name?"

The question seemed to shock the demon, but he recovered quickly. "Getting to know each other, are we?"

Maya didn't respond, merely waited for his answer.

His eyes dipped to take her in, and Maya was more thankful than ever that she had worn a bra that day, her nipples peaked at his attention. She internally grumbled, ready to have a serious talk with her *bits* when she got home.

"Hunter." His gaze traveled back up, slowly, to meet Maya's. "Do I get to learn yours?"

She gave him the tiniest smirk. "Maya."

"Maya," he tested the name on his tongue, and Maya felt her entire body burn, glad more than ever for the chill of the autumn air and the layers she wore. Thigh high boots covering tight fitted jeans, a sweater and leather jacket on top. "Maya,

Maya, Maya," he played with the name on his tongue, each time slower and more seductive. "Tell me, Maya, how did a witch like yourself get a high-level demon power?"

Maya shrugged coolly. "It's a dark power, not a demon one."

"That may be true, but only demons have had it for millennia."

Maya felt her tongue move to lick her lips and lightly bite down on the bottom one, feigning indifference, and watched as his gaze shot directly to her lips. She hadn't realized how sexually it would be perceived until she noticed the liquid desire pool those black depths he called eyes. It was fascinating, all of the emotion that still showed behind the emptiness. He didn't have pupils to dilate, given they were hidden in the black, but there was a light that told her his emotions.

"You said it yourself, I'm a new witch. There's much I don't know." Maya feigned ignorance to the desire in his eyes, and the one racketing her body, and continued on with the conversation as if she were bored.

She watched his eyes take her in, then close as he breathed in a deep inhale. He opened his eyes, and Maya was sure she saw barely restrained desire.

He ignored it, his smirk turning cruel. "You sure Mommy dearest doesn't have something to tell you?"

Maya felt the desire wash away as her features darkened. Nice of him to remind her that he could have had a part of what happened to Loretta just as her body was beginning to boil for him. "You sure you're not just jealous that a witch has a rare high-level dark power?"

He gave a deliciously dark laugh, and the desire bloomed even deeper within her. She felt her panties soak completely through and her nipples peak painfully out, desperate to be suckled. Apparently her mind and her body would be two entirely different entities at the moment.

"Oh, sweetheart." The words were liquid as he breathed in a large inhale of air.

Maya held strong to her composure at the surprise that came with the ring of fire surrounding them. She had not done that. She didn't move but allowed her gaze to slide over the flames that circled them, then narrowed on Hunter. He stared back, features flat, but eyes shining. He was enjoying this, a little too much for Maya's likings.

*She* was enjoying this a little too much for her likings.

The fire dissipated around them, and he began to move, taking slow strides around her, circling her as if she were prey until he stood behind her. Maya didn't move a muscle, knowing he wouldn't sense fear because she couldn't bring herself to feel it. As much as she didn't want to feel it, Maya was excited. She gripped the fabric in her hands tighter, in desperate acknowledgement of exactly where he stood behind her.

He moved up behind her so that his body was only inches away from being pressed against her and leaned into her ear. "I'm not your enemy, sweetheart. Now," he said, voice gruff. "Give me what I want."

Maya couldn't help it, she allowed her head to fall back slightly so the hairs at the top of her head grazed his jaw, then tilted her head to the side so she could get a look at him. She knew he read the desire in her eyes, but she ignored that. "What do you want?"

She couldn't help the suggestive undertones of her question, and she knew he picked up on it as he licked his lips, his gaze glued to her lips before he stepped back and strolled around her once more. Maya's eyes followed him until he was standing in front of her again, this time rather than five feet, there was a little over five inches between them.

He leaned in so his face was maybe an inch from hers. "You know what I want."

And she'd happily give him her body because it was clear he wanted that.

No. No, Maya. You most certainly would not.

Just as the words left his lips, his hand reached for the fabric between her hands. She released it and watched his hand hold an unrolled piece of fabric, nothing within. He took a step back, looking over it before his eyes adjusted to Maya.

Before Hunter could make a move for her, a rock flew through the air and hit him hard against the side of the head. Unsuspecting as he was, the hit dropped him to the ground, blood already oozing from the point of contact. As his gaze shot up to find what had hit him, he met Maya's smirk as her family circled around her and Harry prepared to port them out. Maya gave Hunter a grin to match any of his and a wink goodbye.

Just before porting out, she saw the raw burst in his eyes as he kneeled before her, his fists whitening and trousers tightening. Fuck, she tightened her eyes closed.

---

Harry ported them back to the living room in their house. Vera couldn't help but think over how convincing Maya had been in that clearing and how glad she was that Maya had played the role rather than any one of them. She truly didn't believe either herself or Camilla would have been able to hold so stoically in the situation Hunter had put Maya in.

Vera pushed herself out of her thoughts and focused on her family. No one spoke, but Vera could not help her attention from drifting to her sister.

Eventually, Maya broke. "What!"

"Nothing," Vera answered quickly.

"Vera?" Maya sounded more annoyed than curious.

Vera looked away, catching her breath, then back to her sister. She couldn't meet Maya's eyes. "You were really convincing." Vera forced herself to look Maya in the eyes as she spoke. "If I hadn't known you, I would've assumed you were both demons."

Vera stood, holding her breath for Maya's reaction. She did not expect a smile. A convincingly wicked smile.

"Thank you." Maya eyed her mischievously.

"You're not offended?" Vera couldn't help the disbelief from screeching out of her.

Maya shrugged. "That's pretty much how I act most of the time. It wasn't very difficult. I'm sure you've noticed I'm not the warm and inviting Whittle." Maya laughed at Vera's reaction. "You don't have to worry about offending me. It's not that easy."

In the two weeks she had been living with them, Vera had gotten accustomed to Maya's bluntness, but it still took her by surprise sometimes. Vera gave a hesitant, closed-lipped smile. "Got it."

Harry clapped his hands together, then began to rub them like he was thinking. "Upstairs. We need to figure out how to get that final piece."

"Why? Who was he?" Maya asked.

"Hunter Delvaux. Heir of the Delvaux line, and quite the influential family. Their family is powerful, though you usually just hear of the father and son."

"You could tell that much from just a first name?" Camilla questioned.

He shook his head. "I could tell all that from a first name and primary power. Hunter Delvaux having such rare magic gives that family more power than most demons get."

No one argued, but Vera spoke up, "So you think it best we get the piece away from him?"

"I don't want to consider what they would do with it," Harry simply stated as he began to walk up the stairs.

Maya hauled herself off the couch and followed behind him. "You think the book will have a solution?"

"I sure do hope so," he called out behind him as he made his way to the attic.

They spent the better half of the day looking through the book, taking turns to give their eyes a rest. It was currently Vera's turn once more.

She sat with her back to the wall, the book propped in her lap. Harry sat beside her, his leg pressed against hers, a light distraction.

Maya lay flat on the rug in the middle of the attic, her hands resting on her stomach as she tried to take a nap, or at least rest her eyes. Camilla sat at the other end of the room, textbook in her lap. Though Vera was almost certain Camilla wasn't paying attention to the textbook, rather, staring at it as she got lost in her thoughts.

It had been a relatively quiet day since they'd gotten back from the woods earlier that morning. It had given them a chance to both stress about the possibilities regarding the final piece and rest, the juxtapositions of their situation not lost on them. That is, until Camilla's phone chimed, and Vera glanced up to find Camilla's features darken as she sat up ramrod straight. "Guys." Her voice quivered.

Vera's heart constricted and she immediately pushed the book aside, moving with Harry to Camilla's side. Maya remained lying in her spot, eyes still closed, as she lightly asked, "Yes?"

Vera and Harry looked over Camilla's screen. It was a message from her school.

*Students' Preschool Program have been taken hostage. Authorities are at work to negotiate for the children's safe return. Unable to get any leeway, authorities say the hostage taker will only release the children if he is given his key. No more information has been learned about the details of said key.*

"Oh dear," Harry breathed out.

Vera noticed Maya pop an eye open and look them over,

sitting up immediately when she noticed their reactions. "What now?"

"The preschool for students and faculty with children at my school is being held hostage. Apparently, the only way to release them is to hand over a key," Camilla spoke, a numbness Vera had never heard dripping from her voice.

"You don't think this has anything to do with…" Vera didn't want to voice it.

"Hunter?" Maya sighed as she stood up. "Unfortunately, I think it has everything to do with him. What better way for an uncaring creature to get the attention of witches than take children hostage?"

Vera breathed in, but didn't speak.

"We need to check it out. If it's not Hunter, we'll just port out," Maya continued.

"What? No! We have to help them," Camilla exclaimed, a desperate fire raging in her eyes.

Harry shook his head. "Maya's right. If it's not magically based, we should not get involved. We need to stay out of human problems."

Camilla looked disbelieving. "So we leave the kids to die?"

Harry looked unperturbed to the youngest Whittle. "Camilla, I understand this is difficult, but human matters are for humans to address. We address magical problems only. It's important to remember this, even if we don't like it."

Camilla looked all three of them over stubbornly. "Well, then I hope it *is* Hunter."

Maya rolled her eyes as they all joined hands.

Harry landed them just outside the crowd forming in front of the school's preschool program building. They were hidden in a small alley between two buildings so no one would notice their appearance. The police, ambulance, and news were already on the scene as they waited for the hostage negotiators to do their jobs. Though if it was Hunter, Vera doubted the negotiators would get a connection with the hostage-taker.

Harry, Camilla, and Maya all turned their gazes on Vera. Harry placed a hand to her shoulder. "Do you feel anything?"

Vera looked around the crowds, having a hard time concentrating with all the commotion taking place at the moment. She closed her eyes and breathed in the chill of the air. Her breaths calmed and she tried to focus on the inhabitants of the building. She felt nothing for a moment, then the tingling traveled from the base of her fingertips to the back of her neck and she opened her eyes, gaze locked to the preschool. "Definitely a demon."

## 12

Harry ported them to the hallway right outside where he sensed the children were. The doors were swung wide open, revealing the gym with all the children within. Maya scanned the room. The children were separated, a ring of fire cast around each one, most of them having already peed their pants.

The children were spread throughout the gym, engulfing most of the space, and in the center, lounging in a foldable chair, was Hunter Delvaux.

He looked as if he didn't have a care in the world, legs spread wide as he sat at the tip of the chair, lounging all the way back. In one hand, he held a dagger, playing with it as it twisted around his adept fingers, while his other hand lay carelessly over his thigh.

Maya's bits took notice, but too much of her focus was on the children that she couldn't find an ounce of desire to fill her.

As the four of them entered the gym, Hunter's gaze slowly picked up, and a smile lingered around the edges of that mouth. His hand never broke its game with the dagger as he spoke up languidly, "Look, children. Our friends have joined the party."

"What are you doing?" Camilla demanded as she stepped forward, breaking from the rest of them.

The dagger continued to spin in his hand. He moved it so effortlessly, Maya couldn't help but wonder about those fingers. "Witches are so simple." He broke Maya out before her mind could wander. "You all have bleeding hearts."

"Caring for others isn't a bad thing!" Camilla bared her teeth.

"Au contraire," Hunter teased. "If you didn't care for others, none of us," he pointed at himself, them, and the children with the dagger, "would be in this situation. You've caused quite the predicament."

"Let the children go!" Vera chimed in. "They have nothing to do with this."

Hunter shrugged. "Simple casualties. Of course," his gaze settled on the four of them, "you could make this all go away. Simply give me your two pieces."

Maya forced her eyebrows to furrow. "Two? We only have one. We thought you had the other two."

Hunter's gaze flew to her, taking her in before tilting his head and narrowing his eyes at her. "Really?"

Maya moved her body so she was fully facing him and crossed her arms before her chest, eyes narrowing back. "You took the human piece, and there's one with the demons. We assumed you had that one." She dropped both her features and her tone as if she were speaking to a child. "Or are we having trouble locating the one within our own species?"

Hunter grinned at her attempt to goad him, lazily coming to his feet. He dropped the dagger between his belt and trousers at his back as he took his full height, looking down at them—at her—as he assessed her.

Maya felt her bits wake up with those hooded eyes. Even from across the gym, he exerted dominance. She pushed her dirty thoughts aside, having no time for fantasies with dozens of children in trouble.

"Okay," he sneered. "Let's say I believe you. Give me the witches' piece."

"Or what?" Vera shot out the words.

His gaze moved lazily to meet Vera's as his sneer turned to a cruel grin. "Or there will be a lot of parents burying their little ones."

"You wouldn't kill kids," Vera stated matter-of-factly.

Hunter's eyebrows shot up with amusement. "Shall we test that hypothesis?"

As the final word left his mouth, he brought the fire surrounding each child closer. Maya's heart rate picked up, more thankful than ever that she held the same power. She tried to relax, then moved her power, stopping the flames that were licking closer to the kids.

At the abrupt fault, Hunter flicked his eyes to hers and smirked. "I was wondering when that power of ours would make an appearance."

Maya didn't have time to respond, or even fully process his statement, before she felt his magic overpower hers and continue to bring the flames closer to each of the kids.

When the flames came close to touching the kids, Camilla exclaimed, "Stop! We'll give it to you, just stop!"

Maya internally shook her head, glad she had lied about having the second piece. Of course Camilla would give up the pieces that could unleash true evil into the world to save a couple dozen kids. She was so empathetic; it almost annoyed Maya.

Hunter looked amused as he took in her reaction before she could hide it, then turned to Camilla with a smile, the flames pausing in their movement. "I thought we'd see eye to eye. Now, you have ten minutes to get it to me before this entire building is set alight."

He fell back onto the chair and closed his eyes as he rested his head back. Maya watched Camilla turn to Harry and the two of them port out. She had hidden the demons' piece which meant they could only bring back the witches' piece, playing into the story that that was the one they had.

With the two gone, Maya moved her gaze to her older sister —still kind of odd thinking she had an *older* sister—and caught her attention. With her fire control and Vera's levitation, they should be able to help these kids.

Maya motioned for her sister to try to use her power to move the kids up and away from breathing in the smoke. Vera took a moment to understand, then looked back to find Hunter resting away.

Maya watched Vera focus her attention on each child then try to lift them. Vera had told Maya that she looks for a connection, a tether, and can easily lift with that, but the more she does it, the more energy it takes. The kids all floated a few inches off the ground, when Maya decided to try to counter Hunter and dispel some of the fire. She knew she wouldn't be able to snuff the rings out completely, given he had a lifetime of experience to her two weeks.

That was her mistake.

With her concentration focused on dissipating some of the flames, Maya was slow to realize that Hunter had opened his eyes and was watching them. His booming laugh knocked some of Maya's concentration.

She should have realized that a lifetime of experience also meant he would know if something was affecting his power.

"Clever," he languidly commented through his laugh. As the girls turned their attention away from the children, the glee in his face expanded. "Now we're making this fun."

He ignored Vera as his gaze moved to Maya's and held. He chose one ring of fire and expanded it to engulf the child within. The boy's screams rang throughout the gym, breaking both Maya and Vera from their concentration so that Vera dropped each child from the light hold she had on them and Maya broke away from dispelling the flames.

Hunter dropped his magic around the boy so he was no longer on fire. "Your move."

The girls focused on the child who seemed to have no burns.

"You're sick!" Vera spit out, then continued to throw some choice words at the demon.

Maya ignored her sister and focused on the child. He was completely unhurt. And she remembered that fire control wasn't just making flames occur and grow, but also controlling whether the flames hurt. And like a crash, Maya realized Hunter had no intentions of hurting the child, any of them. It was likely the shock of being on fire that sent that boy into hysterics.

Maya shot her gaze to the demon lounging in the chair, his attention focused on her as if trying to read what she was thinking. She couldn't help but wonder what his true intentions were. He was obviously not trying to hurt these kids, just using them to get what he wanted. Yet he didn't actually care if he did have to hurt one.

But he hadn't planned on it.

It seemed that realization woke her bits up as they took in his lazy posture on the chair, legs spread open as if begging for her to kneel before him and have a taste. Maya tried to hide the hitch of her breath as she pictured it. Just the two of them in a room that blazed around them as she tasted him.

"Keep looking at me like that, *Maya*, and I might come in my pants right here," Hunter spoke up as his gaze traveled her face.

He was trying to goad her. It didn't work, but it seemed to peak Vera's attention as she threw out another round of disgust in her choice of words. Luckily, she did not turn to see in what *way* Maya was looking at him.

The words didn't work in provoking Maya, but they had her thighs tightening to the point of no avail. His eyes slit in heady desire as he looked her over, taking in a deep breath like it was the day after a spring rain and everything smelled divine.

"As Vera said, you're sick." There was no conviction in her voice as she tried to push out the desire.

"Baby, you have no idea." His eyes roamed over her body, then he laid his head back down and smiled to himself.

Maya felt her core tighten, her lust grow. Fuck, the thought of what those fingers could do, how that smile would feel between her thighs. *She* was ready to come right there.

Hunter's smile grew as he took another breath, his trousers beginning to tighten as he moved his hands to cover himself. Now this was an inopportune time for *both* of their bits to talk to them.

Luckily, she was broken out of her reverie when Camilla and Harry ported back to the gym to find a similar scene to the one they had left only a few minutes prior. Except Vera was still throwing her choice words in Hunter's direction, completely oblivious to Maya two paces behind her. She stopped when the others arrived.

Camilla walked straight up to Hunter, who'd opened his eyes when they'd ported in, and thrust the piece at him. "Now release them!"

Hunter smirked at the raging witch before him. He stood and grabbed the piece from her. "I'll send my brother to search for the final piece. Let's hope you didn't lie to me." He finished with a final look over Maya, a gleam of wicked delight in those black depths, before he winked at her and shadowed out of the room, releasing his magic around the children as he left.

With Hunter gone, everyone relaxed, allowing their bodies to drop from their ramrod positions. After a moment to catch their breaths, the girls got the children to gather up so that Harry could wipe all of their memories at once.

With Harry's attention on the children, Vera watched Maya, analyzing her. Maya felt the annoying tingle she got every time

Vera looked at her with something to say and didn't outright say it. "Yes?"

Vera's gaze narrowed on her. "Why does he only flirt with you?"

Maya quirked a brow at her older sister. "Jealous?"

"No," Vera immediately responded, her features twisting at the thought. "Just, odd that he doesn't flirt with anyone else."

"More like a blessing," Camilla cut in. "Plus, it's probably because of the shared power."

Yes, Maya's possessive side cooed, a blessing that she had his attentions all to herself. And oh, what she'd like to do with that attention.

13

Camilla had it figured out that being at Warren's apartment was calming to her. Mostly because they didn't have cable for their TV, so she didn't have to see constant news reports following the mystery of the children that were held hostage then let go with no memory. And because it meant she forgot about the magical world she had been thrust into, one that may be the reason her mother was dead. Things she could not do at home.

She was lying on Warren's bed, waiting for him to get out of the shower and get dressed so they could head to class, and couldn't help but think about how desperately she wanted to talk to her mom about everything going on. She had told Loretta everything before, even more than she ever told Maya, and Maya pretty much knew everything about her. Vera was a part of that group now too.

It surprised Camilla how easily she connected to Vera and the bond that they had already tied, the fact that she saw similarities with Vera that she would never share with Maya. But she still wanted her mom to talk to. About the witchiness that was her life, but also about the Warrenness of her life.

As the thought of talking to her mom about Warren came to mind, he walked into the room, closing the door behind him. He stood before her in only a towel, droplets still trickling down his chest as he walked over to his dresser and took out a pair of briefs.

Camilla's gaze took in every movement as he slipped them on under the towel then turned to face her, removing the towel altogether. With only the briefs covering the indentation of his bits, Camilla couldn't help as her eyes dropped to take him in. Or the desperate cry her bits made for him.

She felt herself flush a bright red, swiftly diverting her gaze to the bedsheets and internally cursing Maya for bringing so much attention to bits and their demand to be listened to.

She saw the cheeky grin he wore as he walked over to his closet and had to press her legs together ever so slightly.

"So." She toyed with the bedsheet as she tried to move the conversation—and her thoughts—away from his body. "My family has this annual tradition of a Halloween dinner. It's basically like Christmas dinner, but on Halloween."

And as she said this to him, Camilla realized why her mother celebrated it so extravagantly—it was a witch's holiday after all. Well, she presumed it was every creature's holiday, demons especially. She shook her head from that thought and focused once more on Warren.

He stepped out of his closet, buttoning his jeans—which immediately got Camilla's attention—and said, "That sounds pretty cool."

Camilla's gaze shot up to meet his and noticed the widening grin and mischievous glimmer in his eyes. He walked back into his closet, and Camilla tried desperately to bury herself into his bed, never to be seen again. How Maya had so blatantly *desired* after Hunter in the clearing *in front* of them she would never be able to understand. Maybe it was easier to control when you were faking it like how actors controlled their feelings on camera.

Must be.

She cleared her throat. "Yeah, it is. Anyway," she pulled herself up to sit, "I was wondering if you wanted to come? It's kind of an important tradition in my family, and I'd love to have you there."

He walked out of the closet, fully dressed, and stalked toward her. He bent, placing both hands on either side of her legs. "If you want me there, I'm there." He kissed her wide grin and pulled her from the bed so they could head to class.

Three hours later, and they were finished with their class and sitting out at the table that Warren loved under the tree with two of his flatmates, Lynus and Dane. The three guys were talking about an experiment they had done in chemistry class the three of them shared, and Camilla sat and listened. When it came to Warren and his flatmates, it was usually more entertaining to just sit back and watch them, especially when they got competitive about experiments.

While watching the boys argue about who was right during the experiment, Camilla noticed something over Dane's shoulder. More like somethings. Hunter Delvaux walked into the Theology building with two lackeys following to either side.

Camilla stiffened as she watched them move, jaws set, into the building. Camilla breathed out a sigh of relief that he hadn't noticed her sitting thirty yards out.

Without raising alarm to the guys at her table, Camilla pulled out her phone and sent a quick text to her sisters to meet her at the quad. Then she turned back to the boys, though most of her attention was now locked on the doors leading to the Theology building rather than the quarreling guys.

It was about a half hour before Maya and Vera found her sitting at the table. Camilla left the boys to continue the same argument they'd been having for at least forty-five minutes and joined her sisters as they walked a couple of yards away from the table.

Huddled together, Camilla told them what, or more importantly who, she had seen walk into the building and not walk back out yet. She realized he may have left some other way, but couldn't be sure why he would be at the school to begin with.

Maya and Vera nodded along, eyebrows furrowing as they listened. When she came to an end, Vera spoke up, "You should go back to Warren. You don't want to be running off every time something happens. We can check this out."

Camilla felt a small bit of tension dissipate at her sister's thoughtful words, but shook her head. "No, I should help."

Maya shook her head. "Vera's right. If you keep running off like that, there won't be a relationship, and your bits will be left unsatisfied, dear sister. We'll check it out."

With a look to each of them, Camilla relented and walked back to Warren as her sisters began to head toward the Theology building. As she went to sit back down, Warren began to stand. "Hey, sorry babe. I just got a text from my dad. I have to go."

Camilla paused short and felt herself perk up. "That's actually fine. I'll just catch up with my sisters." She knew she spoke a little too excitedly about going back to her sisters, but she couldn't help it, she wanted to help them.

They said their goodbyes to Lynus and Dane and walked off hand in hand to the spot Camilla had just stood with her sisters. He took her face between his hands and gave her a slow kiss that Camilla melted into, wanting more—in a much more private setting—immediately.

He pulled away as if he knew what she was thinking and winked before walking away. Camilla controlled her blush then turned and jogged up to her sisters who were almost at the Theology doors. Catching up within moments, she grabbed each sister by an arm and linked the three together. "Guess who?"

Maya didn't seem impressed. "Warren not exciting your bits any longer? Rather fight off demons?"

Camilla rolled her eyes. "No. This time he had to go, so either way, I get to join you guys."

W alking into the building, Vera immediately felt the tingling start at her fingers and rush to her neck. It was slightly more prominent, which she assumed meant more than one demon, given the two other times she'd consciously sensed a demon, it had only been Hunter.

The demons were definitely still there, even if Hunter wasn't. Vera followed her power, understanding that when the tingling grew stronger, it meant she was closer to the demons. Maya and Camilla trailed at her sides, making sure they went unnoticed by the few students milling about.

At the end of the hallway, Maya pulled out a vial of cloaking potion she had been experimenting with a couple of weeks ago when she had still been waiting for her power to show up. Both Vera and Camilla glanced at the vial, but neither moved to take it.

"Your text was vague, so I just grabbed all the potions I had done." She rattled the small bag she had slung over her body as evidence to the different vials still lying within. "Now," she continued, taking a gulp of the potion then handing it to Vera, "cloaking serum, to make sure we're not seen in there."

Vera took the vial and took a gulp, then handed it to Camilla who finished it off. Now invisible to the eye, the three girls held hands so that Vera could lead them and traveled down the hall-way, checking to make sure there wasn't anything out of the ordinary as they walked.

At the end of the hallway, Vera moved them to the only available turn and headed down a flight of stairs that led them to another hallway. Still, nothing suspicious about their whereabouts, but Vera felt the tingling increase as they walked farther into the depths of the Theology building.

At the end of another hallway, they turned left to find a guarded door. Bingo.

They had placed an animal demon to guard the door, likely more a fear tactic, since Vera doubted they were the most intelligent of the demons.

Still invisible, the beast guarding the door did not notice their entrance into the hallway and took no defense as Vera whipped a metal rod toward it, knocking it out. Vera used her power to lift the beast and hide it behind a staircase at the opposite end—another entrance, she presumed—before she turned to her sisters, and they slowly opened the door that was being guarded and walked in.

Inside, they found what genuinely looked to Vera like a potions lab, right out of the movies. A table centered in the middle of the room with cauldrons on each end and different beakers littering the table. And around the room were shelves upon shelves of vials and jars of different ingredients and potions.

Vera noticed the quick shut of the door behind them, then felt her sisters let go of her, likely moving in opposite directions in order to search the room. They'd have to make sure not to touch any of the three creature demons within the room. Luckily none of them were Hunter.

They had luck on their side, given none of the three noticed the slight opening of the door when they had entered. Then luck continued to play in their favor as one of the three left the room. More of a chance for them if there were less of them to fight if it came down to it.

Yeah, Hunter definitely would've noticed.

With the two remaining demons oblivious to their presence, Vera turned her attention to strolling about the room. She read some of the names on the vials and jars, although most were in different languages—demon, no doubt—and listened to the demons who had begun to speak.

"...Asa has gone missing," the burlier of the two said.

"Jonah and Baron too? They must be on a trip. Though those two Lopez girls went missing a few weeks ago."

The burly one leaned into the table with the cauldrons. "Wonder where they're running off to. As if they could get away from the ruling families."

"Why would they want to? No better pay than here."

Vera felt her attention waver, unaware of the basis of the demon's conversation, and felt herself quell the sick building in her stomach when she read one of the jars—fecal matter. Disgusting.

With that thought, Vera stopped reading and looked around the room, gaze landing on the fireplace she stood before. She walked closer to it and stared into the flames, the lick of heat that Maya loved so much.

At a glance, it looked like a normal fire, but Vera's attention noticed a break in the flames as she stared. Like the flames were told not to touch a certain area within the fire, and they obeyed. Given Hunter had better control of fire than Maya, though Vera bet that was merely because he had a lifetime of practice, she wouldn't be surprised if he'd hidden the piece in fire.

Actually, she was quite impressed with the thought process. No one else would be able to control it.

Except Maya.

And he knew that all too well. He also flirted with her all too much, she thought bitterly.

Vera paused as she stared at the piece that lay hidden behind the flames—was he hoping Maya would get past this so he'd have an excuse to be near her again? Vera shivered at the thought. She didn't like the sound of it.

Maya had told them to tap once to get Vera's attention, twice for Maya's, and thrice for Camilla's, so Vera pushed her disturbing thoughts aside and picked up a vial with her power, tapping it down twice.

A responding two knocks came from the opposite end of the room. Vera smiled to herself and used the vial to discreetly point to the flames and motion downward. Luckily, the two demons were too busy discussing the disappearances of their friends.

It took a moment for Maya to understand, or at least a moment for her to take action, but she finally got the flames to simmer down enough for Vera to stick her hand into. She plucked out the piece, surprised at how the lick of flames had not hurt, then remembered Maya could control that too, and threw it into her bag. Now invisible alongside the rest of her, she continued to look around as the flames within the fireplace went back to normal.

She felt a touch to her side and realized it was Camilla reading her thoughts for what was going on. She relayed that the piece had been in the flames, to try checking the other bits of flames in the room for the final piece. Vera was sure Maya had witnessed her taking the piece, so she would know to pay attention to the flames. Vera had a feeling Maya preferred to stay away from the flames because she enjoyed them too much, but at the moment, that enjoyment was needed.

There were little bits beneath the cauldrons, and plenty of little ones throughout the room lighting candles. Four ornaments lay attached to the walls, light flickering from within. Nothing stood out as having a piece within.

Vera's attention to the flames in the room immediately shifted when she noticed color bleeding into life where her sisters were standing—the serum was fading.

Maya ran to one of the ornaments within the room as the skinnier of the demons noticed their presence and grabbed for the dagger at his waist.

Vera shot her hand out, throwing both demons to the opposite end of the room as she watched Camilla run toward her calling out for Harry. Maya reached into the ornament, then pulled away with what looked like the final piece to the Hell's Gate key, the human's top piece.

Harry landed beside them as the demons came running, and together, the four ported out.

Landing in the foyer, Harry looked them over before his gaze dropped to Maya's hand. He turned toward her and Camilla. "You two don't have the other piece, right!"

More a demand than a question.

Before Vera could answer, she noticed the piece within Maya's grasp begin to light up and vibrate. Maya's grip tightened on it as it shook within her hold. Then Vera felt her bag begin to vibrate.

Oh no.

With no chance to stop it, the hidden piece flew across the house as the one in Vera's bag ripped straight through the fabric, and the three pieces attached together in Maya's hands.

The vibrations stopped, and a shine bled from the key for a moment before dimming to a shimmer as the key awakened in Maya's hands.

Vera was now more sure than ever: Hunter had seen Camilla. He knew she would call reinforcements. He knew they would get in undetected and that Maya would be able to get the pieces. He knew that the pieces would come together when they were within reach. He knew, and he played them well.

With everyone's eyes on the key, about the size of Maya's forearm, they breathed out in unison. "Oh, crap!"

With the key now beautifully assembled, a mix between an old medieval key and a fantastical dagger, Vera felt the panic embed into the house. Maya, for her part, kept her composure and looked down at the key still gripped in her hands. "Stop! We'll simply hide it the same way Mom hid the book. I think I know what spell she used. We'll do the same thing. No one else will be able to get their hands on this."

Vera faced the determination in Maya's eyes and felt a calmness wash over her—Maya may be faking it, but it was definitely helping the moment. They all nodded obediently and followed her as she walked up to the attic.

It was moments like this that Vera was glad Maya had instantly gotten a fascination with the book and learning everything within. And moments like this that convinced her it may be time to do the same.

Maya moved straight for the book, flipping to the page she needed, as the three of them began pulling out salt and candles, the common ingredients.

With the page open before her, Maya delegated the required ingredients and what was to be done. Harry drew a pentagram out with the salt as Camilla placed the candles at each point. Vera took the required dried herbs and filled the gaps throughout the circle surrounding the pentagram—sage, blessed thistle, yarrow, white willow bark, and hyssop. Throughout the gaps within the pentagram went the hearts of five animals—a pig, a goat, a rabbit, a snake, and an ox. Lucky for them, their mother had a supply of ingredients hidden away in a chest in the attic. Vera had found them in an unfortunate scavenger hunt throughout the house when she'd first moved in.

At the center of the pentagram would go the droplets of blood from each of the three of them. Maya grabbed a dagger and moved her way carefully into the middle of the pentagram, cutting her hand and squeezing to allow the drops to puddle the ground.

She stepped out, wiping the dagger clean on her jeans, and handed it over to Vera. Vera followed in her sister's footsteps, then handed the dagger to Camilla, who seemed to hesitate for a fraction of a second before following in their leads.

With all three done, Maya placed the key above their droplets, and they each took their positions around the circle of the pentagram. Hands spread wide, they recited the spell that Maya had taught them as they prepared their blood.

As the spell began to come to life, the electricity of their powers gathered around the circle, and with a gust of wind, the spell was complete.

As the smoke disappeared, Vera looked down into the circle to find everything within, including the key, gone.

## 14

Vera was with Harry in the kitchen preparing for Halloween dinner. Maya and Camilla had gotten most of the traditional meals prepared and left making desserts for the newcomers.

Vera had racked her brain for Halloween desserts and settled on mini pumpkin cheesecakes and a chocolate ghost cake. Harry was there to help in any way he could, which mostly meant taking her direction on decorating the cakes.

"Why are you so good at this?" Harry's British accent accentuated as he spoke through his laugh at the horrible excuse for a pumpkin he'd drawn on one of the cheesecakes.

Vera laughed along at the sight of the sad festive cake and shook her head. "Oh, Harry. You're useless."

"With baking!" he defended himself. "I could have beautifully helped your sisters with the food."

Vera smiled at him but said nothing as she finished the glazing on the ghost cake.

Harry finished another mini cheesecake, this one not too terrible, and looked up to her. "You didn't answer my question."

Vera smiled and settled her gaze on the cake as she

answered, "I used to bake for my dad all the time. It's just in me. I love it. Kinda like playing the piano. It soothes me."

"It does quite the opposite for me," he muttered as he made another attempt at a pumpkin.

Vera stopped her glazing and looked up to Harry's concentrating face as he moved on to a fourth mini cheesecake. "I've wanted to do this for a career. Freelance baking."

Harry paused and looked up. "Why haven't you?"

Vera shrugged and went back to glazing, this way she didn't have to look at him. "Fear, maybe. I always said it was because I didn't have the money or the time, but they were excuses."

"I think the fact that you've accepted that means you're ready. Try it out. *Believe me,* people would pay to eat your sweets."

Vera didn't look up as she felt the light blush take a hold of her, and the smile began to blossom. "Thank you," she replied meekly.

The doorbell rang just as she looked up to find Harry smiling at her. Maya walked into the kitchen and looked over his shoulder. "You call that a pumpkin?"

"Oh shut up," he mumbled, then got back to concentrating on his designs.

Vera looked at Maya, and they both laughed as Camilla walked in, pumpkin pie in hand, with Warren. Vera smiled at the pie. IIt was sweet of Warren to have brought something.

It was about a half hour after Warren's arrival before they settled in for the traditional Halloween dinner—which truly was just a 'festive' dinner, one her father had tried with her throughout the years—and another hour after that before it was time for desserts.

Vera moved from the formal dining room, where they had set up their dinner, to the kitchen to pick up the ghost cake and plate of mini cheesecakes. Picking up the plate with the mini cakes, Vera used her power to levitate the ghost cake from the other end of the room.

Her magic picked it up, then immediately dropped it.

Vera paused and looked over to it. She tried again. Then once more and watched the plate fall back down.

Maya walked in just as she was ready to try again. "What's that noise?"

"I don't know what's going on." Vera panicked as she tried her magic on a glass Harry had left on the island. Again, it lightly lifted off the counter, then fell back down. "My magic. It's not working."

Maya's eyebrows furrowed, then she lifted her hand. The fire came to her hand, then vanquished almost immediately. From the look in Maya's eyes, not by choice. She tried again, the concentration to hold the fire burning evident on her features, and she was only able to hold it on her fingertips.

Maya looked up to Vera, eyebrows drawn and lips pursed. She called Camilla and Harry, asking Warren to stay behind for a moment, and walked them to the far end of the kitchen so Warren wouldn't be able to hear a thing.

Together, the two elder Whittle sisters told them about their depreciating powers. Vera tried to lift the glass once more, and Maya tried to conjure a flame. Both as deplorable as before.

Camilla's eyebrows drew together as her hand went to grab for Vera's arm, then again to Harry's. "It's a small whisper of a thought. Nothing like it was before."

Harry didn't seem to know what was happening, which concerned Vera even more, but he jumped into mentor status anyway, even though he'd told them time and again that he was no mentor. "Okay. We need to remain calm and think about this logically. How were your powers earlier?"

"Perfect," Maya answered immediately. "I lit all the fireplaces early this morning, then controlled the candles in my room before coming downstairs. I had no problems."

"Same with me. I could read all of Warren's thoughts perfectly."

They turned to Vera.

She shook her head. "Harry saw me use my powers while we were baking. They were working fine."

Harry opened his mouth to make a comment when Warren walked in. "Hey, sorry, I know, family conference, but do you have another bathroom I can use? This one isn't working."

Camilla smiled at him. "Yeah. Across from my room upstairs."

Warren smiled thankfully and headed out. They waited a few moments to make sure he was out of earshot, then continued whispering to each other.

"Okay," Harry began, "that means something changed between the time we ate and now. Something in the food?"

"No," Maya insisted. "We followed Mom's recipes. And the desserts were from Mom's recipe books too. Something else changed."

"Maybe having Warren here for Halloween dinner?" Vera thought aloud. "You said this was a traditional dinner. Maybe having a non-magical creature here is offsetting the tradition?"

As Harry and Camilla considered the point, Maya interjected. "No. It's not that. Mom once had a couple of co-workers over, and I'm almost positive they were human."

"Almost isn't positive," Camilla argued.

Maya completely ignored her little sister as her eyes raked over Harry, then her, taking everything in, before moving onto Camilla. Her gaze paused on Camilla's hand. "What is that?"

Camilla looked down to her hand. "Um, a ring?"

Maya fixed her gaze to the youngest of them. "I haven't seen it before, and I would know, I go through all of your black rings."

Camilla scrunched her nose as she looked back at the ring.

"Huh, I could have sworn it was pearlescent earlier. It's probably a mood ring."

Maya's eyebrows drew together. "From?"

"Warren. Like a Halloween-instead-of-Christmas present. He said he saw it at an antique's shop, and it reminded him of me."

"Take it off," Maya demanded.

"Excuse me?" Camilla looked bewildered.

"If Warren found it at a shop, it could be magical. Like when Vera found the book. It could be what's draining our power. Until you put that ring on, we were all fine. Take it off."

Vera couldn't help but agree with Maya.

Camilla looked to Harry then Vera for assistance, but found none. She grumbled as she took the ring off and held it up. It remained black.

Maya lifted her hand once more, trying her fire and finding it was still mostly just the tips of her fingers that held.

Vera turned to the glass and tried to lift it once more, still shaky and unstable.

Camilla widened her eyes at them as if to say 'I told you so' and went to put the ring back on just as a shadow shifted at the end of the kitchen, and low and behold, Hunter appeared.

How the hell he had come into the house without first being invited was a whole other concern.

He stood smug, taking up the expanse of the entrance to the kitchen as his gaze took them in. "I came back from a business trip to find you girls have caused another mess."

Flames took a hold of his arm and lit from his elbow to his fingertips as he watched them, cocking his head back with a smirk.

Before Camilla could put the ring back on, Maya ripped it from her sister's hand and wrapped her hand around it, letting what little power she had left burn the piece of jewelry.

Camilla turned angry eyes on Maya, as if there wasn't a

powerful demon in their kitchen, and opened her mouth to yell as Maya held up her hand and flames shot up. She looked at Camilla smugly. "Told you."

In her distracted state of watching her sisters, Vera didn't notice the fire bolt coming her way until it was too late. Luckily, Maya was quick to catch on, allowing her magic to take hold and deflect the flames so they didn't hurt when they touched Vera's skin. She dissipated the fire immediately, eyes already latched onto Hunter's.

Vera felt the shiver of disgust roll through her at the heady look Hunter gave her little sister. He was definitely here for more than just the key. Thankfully, Maya felt no need to fake interest like she had that time in the woods, her chocolate browns promising death.

He seemed to like that. *Dis-gus-ting.*

And it seemed things could only get worse when Warren chose that moment to come back downstairs and find Hunter and Maya both with arms aflame and staring one another down.

"What the hell is going on here?" he demanded, and Vera was shocked to find there was no confusion or fear in his tone or gaze.

Hunter smirked, gleaming eyes still holding Maya's, though they were amused rather than ravenous now, as he responded, "Well, Little Brother, it looks like the ring worked. Too bad my girl figured it out."

His final words loosened with another bolt of flames toward them.

---

Camilla's mind moved into slow motion as she took in Hunter's words. Little brother. He'd called Warren brother. A brother he had mentioned before. A brother that would check to make sure they didn't have the final piece. A brother who happened to have a piece hidden in his room. A brother, Camilla realized, that just spent a *long* time in the bathroom upstairs.

Camilla's gaze moved to Warren as her sisters and Harry fought Hunter around her. Brother, she thought. Warren was Hunter's little brother. Warren was a demon.

She should have known. Warren Delvaux. He'd said his father lived in a French estate, so she hadn't connected the names. She hadn't even thought of Warren when she'd heard Hunter's family name *and* the fact that he had a brother. She'd been so naive.

Camilla came out of her thoughts to find her sisters and Harry thrown haphazardly around the kitchen, Hunter's attention focused on her. He held a cruel smirk that said he knew what she was thinking and was glad for what it was doing to her.

As he moved to attack her, Warren jumped out of his frozen stance and knocked his brother to the side. Maya, Vera, and Harry moved to stand beside Camilla as they all watched the brothers shadow around the kitchen, taking turns in knocking each other over something.

The two finally stopped against the fridge as Warren held his brother against the doors. Hunter's fists balled in his brother's shirt. "You're really going to fight me, Warren? Your brother?"

Hunter pushed off the fridge, and the two held their positions, nostrils flaring, teeth baring, and eyes glaring.

Neither one backed down. Then they shadowed out of the kitchen completely.

The Whittle family remained glued to their spots, waiting to see if anything else would happen, waiting to see if they had just imagined it all. But Camilla knew it to be true—Warren was a demon.

Her gaze was unfocused as her family moved around her, taking in the mess of the kitchen before landing their gazes on her. Vera stepped forward and placed her hand on Camilla's shoulder. "Cam."

Camilla screwed her eyes shut, then reopened them and took in the state of the kitchen. "I don't get it. I've read his mind multiple times."

He had been eager to hear what Lana had to say, to learn what secrets it was that their mom had with Lana.

Vera gave her shoulder a squeeze. "I never sensed him either, Cam."

He had left her to go to the Theology building, knowing they would get the pieces to the key.

Maya tilted her head as she took Camilla in, sighing. "He's a demon, Camilla. He knew about us. He probably manipulated his mind every time he was around you. Made sure you heard what he wanted you to." She turned to Vera. "I don't know how he got past that one."

*Please say you wanna leave. Let me take you back to my place.* He'd wanted to be with her.

"My job is to fight evil," Camilla whispered through her blurred vision as her family turned to the mess of the kitchen.

*They're important to you, and you're important to me.* He wanted to be involved with her family because that mattered to her.

"I should've been able to tell evil and good apart!" she whisper-yelled to herself as her eyes watered around her unfocused vision. But she did not cry. Would not.

*If you want me there, I'm there.* He'd lied to her.

"We all fell for it, Cam," Maya interjected.

Camilla looked at her sister, taking in that this was not her fault, though she didn't believe a word of it, and began to clean.

It took them over an hour to get the house—mostly the kitchen—cleaned up. They had taken their teas to the living room and seated themselves silently around the room. Maya lay lounging on the long ottoman in front of the fireplace, Vera and

Harry took one couch, and Camilla huddled into the corner of the opposite one, gripping a pillow.

Camilla stared at Maya's back as her sister faced the fire, playing with her magic. The silence rang through the air, even Vera not breaking through the tension that had built—no one knew what to say.

In the quietude of the space, a shadow appeared by the foyer entrance to the living room, and the three facing forward stiffened immediately. Warren's eyes went straight to Camilla's and he opened his mouth.

Before he could get a word out, Vera whipped her arm out, throwing him through the air and into the wall of the foyer. Maya jumped from her lounge at the crash and turned to see Warren crumpled in the foyer. She took a stance, engulfing her hand in flames, her gaze focusing on him.

Warren stood, motioning his hands up in defeat. "I'm not gonna fight you guys."

"Why not?" Maya seethed. "Make this fun for us."

Warren ignored Maya's jests and turned his full attention to Camilla. "Camilla, please, you have to listen to me."

Camilla's grip tightened on the pillow, then she threw it aside and stood. "No, Warren. I don't."

Warren took a step forward but stopped when Maya and Vera stiffened from their standing positions behind her. Harry looked ready to defend her, though his stance remained calm, likely a century's long practice that kept him so.

"You've known what I was this entire time. Our entire relationship was a sick game!"

"No!" Warren pleaded. "I didn't know what you were until after you found out. I was just as surprised when my family told me my girlfriend was a witch."

"But they figured 'Perfect, let's use this to our advantage,' right?" Maya snickered. "Do not lie, Warren. It's exactly what I would have done, it's exactly what any sane person would do."

Warren looked ashamed but tilted his gaze to Maya. "Yet you still judge me?"

Maya's fists grew white beneath the flames as her nostrils flared. "You were to say no! Just because I'd like to take advantage of your situation does not mean you must agree."

Warren slouched in his spot, hands hanging to his sides.

"Your family tells you to play with me, and demon boy runs to do their bidding?" Camilla spit out. "You're worse than your brother. At least he doesn't pretend to be something he isn't."

"Camilla," he pleaded. "You've told me a thousand times that family is more important than anything. I was doing this for them. But I couldn't go through with it."

Scoffs radiated from behind Camilla's form.

"You seemed to be going through with it just fine," Harry interjected, his stance stiffening. "Even had the girls' power drained."

Warren attempted to hold his posture. "I was coming down to break the ring and tell you everything."

Camilla ignored the pained expression taking a hold of his features.

Vera spoke up, "How did you do it? Come into our lives as a demon? I can sense demons. I can't sense you."

He faced Vera. "I'm half-demon. Hunter and I have different moms. Mine is human. The demon sensing power only works on full-blooded demons."

Camilla couldn't help but be relieved that intrigue didn't light his eyes at learning of Vera's new power.

"Just makes you the perfect little boy for infiltration, doesn't it?" Maya ridiculed him.

"You said your father lived in a French estate." She wasn't sure why that was the thing that came out. Out of all his lies, that's what she focused on.

His gaze drank her in before he slowly responded. "He does. He lives in a French-designed estate out of town."

Camilla scoffed at the response. Perfect out. She should've guessed.

Warren watched her and tried again. "Camilla, I promise you, I am done with them. All I've done my entire life is try to please my father, but I don't care about that anymore. I love you, Camilla."

She couldn't help the hitch of her breath at hearing the words she had so longed to hear. Couldn't help the tears that stung her eyes that she did not allow to fall. "Get out."

Warren deflated. "Camilla, please…"

"Get out! I don't want to see you again, Warren."

His Adam's apple bobbed and his chin lowered, but Warren kept his eyes on her as he shadowed out.

Camilla allowed a single tear to slip before wiping it away and turning back to her spot on the couch. Luckily, her family did not speak.

———

Maya was never one to comfort. That had always been Camilla's position in their family. And when Camilla needed the comfort, their mother had been around. Luckily for Maya, Camilla didn't seem to want the comfort.

They'd all gone back to their positions around the living room after Warren's departure, Maya leaving the ottoman to take the other corner of Camilla's couch, closer to the fire. She faced the foyer, where Warren had been standing only an hour before.

Maya couldn't help but understand his position. Had he not broken her sister's heart, Maya would've defended the kid.

She enjoyed the calm the silence brought with it.

That is, until she noticed Harry and Vera stiffen across from her just as a hand snaked around her face and latched onto her neck.

Sandalwood and bergamot and musk.

Her center filled with liquid at the scent, but she stiffened in her seat as her family stood and faced them, their defensive stances taking a hold of their bodies as they assessed whether they could do anything to Hunter without hurting her.

His grip didn't hurt, rather toying with her neck as he pulled her up to stand before him. "This was fun when we started." He sounded angry, and Maya couldn't help growing wetter at the sound. "But now you've become bothersome. Give me the key."

He pressed her firmly against his form, and Maya could feel every ridge of him, every muscle as he tightened his grip around her neck. Still not enough for pain, but enough to control her movement. She could definitely not get out of his hold.

And it seemed Maya's bits decided this would be the perfect moment to draw up a fantasy of Hunter gripping her by the neck and standing behind her as he bent her over his desk—which she assumed was the dark wooded masculine sort—and fucked her. Her thighs drew tight together, slightly moving against him.

"We don't have your stupid key," Camilla spit at him, hatred plain in her eyes.

"Oh, I know," he rebuffed. "I want to know where you hid it."

"Tough," Maya commented against his hold.

Hunter laughed against her neck, and fuck, did that bring her right to the edge. He bent his head closer to her ear so only she could hear his next words. "Love, I've a lifetime of stealing powers behind me." One of the fingers around her neck began to move slowly, teasing her. "I stole this one power a couple of years ago. It lets me detect scents. So you can fight me as much as you want, but you and I are both very aware of what your body wants."

His fingers grazed his neck, though the hold remained. His cock, now completely hard, pressed firmly against the back of her. Maya tried to ignore his comments, his movements, but couldn't help the change in her breathing. It seemed he noticed as well.

A glance at her family showed their stances growing stronger. They thought he was antagonizing her. Thank the lords.

She took the opportunity of his distraction, staring at her chest to elbow him in the gut and move from his grasp just as Warren shadowed into the room beside her family, holding the staff they had seen Hunter with in their first meeting.

Hunter caught his breath quickly, reaching out to grab her arm just as Warren began to stomp the staff against the ground, chanting.

The ground began to rumble and open beneath Hunter before they had a chance to react. His hand slipped down her arm, her fingers interlocking around his subconsciously.

"An opening to Hell's Gate." Harry's frozen stance and astonished breath caught Maya's attention as she realized what was happening. Warren was going to send Hunter to Hell's Gate—both Hunter and her.

Her gaze shot to Hunter's as the pull from beneath tugged them, and his widening gaze told her they could not get out of this, his shadowing ability not working above the opening. He would not be able to protect them—because somehow she knew he would not leave her—from this.

Her family yelled to Warren to stop, but it was too late. The chanting and stomping over, the portal sucked them into Hell's Gate, and Maya couldn't help but now feel true rage toward Warren. He had sent them to Hell's Gate. He had come to send his brother to Hell's Gate—fucking ridiculous.

15

Free falling was a lot less fun when you had no idea when, or if, you'd land. Where you'd land.

Through a tight grip, Maya and Hunter's hands never parted as they fell.

They landed on a dirt-ridden ground. She felt the impact, but most of it was broken by Hunter's body half-beneath hers. She could only imagine how much worse that landing was for him.

She rolled off of him and they laid there, unmoving, for long moments, allowing the air to reach their lungs once more.

Grunting as they picked themselves up off the ground, they slowly stood and looked around to see where exactly they had landed.

Maya turned in her spot, but all around her she saw the same thing: pillars that looked to be holding them in a cage, and beyond that, nothing. She only saw fire surrounding their cage from all sides. She reached out with her power to see if she could control the flames and found nothing.

"Yours powers won't work in here." Hunter cut into her thoughts. "Hell's Gate was designed so that creatures can't use their powers. One of the ways to toy with them is to take their power away. It's ingenious."

Perfect, Maya thought to herself.

"But what will work in our favor," he turned to face her, "is that both of our primary powers is fire control, meaning our bodies will be immune to the flames. It cannot be used against us."

Maya felt her body sag as she turned from him to the depths beyond the pillars, once again grateful for her power.

It seemed, though, that Hunter was not done speaking. "Being immune to the fire will work in our favor, but that may only mean the psychological pain will be worse." Maya turned back to meet his gaze. "From what I've heard, Hell's Gate thrives on psychological pain. The only form of physical pain they have is the fire."

Maya breathed in slowly, trying to remain calm. "Psychological pain. So they're going to make us think things are happening that aren't actually?"

Hunter looked out to the flames beyond the pillars and shrugged. "That's likely to happen to me. You on the other hand, my bleeding heart," he turned his full attention to her, "have things that can be used against you. Very real things. Any insecurities, hidden desires, suppressed traumas, anything regarding you and your feelings in any way can and will be used against you."

Maya stared into his black eyes and read the truth of his words in them. She pulled her gaze away and spun slowly in her spot, taking in the nothingness beyond the cage in every direction.

She was officially terrified.

———

Maya was in Hell's Gate.

Warren had sent Maya to Hell's Gate.

Albeit, Camilla knew he hadn't meant to send her. She felt the fury build within her.

A second before the portal closed, taking Maya away, the staff within Warren's grasp had flown to the center of the hole and been sucked away. They'd stared in disbelief for a few seconds before Harry had explained that the staff can only be used once, then he turned for the attic.

Camilla followed Vera and Harry as they raced up the stairs, but stopped mid-step when she felt Warren follow them. Turning to face him and placing a hand to his chest, she allowed her anger to show. "Leave. We don't want any more of *your* help." Warren opened his mouth to argue, but Camilla stopped him. "You've done enough. Get out."

It seemed the message was clear in her eyes because he stepped back and shadowed out of the house. She breathed in a sigh of relief that he hadn't made it harder on her, then turned and raced up to the attic.

Vera and Harry were already at the book, looking for the spell they had used to hide the key. Harry looked up to Camilla. "Would *you* happen to remember which spell you three used?"

Camilla paused before them. "No. I didn't even think to check on it. I trusted Maya."

"We all did," Harry responded. "Until we can find that spell, we won't be able to get that key back."

Vera's frustrated tone broke the air as she faced Harry. "Aren't you meant to be the mentor? You should've paid attention!"

Harry's eyes bore pain and fury as he met Vera's, unbreaking. "I got distracted. Rest assured I'll make sure *that* doesn't happen again."

Camilla watched them stare at each other for another

moment before breaking their argument. "Now is not the time, you guys. We need to find that spell."

Both took another second to stare the other down before turning to the book and beginning their search.

It took hours of meticulous scrolling, hours far too long, to find the spell they were looking for. Although distracted as he was, Harry seemed to remember some of the lines, and they all remembered the ingredients, which made the search a tinge easier.

Vera read out the second page to this section—how to get the item back—and all three came to an abrupt halt. "Everyone who contributed to hiding it must contribute to finding it."

"We need Maya to find the key," Camilla concluded breathlessly.

Harry kicked himself out of the shock and began to pace the room before stopping. "No," he declared, catching Vera and Camilla's attentions. "Maya knew what spell she had chosen. She would have made sure there was a precaution in case all three of you weren't available. There's a loophole to that spell. We just need to find it."

The determination shining through his eyes brought hope into Camilla, and she turned to her sister.

Vera turned back to Harry, her gaze already readying the apology she would not voice. "You're right. Maya's dark side would have thought about a situation like this and created a loophole. We just need to find it."

Camilla snorted and looked down. "Damn, Maya. Of course you chose not to share this bit of information with us."

Vera turned to the book. "She was obsessed with this book. I'll check it. You guys check the house."

Camilla nodded. "I'll take her room."

"I'll take the rest of the house," Harry chipped in, and they left the attic.

Camilla walked into Maya's room, finding the darkness all consuming, unaware of how Maya found it relaxing.

It was clean. No clothes on the floor or on a chair, no things thrown haphazardly around. If their mother had taught them one thing, it was their need for cleanliness.

Camilla did a once-over of the room and found that it looked the same as it always did—queen-sized bed on one end, with a large dresser across from it, a mirror on top, and an old armchair in the corner made up the majority of the small room. This would make it harder to find whatever it was she was looking for.

Great.

Thanks Maya.

She walked in and went straight for Maya's dresser, taking a look at the things sitting on top, and found a small mirror - Camilla wasn't sure why. She had a large one right above the dresser—some vials, and Maya's graphic design equipment. Camilla looked through the dresser drawers and found nothing out of place, nothing hidden within.

Turning to face the rest of the room, she began her search.

She checked within the bedside table, under the bed, throughout the bedsheets, and between the mattresses.

She checked behind the frames and mirrors on the walls, the bottom of the chair, and Maya's closet.

She checked inside shoe boxes and bags, in the pockets of all the clothes, and still, nothing unusual. And she would know, she'd been stealing her sister's things and sneaking into her room for almost two decades now.

***

Harry had begun his search in the kitchen, as it was the room they spent the most time in outside their respective bedrooms. Everything seemed to be in place.

He then moved to the living room, given it was the next most used room. Again, everything seemed to be in place. He even checked within the fireplace, since Maya had a love for fire, but found nothing.

Seeing as the rest of the house wasn't used as often, Harry paused in the foyer, then turned and headed down the hall to the office at the other side of the house—the other room where Maya had spent plenty of her time.

It was where she went when she was getting her freelance graphic design work done. It had been Loretta's office before, where she did all of her magical-creature-related work.

Harry walked in and again, seemed to find nothing out of the ordinary. Though why he was surprised at his findings, he did not know—Maya would not so blatantly have left whatever they were looking for out in the open.

He did notice, however, that Maya had not changed it since Loretta's death. Harry had been to the house only a few times before the girls found out about their powers, before Loretta's death. A large oak desk took up the expanse of the room, with a chair behind it and the fireplace beyond that. Two smaller chairs sat before the desk, and a chaise was off to the side of the room.

The room was dark. Loretta had always said the deeper tones made her concentrate, whereas livelier tones knocked her attention to the life around her. That's why the rest of the house was livelier. Likely another reason Maya preferred this room— the only other dark room in the house apart from her bedroom.

As he walked through the room and checked different areas, he came to a stop at the fireplace. On the mantel, he saw a photo of Loretta with a little girl he had forgotten all about. Lila had been the daughter of one of Loretta's friends. Harry felt the twist of his features at the memory, but couldn't help the smile at Loretta's sentimentality before he continued his search.

He left the office after finding nothing amiss and began

choosing rooms at random, as Maya spent almost no time in any other room. He even checked his own room, remembering to ask the girls to check their rooms in case Maya had chosen to place the hints there.

Nothing out of the ordinary was found. Harry stood in the middle of the hallway and sighed to himself. Oh, Maya, what did you do?

## 16

Maya couldn't be sure how much time had passed but guessed it had been about four or five hours. She could be wrong. There was no concept of time within the cage.

And yet, nothing had happened.

She'd walked laps around the cage for a while, but had gotten tired of that, rather, choosing to move to the middle and lie down while she tried to ignore Hunter, who had decided exercising made sense at the moment.

Jumping jacks must've been helping the adrenaline he likely felt that told him to get out of the cage. She felt the same rush and tried to close her eyes and find a calmness.

It was peaceful to get to shut her eyes and forget about this entire situation. So peaceful, Maya didn't realize she had drifted to sleep.

*Maya wasn't sure how she got there, but she was home. Though it looked different now. All the pictures of her and her family were gone, now replaced with only her mother and Vera and the man Maya knew to be Vera's father.*

*She gasped to herself, realizing she was dreaming into the past.*

*Hunter had said everything was fair game in Hell's Gate. It seemed that rule still held for memories she was not aware of.*

*Maya was standing to the corner of the living room when Loretta walked in, heavily pregnant. And from what the pictures indicated, Loretta was pregnant with Maya. Apparently to Hell's Gate, this still counted as* her *memory.*

*Loretta seemed to be alone in the house, and Maya couldn't help but wonder where Vera was, how long had it been since she'd seen her first daughter? Had she and Bishop separated yet? How long had it been? Maya had so many questions.*

*Pushing the thoughts aside for the time being, Maya paid attention to the scene before her. It was her mother, pregnant with her, and she looked happy as she rubbed her stomach.*

*Maya watched Loretta as she waddled around the living room, cradling her belly. The peace of the moment, unfortunately, was taken when another woman walked into the room. A dirty blonde with eyes verging between green and dark brown. She looked frantic.*

*Loretta turned to the woman. "Althea, dear, what is it?"*

*Althea looked at her fellow witch, terror bleeding through her eyes. "Loretta, I had a premonition." Her gaze dropped to Loretta's stomach. "About your daughter."*

*Loretta grew still, staring at her friend, the fear evident in her tone. "What is it?"*

*Althea looked into her friend's eyes. "She's a demon."*

*Maya's eyes popped out as she watched the transaction. What was this woman talking about?*

*Loretta looked equally flabbergasted. "Excuse me?"*

*"The child," Althea explained, "I saw her power. She can control fire. That is a high-level demon power, Loretta."*

*Maya noticed herself sighing in relief alongside her mother as Loretta spoke, "Oh, Althea, dear, it is not a demon power. It is a dark power. Witches have dark powers as well."*

*"It is a rare high power, Loretta. That child is a demon." The disgust in her tone had Maya tightening her fists. Bitch.*

"Althea." Loretta's tone turned demanding. "Enough. The child is as much a witch as you and I. Her dark power will not change that."

"It is a demon child!" Althea yelled back, growing more and more frantic the longer the conversation went on. "We must exorcize it!"

Maya watched her mother's indignant friend and wanted more than anything to smack her. The bitch was trying to kill her.

Maya looked past that bitch to her mother and cracked a grin, glad to know her mother wanted to keep her despite knowing the powers she'd have.

"Loretta, listen to me," the bitch continued, "the coven has taught me how to do this. We don't have to go to anyone else. We'll get rid of it, just you and me, and we'll tell everyone it was a miscarriage. No one will find out about that abomination."

Maya gasped at the same time as her mother. She was really getting tired of this witch. If only she could use that demon power on her at that moment.

Loretta looked to her friend. "That's enough, Althea. I am not hurting my child. You need to leave."

Althea's face dropped, determination growing. Even faster than it had before.

Using her powers, Althea pushed Loretta into the armchair by the fireplace, holding her down with what looked to Maya like invisible ropes.

Maya screamed for her mother, tried to run to her, but nothing happened. They could not hear her, she could not move. Stuck in her spot, she watched as Althea walked up to Loretta. Felt tremors rock her body as Althea stepped closer to Loretta.

This witch—their ally, one of their own people—scared Maya more than any demon she had seen. Althea's face turned dark and serious as she raised her hands to her sides, calling on the angels to aid her in ridding the world of the demon child.

Maya watched as her mother struggled in her spot on the chair. Watched as Althea ignored the terror in her friend's face and began to recite her spell.

*Loretta called out desperately, Maya catching the faint hints to Harry's name. He didn't show. Unsurprisingly so, since Maya had barely been able to grasp the name.*

*The spell had begun to take place as Loretta called out in pain, and Maya urged her body to take action. Instead, she stood in the corner of the room and watched her mother beg her friend to stop through gasps of pain.*

*Feverish eyes met with uncaring ones as Loretta tried calling to Harry once more. This time, he popped up right beside where Maya stood at the corner of the room.*

*Maya sighed out in relief.*

*Harry's eyes widened at the scene before him, and he moved quickly, pulling Althea away, though it seemed the witch was rooted to her spot, ready to kill the baby within Loretta's stomach. Harry tried once more, though it was evident he was running out of options. Althea would not budge.*

*He pulled the poker by the fireplace and stabbed it through her back, straight through her heart, halting the exorcism immediately.*

*Maya felt the rush of relief ooze out of her, falling back into the wall, even though she knew nothing would have come out of it: she had been born, and Loretta had been around to raise her. Still, she watched Althea crumple to the floor and couldn't help the joy that ricocheted around her heart.*

*Loretta breathed in as she checked on her belly, finding the child kicking as aggressively as she had been that morning. Harry stormed over to her and placed both hands on her stomach. If Maya hadn't already seen Harry as a brother, she would have found his commanding presence attractive. He used his magic to make sure the babe was fine, then looked to Loretta, who cried out in relief.*

*"She's my magic baby, my Maya."*

*Maya felt a tear slide down her cheek as the image vanished before her.*

She woke from her dream in a cold sweat and looked around frantically, finding that she was back in the cage, Hunter at the edge with his back to the pillar, staring into space. She sat up slowly and stared ahead at the fire beyond and found that she felt more relaxed the longer she looked at it.

She wasn't sure what to make of her dream, didn't know if what she saw was real or if it was a beautifully torturous rendition created by Hell's Gate, but she couldn't help but *know* it was real. Hunter had told her that any past traumas could be used, and although she had not been alive, it had been her earliest trauma.

The only way to know for certain was to ask Harry when her family got her out of there.

As the memories from her dream came crashing back, she felt the adrenaline in her body spike. She threw herself up and began taking quick laps around the cage. Maybe Hunter had known what he was doing after all. But she couldn't get it out of her mind, that it was her fault her mother had gone through that experience. If she hadn't had such a powerful dark power, her mother wouldn't have had to experience that.

And yet, in her selfishness, Maya couldn't get herself to think poorly of her magic. She loved her fire power dearly and couldn't imagine a different primary.

She paused at the opposite end of the cage to Hunter and wrapped her arms around two of the pillars as she dropped her forehead between them, looking into the fire.

She wasn't sure whether or not that dream had actually happened, but there was one thing she was beginning to understand—not all witches were their friends. She would not make the mistake of blindly trusting one.

---

Maya had gone back to the middle of the cage after some time, unaware of how long it had been. She now sat cross legged in a meditation position and stared at the fire beyond as Hunter walked laps around the cage. Surprisingly, they had yet to speak to one another.

She focused her attention on the constant blazing beyond the cage with an interruption every time Hunter walked past her for his lap.

It must have been a few hours since her dream. That or time was working all too fast or all too slow. Maya truly wasn't aware any which way. She had decided there wasn't much else she could do but wait for her family, so she decided to meditate to keep herself calm.

Meditation, though, was a lot harder than anyone could imagine, and she got the constant reminder of that fact with each thought that rooted itself within her mind.

She continued to attempt it though, eyes open now so she had something specific to focus on. Though Hunter's constant interruptions weren't exactly helping.

With the annoyance toward Hunter fresh on her mind, a voice popped into her head. *It's his fault you're here.*

The voice came from her right, but as she jumped and looked to the side, she found nothing there.

Maya took a breath and focused her attention back to the flames beyond as the voice came back. *If he hadn't come into your life, you'd be with your sisters now. Better yet, if he hadn't pulled you into the portal with him, you would have had the satisfaction of knowing he was down here on his own.*

Maya brushed the voice aside, knowing this was more Warren's fault than anyone else's. He had seen her standing right beside Hunter. For him to even open the portal was stupid. On top of the fact that knowing Hunter was an ass still did not make him deserving of getting sent to Hell's Gate.

*Yes, let's kill the small one first. We can play with this one.* The voice came back, apparently responding to her thoughts.

*Aw, we sure can.* Another voice popped up, this one felt like it was talking to her from behind her neck. *He sure is orgasmic to look at.*

Maya grimaced at the swoon in the second voice's tone.

*Oh deary,* the second voice continued, *you cannot deny that. We are in your head after all.*

The first voice took this opportunity to jump back into the conversation as Maya attempted to regain her focus on the fire, Hunter brushing past her concentration once more. *Yes, we are in your head which is why I can say that if he hadn't come into your life, you wouldn't be in this predicament. And you sure wouldn't have Lust whispering down your neck like that.*

The voice finished, and Maya realized what these voices were—the seven deadly sins. Lust was behind her, which meant one of the other six was on her right shoulder. The voice on her shoulder sounded quite miserable, probably Wrath.

Lords, let there only be two.

It seemed she would not be so lucky, as another voice joined next to her left shoulder. *You know you don't have to like him to use him.*

*Ugh, Gluttony, anything to get more, more, more,* Wrath scorned from her other shoulder.

Maya pulled her legs up and shoved her head between her thighs, screwing her eyes tight. The voices laughed at her—as if closing her eyes would make them go away—just as Maya snapped her head up at the sound of Hunter falling to all fours.

***

Hunter was breathing hard as he held himself up with both arms. On his hands and knees, he tried to control his thoughts, knowing that everything he was feeling was a figment of his imagination. Nothing was actually happening to him. It seemed useless since knowing that did not change the way his body convulsed.

He grit his teeth and ground his hands into the dirt as his mind experienced another one of his ribs being turned up. It was an old, archaic torture mechanism Hunter had read of—the 'Blood Eagle.'

Hunter bit down as much as he could, but the crack of a rib completely turned around—though he knew none of it was truly happening—had him screaming.

Eyes closed desperately as his voice droned on with scream after scream as more of his ribs were turned around. He'd broken ribs before, but somehow this felt worse. Hell's Gate power, no doubt.

He felt his hands give out by the sixth rib.

On his forearms, he held himself up until the thirteenth rib.

Between thirteen and twenty-four, he dropped from his forearms to his chest, too weak to hold himself up, too much in pain to care.

By the time the last rib was upturned, Hunter's voice had broken, and he lay crumpled on his stomach, his arms spread around his head.

Just as he thought the mental torture was over, his mind took all twelve pairs of ribs and shoved them back to their original positions. Hunter barely lifted himself to his forearms as a final roar escaped his body.

With the end of the mind fuck, he lay on his stomach, sore and unable to move. His lidded eyes found Maya, who was holding onto one of the cage pillars with a death grip as she watched him. Her eyes bled no pity, which Hunter was glad of. Instead, he saw concern, like she wanted to wrap him up.

Hunter couldn't help the weak, dry laugh that pulled from his lips as his eyes drooped closed and he thought of his bleeding heart sitting across the cage.

He'd drifted off to sleep without realizing it, thankful for the peace he had gotten in those moments. He dreamt of nothing, and for that, he was particularly grateful.

On the other hand, he was not happy about the uncertainty that tinged him with fear at being awake. As he attempted to lift himself up, his sore and limp body refused to cooperate, and he fell flat to his stomach.

*Get up, you fool.* Hunter heard a voice come to him from his left shoulder. At seeing nothing, he cursed himself, knowing this would be another mind game.

*Get up.* The voice came back. *You worthless excuse, get up. You call yourself a powerful demon. You're letting that little bitch see you crumpled like that. Up, you pathetic waste.*

Hunter tried pushing that voice aside as he attempted to lift himself once more. His abs and arms were sore from trying to hold himself up earlier, and everything felt like jelly.

Failing a couple of more times, Hunter eventually pulled himself up to a sitting position, effectively shutting the voice up as another joined the party.

*Oh, Pride, don't be so tough on the boy. The little witch can see him any way she'd like. Especially if they were naked.*

The second voice sounded giddy, and Hunter stiffened as he realized what was happening. It was said that the three sins you relate to the most have been known to infiltrate the mind of creatures. It seemed he had Pride, and if he had to guess, Lust. Although he would never have guessed Lust would be one of his. It likely worked based on which sin affected you the most in the moment, because lust had become his constant companion since meeting that witch of his.

All of this just meant he should be expecting another, and it seemed the third would not disappoint. The voice was laughing as it joined in. *Yes, take her and fuck her. Yes! Come in her again and again and again, then take her power!*

Hunter rolled his eyes. Here was the other sin he had been expecting—Greed. Though Hunter would swear Greed sounded a lot like Lust.

Yes, Pride and Greed he had expected. Lust was definitely a manifestation from these past couple of weeks, and yet, this entire conversation seemed to be revolving around it. Guess it was also based on which of the three affected you the most in the moment.

Hunter looked over to Maya sitting with her back to the pillars, legs bent and spread before her as she rested her arms on her knees and stared at the ground.

*Well, would you look at that,* Lust gleefully announced, *she's ready for you. Look at the way she spread herself for you.*

*Oh, yes,* Greed joined, *imagine how much you can take from her! She's so ready for you.*

Hunter screwed his eyes shut and rubbed them with the palms of his hands.

*Yes, show the little bitch what you're made of.* Apparently, Pride was also horny.

Hunter opened his eyes to find Maya's gaze on him, and all three voices broke out at once.

*Take all that you can from her!*

*Show her who holds the power!*

*Oh yes, get a taste of every inch!*

Hunter felt his eyes dilate as he imagined stripping her right there in the cage and shoving her against the pillars as he suffocated between those legs. Imagined the marks the pillars would leave and her broken voice after the screams he'd evoke. He imagined sliding into her until the very hilt and watching her eyes widen in unbearable pleasure. He imagined coming inside her so hard he'd have nothing left in himself.

Hunter shot his gaze away and turned his back to her as he got up and walked to the end of the cage. He leaned his arms against the pillars and rested his head on his forearms. The voices continued screaming at him as he held himself rigid, trying to rid the hardness between his legs, while also trying to ignore them.

---

Maya was sure Hunter had been standing in that rigid position for days before he peeled himself off of the pillars. Bored with sitting about, she'd begun to walk laps around the cage when he pushed off and turned, crashing into her.

She stumbled from the impact and felt his hand reach out for her arm as his other hand wrapped around her, holding her from her lower back, and pulling her into him. He steadied her against his chest, and they looked each other in the eyes as they caught their breaths.

He pulled away abruptly, fully relinquishing his hold, and walked to the middle of the cage, lying on his back and closing his eyes.

Maya remained glued to her spot as she watched him lie there. She was eventually sucked out of her frozen state when Lust came back screaming, followed closely by its two friends. *Oh, how glorious he felt!*

*He did! We should feel more. More, more, more!* It seemed Gluttony would remain on Lust's side.

Maya pushed the two aside and continued her lap. Gluttony and Lust continued their comments, though Maya was glad to see Wrath on her side. She had just finished another lap when her luck fell.

*I think we should listen to them.*

Maya abruptly stopped as Wrath took the sins' side.

*I thought you hated him!* Maya argued back in her head.

*I do,* Wrath responded calmly. *But hate sex is amazing sex!*

Maya rolled her eyes, he sounded almost giddy with excitement. She grumbled to herself as she continued her trek around the cage, attempting not to allow her gaze to fall to the man in the middle. The last thing she needed was to give the sins ammunition.

Maya walked her laps around the cage as the three continued on with their comments, moving on from convincing her to fuck him to imagining the different positions he could take her in. A delicious thought of gripping her hair as he shoved her onto the ground, ass up, and pounded into her had Maya grumbling.

She made the mistake of sending a death glare over to Hunter's innocent form. Big mistake. She should not have looked his way. The sins were all too happy for that misstep.

*Look at those lips. Imagine what they taste like!* Lust whispered down her neck.

*Yes, you should find out,* Wrath contributed.

Gluttony laughed. *Yes, get a taste. Then find out what that tongue can do.*

Ridiculous. They were all beginning to sound exclusively lustful.

She shot her gaze away, but it was too late. They had their ammunition. She closed her eyes and tried to throw them out of her mind as she fell to her knees. Her hands flew to her head, messing into her hair, as she internally begged them to leave her alone.

*Kiss him,* Lust whispered.

*And we're gone,* Wrath agreed.

*Get a taste, and we'll leave you.* Gluttony tickled her neck.

She was beginning to see that it was less about the individual sins and more about what tortured her the most. Maya turned to the pillar beside her and banged her head against it lightly.

*That won't get rid of us.* Gluttony laughed at her.

*Only one way,* Wrath threw in.

*Get that tongue in you, deary,* Lust teased her.

Maya let her forehead hit the pillar. She didn't know how long the voices had been in her head, but it felt like hours. She couldn't take it any longer. She had to get them out.

Resolved, Maya quickly lifted her head off the pillar and turned to find Hunter unmoved. Before she could back out, she speedily crawled over to him and fisted her hands in his black button up, the jacket having been thrown to the edge of the cage when they'd first arrived to Hell's Gate.

His eyes popped open at the sudden attack, but before he could react, Maya had him pulled up against her, meeting his lips in the middle.

She recognized the half second of shock pass through him before he caught on to the situation and kissed her back fervently. His hands were equally as immediate to react as they found themselves on her, reaching into her hair and holding onto her hip. He pulled her closer, reaching for her thigh and holding tightly to the cusp between her thigh and ass.

*Mmm,* Lust moaned in her ear, *delectable, isn't he.*

Hunter sat up completely and pulled her closer, meshing their bodies together.

*More, more, more.* Gluttony giddily circled around her.

Maya pulled her leg over his lap so that she was straddling him and let herself fall onto him. They both moaned as she landed on his hardening member.

Hunter's tongue slipped into her mouth as his hand reached to grab her ass. Again, they moaned from the pleasure.

*Yes!* Wrath was demanding.

*This is glorious.* Lust sounded orgasmic.

It sure was, Maya thought to herself as she rocked against him.

Hunter tightened his grip around her as he guided her against him and thrust a hand into her tangles, pulling at the roots. Maya moaned as her hands found their way around his neck, leaving marks as they slid into the back of his shirt and scratched their way up.

*More!* Gluttony was reaching Lust's tone. *More, more, more!*

Hunter flipped them so Maya's back hit the dirt ground. His hands found new positions as one moved to cradle her neck and the other glided over the bit of skin between her shirt and jeans. Their tongues fought, and her body arched up to him, wanting more of him on her, in her.

Her hands found their way to his button up as their lips broke, and he licked down her jaw. She ripped the shirt apart, buttons flying around them.

Hunter groaned in pleasure as he sat up on his knees and looked down at her, a smirk wicked and glowing on his features. With his shirt thrown open, Maya had a clear view of his chest. Built from doubtless hours spent training, there was no six pack but a glorious set of muscles—just the way she liked it. And he hadn't cleaned himself entirely, leaving a light trickle of hair from his chest leading down, a true happy trail.

She watched him hover over her; her breathing growing more ragged at the anticipation, her center growing more damp at the knowledge that they were only a couple of layers away from meeting.

Her gaze racked his chest, and she wanted more than anything to mark him. And it must have shown on her face because his smirk grew in that moment and he lowered back down to her, holding her down by the throat once more as his tongue slipped into her mouth. "You're my witch," he said through a possessive growl.

Maya moaned as her hands found bare skin and her nails raked over him, leaving the marks she had been fantasizing about behind.

Hunter lowered his bottom half onto her, riding as if he was inside her and rubbing against her clit through their layers of clothes. Moans, deep and guttural, escaped from deep within them both.

Maya's legs moved to cling around his waist as he ground into her again, her clothed chest grazing his bare one. Her nipples tightened and she raked her nails down his back to appease some of the wanting.

With another thrust, Maya's body arched further into him, grinding to match his movements as his tongue moved from her mouth to her jaw, making its way lower. He gave a guttural groan as she rocked against him, and he bit down on her neck.

He sucked down on her neck at the sound of the unhinged moan Maya could not hide.

Another thrust had her seconds from coming, when her thoughts came back to her all at once.

Or lack thereof.

The sins were gone.

As the realization hit her, she gave an immediate pause to her actions, stiffening. Hunter noticed right away and paused his motions. He looked up as she caught her breath.

"Stop," she said inaudibly.

He remained above her and watched her catch her breath as she tried again. "Stop." It was barely above a whisper, but he picked up on it and pushed himself off of her. He rolled to her side and lay flat on his back beside her. They remained lying there, only a couple of inches apart, staring up into nothing.

It took about a minute before the accusations assaulted her. How could she do that? With Hunter Delvaux. How could she throw away everything she knew about him, everything she had seen? And be the one to *initiate* the kiss.

That wasn't a kiss.

That was *way* more. And she had enjoyed it. She had more than enjoyed it. She was ready to combust just thinking about it.

Maya squeezed her eyes shut and shook her head. She tried to remember him as he stabbed a priest with the staff. As he burned a child, as he held dozens of children prisoner. As he fought her sisters, almost hurting them. As he fought her in the kitchen before Warren intercepted.

No, it had all been the sins' influence.

Except she could not lie to herself. What had happened was all her doing. It was all she'd wanted since the moment she'd seen him in the church. It was all she'd thought about since he'd stood behind her in the woods. And she still wanted more.

Worse. She now knew how it felt. She *needed* more.

H unter was holding all of his concentration on fixing his breathing and chasing away the stiffness between his legs.

She'd kissed him. She'd made the move he'd been waiting for since she'd feigned nonchalance in the woods. And fuck did he want more.

She'd tasted dark and rich and like his new favorite flavor to exist. He could only imagine what *she* would taste like.

She'd sounded haughty and exulted.

She felt desperate and needy.

She looked luscious and ready.

And fuck, Hunter could not get his mind off of what had just happened. Of grinding into her and feeling her move against him, matching his pace. He wanted more. He needed to be inside her.

Yet he knew he would have to wait a bit longer for that pleasure.

One thing was for certain—he was thankful to Warren for sending them down there. Without his annoying little brother, Hunter never would have gotten that moment with Maya. Of that much he was sure. With her sisters around, Maya never would have given in.

And she had given in and almost come right beneath him.

Hunter felt his fingers reach out for her, but kept his hold on his body—no more touching. She had stopped them.

He knew it was her conscience coming back, but he couldn't help but wait restlessly for her to give in again. And give in she would. Of that much, Hunter was also certain. Until then, he'd have to rely on his hand and the glorious memory of rocking against her, of her fingers raking over him, of suckling her neck, tasting her skin, devouring her mouth.

The stiffness between his legs would not be going anywhere anytime soon.

"Hunter?" Her voice was low, like she was deep in thought.

"Love."

"I hate you."

His heart jumped and his lips quirked up. "Good."

## 17

era followed Harry into the living room where Camilla was watching the news on her laptop. Vera had spent the last ten minutes watching Harry quietly make them tea as she let her frustration out on him. He seemed to be taking it well, allowing all of her anger to get thrown on him.

It had been over a week since Maya and Hunter had been sent to Hell's Gate, and Vera's resolve was beginning to break. She felt hopeless.

Harry, for his part, had tried comforting them with the knowledge that the point of Hell's Gate was that you would be there a *long* time, so too much shouldn't have happened to Maya yet.

This gave them little comfort.

Especially since they were still at a loss as to Maya's plan for getting the key back without all three of them present. They had surprisingly remained hopeful that Maya did, in fact, have a plan for them.

Vera paused beside Harry as he stopped behind Camilla at the couch and watched the news over her shoulder. "We should be looking for a clue to get Maya out of that prison, *not* watching the news for some human problems."

"This is a magical problem too," Camilla argued, though Vera knew Maya's loss was hurting Camilla more as they'd grown up together. "They're still talking about those kids that came out with no memory and no evidence to the hostage-taker."

Vera rolled her eyes. "Yes, well that's the thing about magic. They're not gonna find anything. We need to focus on Maya."

Camilla sighed in defeat, tears on the brink of her eyes, but Harry interrupted before she could say anything. "Look there!"

Vera snapped her attention to the screen to find footage of a couple of children from that day in the gym. Nothing new on the screen. "What?"

Harry bent over and pointed at the text written beneath the children. "Not this story. The one coming up. Siblings that found each other because one donated blood and the other got it." Harry stood up quickly. "That has to be it!"

Vera caught Camilla's gaze and read the equal confusion there. Harry left the room for the stairs and the girls followed behind.

"Mind filling us in, Mr. Mentor Man?" Camilla said when they walked into the attic to find Harry hurrying over to the pedestal for the book, already opened to the page holding the spell that would bring the key back to them. He looked up with a quizzical glare, and Camilla raised her arms in defense. "Maya's not here. I'm playing her role to lighten the mood."

Harry ignored it, and looked the spell over, and stopped on the last ingredient. "The blood of all the castors!"

"Yes, Harry. We each used our blood," Vera commented slowly.

"Yes!" Harry exclaimed. "That must be it. You're not all needed in order to find it, just the blood of all three of you! If I had each of your blood, I should be able to recall it as well. It says nothing here about those who cast the spell, just those who contributed to it."

Vera felt like she'd been hit by a truck as understanding dawned on her. "So we just need some of Maya's blood? Okay, that'll be easier than actually having her here, but how are we supposed to get that without her here?"

Camilla snapped to attention. "Her room!" She turned to Harry. "You said she would have made sure to leave behind how to find the key without all three of us being present. When I was searching her room, she had three vials of this dark liquid on her dresser!"

She rushed out without another word and zoomed back before either she or Harry could follow. Camilla handed the unlabeled vials to Harry.

Vera allowed her gaze to land on the vials for only a moment before nodding and turning to the chest. "Let's get this spell set up!"

They took out the same ingredients they had used previously and began to arrange them. Everything remained the same, except now they placed the herbs inside the gaps of the pentagram and the hearts in the gaps within the circle surrounding the pentagram. Harry would have to restock their supply after this; the hearts were beginning to run out.

Camilla stepped into the circle and cut her hand, allowing the blood to drip into the center. Vera followed after her sister, then walked out and waited for Harry to orchestrate the rest. He chose a vial at random and walked in and released a couple of drops into the center of the pentagram so that each of their blood lay separately, as they had before. In retrospect, they could have made a drop from each of the vials rather than cutting their flesh anew, but they wanted to take every precaution to make sure this worked.

He stepped out and stood at the end of the room. Vera took her spot at one end of the circle, and Camilla took the other, as they raised their hands and began to chant the reversal spell.

Nothing happened.

No smoke, no energy, no magic.

The three looked to one another, then to the vials sitting on the pedestal beside Harry. "Well, I guess that wasn't the right vial," Harry commented as he walked over to the center with a handkerchief and wiped the unknown blood from the pentagram's center.

<hr>

Maya was lying on her side, head resting on an outstretched arm as she watched Hunter from a foot away. She couldn't be sure, but if she had to guess, it had taken about five hours after their kiss for Hunter to get his next round.

They hadn't said much after their kiss, just laid there, until eventually, she had turned to her side and watched his chest rise and fall. After some time, he'd followed suit, and they'd laid staring at one another, their eyes saying more than their mouths ever could. Things like how much they both wanted more. Like reassuring her that he was going to wait for it. Like admitting to him that she would definitely give herself over. Words that could never be spoken.

Then his back had arched and he'd flipped to his stomach.

He was lying face down with his features scrunched up in pain as he gritted his teeth. His arms shook as they tried desperately to grab a perch on the dirt ground as he endured whatever was happening in his mind. Maya had no clues what those horrors were.

She wasn't sure if she was glad that she didn't receive the same type of torture as Hunter, or if she wished that was all she received. Just as she gave into her bleeding heart, as Hunter so loved to refer to it, reaching out to comfort him, her eyes drooped closed, and she was sucked into a dream.

*She was in a dungeon.*

*It was filthy, and she swore she saw a rat crawl past the light overhead.*

*Maya stood in the shadows and watched as someone was brought into the room. The person dropped to the ground and was chained by her wrists and ankles to the floor, facing up. When she turned, Maya realized that it was her mother—Loretta Whittle was chained to the floor.*

*Maya gasped and tried to move toward her, though as she was beginning to learn, her attempts were futile in these dreams. She could not move.*

*The door opened, and a demon walked into the room. It was cloaked, but Maya guessed the awful thing would be a demon as it walked just out of Loretta's sight. As Maya watched, the demon pushed the hood of its cloak back, and Maya felt her heart drop as she recognized Vera standing before her.*

*Maya shook her head, already afraid of what she was about to witness from the sister she had just met. The Vera look alike strolled up to Loretta and spit in her face. Loretta turned to face it and cried with relief. Maya felt her heart constrict.*

*"Oh, my first born, I've missed you so much! Leaving you was the hardest thing I've ever done."*

*The thing—for Maya would not believe it was Vera—smirked cruelly down at Loretta as it pulled out a hammer. "Killing you will be the easiest thing I'll ever do."*

*It sounded just like Vera.*

*It lifted the hammer above its head, and anticipating the blow, Maya tried to close her eyes, but they remained open, forcing her to watch as her new sister slammed the hammer into their mother's head.*

*Maya reminded herself this was an imagination from Hell's Gate.*

*As she attempted to steady herself, her mother began to breathe again and looked over to her corner of the room once more. Maya's* sigh of relief was short-lived as another cloaked figure entered the room. It pulled its hood down.

Camilla.

The thing, as Camilla, strolled up to Loretta and kicked her to grab her attention. Maya couldn't help the intensity of her gasp. Witnessing Vera had been difficult, but it was easy to compartmentalize about a sister she hardly knew. Camilla was her baby sister. They'd grown up together. With their mother. Maya could not compartmentalize this.

Loretta gasped from pain and turned to see Camilla staring back at her. "Camilla, baby..."

Before she could get another word out, the thing kicked her in the face. "I am not your baby anymore, Mother."

The revulsion in her tone had Maya reeling. She was not seeing this.

Maya tried desperately to turn around, but again, she had no control over these dreams. She watched as the thing that looked like her baby sister took a knife out from under its cloak and sunk it into their mother's heart without a moment's hesitation.

She was going to be sick.

Maya was sure she couldn't take any more of this when the room blacked out and she was now standing on the other side, watching her mother stare at the corner she had just been standing in. Her body moved, but she had no control over it.

Oh no.

Maya tried to push her body back, to throw herself against the wall, but it was all to no avail.

She felt her arms raise and push down a cloak as Loretta's eyes turned to face her. Her foot picked up and stomped down on her mother's knee, snapping it.

Maya internally gasped. She could feel herself hyperventilating on the inside, but her form remained stoic.

It was her turn to kill her mother, and she would be getting a front row seat.

*Loretta turned to her middle child with a weak smile that shattered Maya's heart. "My little fire, I've missed you."*

*"You were a terrible mother." She felt the words slip from her mouth. Maya tried to reject what she'd just said, but found she could do nothing.*

*The weight of an object in her hand stole her attention. Her arm raised, and Maya noticed an axe in said hand over her head. With horror, she realized what was about to happen, and again, none of her pushing and thwarting would help. She was going to do it.*

*Her arm came flying down as she stared at the eyes of her crying, loving mother and beheaded her. Blood splattered everywhere as Loretta's head rolled to the side, coming to hit her foot.*

*Maya looked down and felt her mouth open in a cruel, disturbed laugh as she internally screamed.*

She woke from the dream, still on her side, with tears falling down her face. She felt numb to them.

Hunter was still lying on his stomach with slightly controlled breaths coming in and out.

He was watching her, a pain evident in his eyes that she had never seen before. She fixed her gaze to his, finding she preferred the black depths of his eyes to the depths of nothingness beyond the cage.

He had a hand behind his back, holding onto the one she had reached out with before falling into that dream. He was trying to comfort her. Or maybe he was only trying to take the comfort she had tried to offer. Neither truly mattered to Maya.

---

Vera watched Harry choose another vial and drop the blood into the center. He stepped back out and watched them as they attempted the spell once more.

Again, nothing.

Without a word, Harry moved with the final vial and a clean

handkerchief. He wiped the spot clean and poured the last vial in its spot. He stepped out of the pentagram and retook his place by the pedestal.

Vera looked to her sister as they reattempted the spell.

And felt the hope she hadn't realized was beating her heart break. Nothing happened. They waited a few moments to be sure, but when everything remained calm, they all fell back against the walls.

"There has to be something we're missing." Vera pushed off her wall and began picking up the now empty vials.

In picking up the second one, the vial came near her face, and she got a sniff of the contents. Vera paused and pushed the vial closer to her nose, then tried with the other vials.

She looked up as Harry crouched beside her.

"Vera," Camilla commented. "*What* are you doing?"

"These vials aren't filled with blood."

Harry looked at her, eyes gleaming as he pulled a vial to his nose. He broke into a grin as he pulled another to his nose. "She's right."

Camilla pushed off the wall, and Vera saw the hope begin to bloom in her youngest sister once more. "What is it supposed to smell like?"

"It's a metallic odor," Vera answered. "And this isn't blood. Which means we have to find the blood. And I think we begin by searching the attic. It's the only room we haven't fully searched."

All three pairs of eyes locked onto different areas of the room without another word and began their search.

After about ten minutes of rummaging through chests and drawers, playing with loose floorboards and wall hangings, tumbling with pillows and stuffed animals, Vera stumbled upon a framed photo. The photo consisted of three cut outs of her mother as she was pregnant, each time holding a different daughter.

Vera smiled as she picked up the frame and realized how thick the casing was. She shook it lightly and heard the rumble that could only be vials hitting one another.

Vera found a latch at the bottom of the frame and opened it to find three identical vials within. She couldn't help the wide grin that ate at her face. "I found it!"

Harry and Camilla stood at her shoulders as they all looked down at the framed photos. "A photo of each of you above your vial. Clever," Harry remarked as he pulled the one on the right out.

Of course Maya would not have put them in order. Only someone who knew which daughter Loretta was pregnant with would know which to grab.

Harry bent at the center of the pentagram and wiped all of the blood off, starting fresh with this vial. He stepped out and took his place at the pedestal.

Camilla stepped up and cut her hand once more, letting some of her blood fall into the center. Vera took her turn, then once again took her position at one end of the pentagram. She looked to her sister, and they raised their hands.

This time, the same energy and magic she had felt when hiding the key emerged. With a burst of smoke, the girls stepped away and waited for the air to clear. The ingredients were gone, and in the center of the pentagram sat the Hell's Gate key.

Vera rushed to take the key and looked to Camilla and Harry in turn. They all smiled, then ran for the door, heading to their backyard. Harry had explained to them the night they had found the witches' piece the way the key was meant to be used.

Nervous, Vera and Camilla walked to the middle of the yard, and with both of their hands on the key, they thought of Maya and shot the key into the ground as they screamed her name. And the key did its job as the ground immediately began to rumble.

Maya had been lying stoically on her back for some time. Hunter, the same to her right. They lay a mere two inches from touching as they stared up into the fire surrounding the cage, finding the peace they desired within the flames, though the nothingness behind it still bothered Maya.

With their hands resting lightly on their stomachs, they timed their breathing in and out.

Maya thought of her sisters and fought with every fiber in her to thwart the new memories those names brought with them. She thought of Harry, her new family.

She knew they would figure it out.

A couple of tears fell down her cheeks as she thought of her family. Of Camilla, loyal and loving. Of Vera, open and accepting. Of Harry, patient and understanding.

As another tear fell off her cheek in the silence, Maya felt the ground beneath her begin to rumble. This was new, and Maya was afraid of what it could mean.

She let her hand fall between their bodies and felt Hunter's fall immediately into hers, their fingers interlocking. She held his hand in a death grip and felt him return it—they would not be leaving one another.

Staring up into the flames, Maya felt the fear in her heart calm ever-so-slightly at the light strokes Hunter's thumb ran over the top of her hand. His fingers never relinquished their hold, but his thumb played with her, stole her attention and helped her cope.

The ground beginning to shake caused them to tighten their grips to a breaking point until everything went black.

18

*H*arry, Vera, and Camilla remained glued to their spots as the ground beneath them shook harder and harder before coming to an abrupt stop. Their yard had filled with smoke, and as Vera pushed the smoke out of her eyes, she found two bodies lying unconscious on the grass.

Maya and Hunter were *both* back.

Not giving themselves time to think, Vera and Camilla ran up to their unconscious sister, but came to a stop at seeing their conjoined hands. Harry came to join them and focused his gaze on the same spot.

Why were they holding hands?

They were dirty, like they'd tumbled straight through the ground and picked up the dirt on the way out.

Camilla sighed. "Well, I'm not excited to have him back."

"Why is he back? We didn't call to him," Vera asked.

"I haven't a clue." Harry hadn't moved his gaze from their interlocked fingers. "But until we find out, we shouldn't move them from one another."

Camilla grumbled her disapproval but agreed with Harry's

comment. Vera, too, didn't like the idea of Hunter topside, but she wanted to make sure nothing else happened to her sister.

She used her magic to levitate both bodies into the house and kept them together as she moved them up the stairs and into Maya's room where she dropped them onto the bed.

Settled onto the bed, Hunter and Maya's bodies fell so they were facing one another, hands still interlocked between them.

Vera couldn't help but wonder what had happened to them down in Hell's Gate. Would she still be the sister Vera had just been getting to know? And she knew without a doubt that Camilla and Harry were wondering the same thing.

Vera watched her sister, her gaze falling until they settled on the marks around Maya's neck. She had long bruises down the side of her throat, and Vera would guess there was something on the other side as well. In Maya's current position, she couldn't be positive.

Afraid for what it meant, Vera remained silent and watched her sister sleep beside the demon. She wondered how long it would be until they awoke.

Hunter was in a dream of nothingness that he found so comforting, he felt his body settle. He was safe. He waded in the blackness around him as he relaxed.

He felt good.

Better than he had the entire time in Hell's Gate, and he was scared to think it, but it felt like he was lying on a bed again.

Afraid to end the calm, but knowing there was nothing he could do about it, Hunter opened his eyes.

His gaze immediately settled on Maya's relaxed features as she breathed in and out in a calmness that matched his. She looked beautiful.

Hunter memorized the look of serenity, those fluttering

eyelashes and slightly pouted lips. He wanted to trace every inch of her face.

Peeling his gaze from her, he allowed his eyes to wonder down to their joined hands and noticed that they were not resting together on the dirt ground. Instead, they were on a soft landing.

Hunter shot his gaze over Maya's shoulder and noticed black curtains and a chair in a corner. They were out. They'd left the same way they'd entered, hands gripped tightly together.

His breath slipped completely out of him as he allowed his body to take in the fact that he truly was safe and out of that cage. He closed his eyes a moment at the thought, then opened them once more and settled his gaze on Maya.

He moved his thumb, grazing the top of her hand the same way he had when the rumbling had begun in the cage. It was likely only a couple of minutes—though Hunter's perception of time was still slightly skewed in the darkness of the room—before Maya opened her eyes. Her gaze landed on Hunter's immediately before she closed them once more with a single word. "Damn." The grogginess in her tone had his lips quirking up. "I thought my sisters had gotten me out."

"They did," came his throaty response.

Her eyes sprung open and landed on him. She let her gaze wander over him before moving to the rest of the room. Hunter watched the smile blossom upon her lips as the realization filled her. He wanted to kiss those lips again.

She turned her gaze on him. "Why are you here?"

He didn't break his gaze from hers as his lips broke into the grin he had been fighting. There was no malice in her tone, just plain curiosity, and he gave her hand a light squeeze as an answer.

She seemed to be considering it when her family walked into the room, breaking his moment with her.

Camilla walked in holding a tray of tea, and a smile bloomed on her face. "Ha. I knew the smell of tea would wake her!"

Maya smiled in response and pulled her hand out of Hunter's as she began to sit up against the headboard. Hunter followed her movements and rested his head back on the headboard as he smirked at the three members standing at the end of the bed.

Camilla tried to ignore his presence as she turned to prepare a cup of tea with honey and handed it to Maya. He watched as she made a cup for Harry, then Vera, then herself, blatantly leaving him out of the equation. Hunter rolled his eyes and saw Maya try to bite down on her laugh—she had noticed as well.

"That's very mature of you, Little Sister," he remarked, knowing it would annoy her.

It worked. "I am *not* your little sister."

Hunter smirked down at her. "Oh? But my brother is so very in love with you. You're basically family."

Camilla scowled at him. "Fuck you and fuck your brother too."

Hunter noticed the shocked faces all around him. Apparently his little sister wasn't known for speaking out like that. He went to respond when Maya cut him off.

"So, you guys finally figured it out, huh?" Maya took a sip of her tea.

Vera's eyes moved to meet her sisters. "Yup. Would've been a lot faster had you let us know beforehand."

Hunter had no idea what they were speaking of. Likely the way to find the key they'd hidden.

"Where's the fun in that?" Maya responded, a quirk to her lips.

Hunter felt the smirk grow on his face. He'd go through it all again to get those minutes with Maya.

"The fun in that," Harry jumped in, reprimanding her, "is next time, it wouldn't take us so long to get you out."

"How did you get our blood anyway?" Camilla asked before Harry could finish his comment.

"I found a spell in the book that helps cut without pain and another that heals small cuts. You guys were asleep."

"That's creepy, Maya." Now Camilla was reprimanding her.

Hunter had to bite down on a laugh, though Maya was evidently allowing a small smile to remain on her face as she hid behind the cup she brought up to her lips. "How long did it take?"

All of their eyes landed on the two of them in the silence, then Camilla asked, "How long did it feel?"

Maya shrugged as Hunter pulled the half empty cup out of her hands. "Sometimes it felt like forever. Sometimes it felt like a few hours."

Hunter took a gulp of Maya's tea then spoke, "Boredom slows down time, and there was a lot of nothing happening. I'd wager a few of days."

The three remained quiet, then Vera said, "It took about ten days. It's the ninth today."

Hunter and Maya nodded in unison as he commented, "Not bad."

He hadn't been far off.

Camilla's eyes narrowed on him. "How did *you* get out? We called to Maya only."

Maya took the cup from Hunter's hands and finished the remaining bit, then wordlessly handed her cup out to be refilled. Vera took it and refilled it before handing it back. Maya held the steaming cup in both hands as Hunter allowed the silence to carry. It made them uncomfortable, which amused him. He finally answered, "Well, dear sister, yours truly here," he bobbed his head to Maya at this side, "just couldn't seem to leave me behind."

He bit down on his lip as Maya rolled her eyes. Her family watched her instead for an explanation. "We didn't know what was happening. We were lying on the ground and it began to shake. I didn't know what to expect so I grabbed his hand."

Harry nodded in understanding. "Comfort from a demon is still comfort."

Maya nodded and took a sip from her cup, before Hunter pulled it from her hands again. They remained quiet after that, each drinking their tea.

Vera broke the silence. "Maya," she called out lightly. "What happened to you?" Her gaze glued to Maya's neck.

Hunter's eyebrows furrowed and he turned his attention to Maya's neck. His eyes widened. He nearly spit out the tea he had just taken a gulp of. He hadn't noticed it before with her hair covering and his attention on being out of Hell's Gate, but she had bruises lining the entirety of her throat.

Hunter could make out exactly where each of his fingers had gripped her, where his palm had pressed into her, where his tongue had focused its attention. If he focused, he could even see the light indentations of his bite.

He couldn't help the wicked grin that took over him at seeing her marked. He wanted to do it again. To every inch of her.

Maya's eyebrows scrunched together. "What are you guys looking at?"

Hunter tried to hide his wide grin but found it far too difficult. He was sure she could see the gleam of joy in his black eyes.

She turned back to her family as Vera handed her a hand mirror. Hunter watched the immediate burn of a light blush take a hold of her features as she, too, remembered exactly how she had gotten those.

Her gaze momentarily hovered over to his chest, then shot back to the mirror as she feigned innocence with a shrug. "I don't know."

Hunter looked down at his chest and found his shirt still

open from when Maya had ripped the buttons off, and on his chest, he saw a couple of light scratches marring his skin. He couldn't help the desire that grew in him at the memory of how he'd gotten those. Couldn't wait to get home and check out his back.

Maya kept her gaze away from Hunter, and he elated in knowing it was because she wouldn't be able to feign ignorance while looking him in the eyes. He took another sip of the tea, ready to offer some insight. "You sure? I think you got that from…"

Maya moved in her spot, adjusting her position ever-so-slightly so she was seated pressed against him, and jabbed her elbow into his ribs.

He stopped immediately and laughed. "You're right actually, I can't seem to remember." He found true joy in his laughter as she begrudgingly took the cup from his hands.

This new position gave Maya's elbow ample opportunity to shut him up in further conversation, but he didn't care if it meant he could enjoy having her pressed against him.

Camilla brought him back to the room, turning her attention to him. Apparently, he would be her punching bag to keep the inquiries off of her sister. He couldn't argue with that. He would take it all if it meant Maya could relax from her time down below, especially so soon after finding out she was a witch. At least he'd had his fair share of torture before. She was still a baby in supernatural views. And being completely undeserving of going down to begin with didn't help.

"Why did you want the key? Who are you trying to take out of Hell's Gate?"

Maya stiffened beside him, but she didn't move away. Hunter took the empty cup from Maya's hands and looked into it. He lifted the cup up for another refill and smirked as Camilla quirked a brow at him. Harry walked over and took the cup, seemingly begrudging, as he refilled it.

Hunter answered, "I'm not trying to free anyone. I don't want to use it."

He couldn't fight the spring in his heart as Maya relaxed into him once more, though everyone looked at him with suspicion. He smirked at their reactions, not elaborating any further.

Camilla handed the cup Harry had just finished preparing to Maya, gaining another eye roll out of Hunter, and a poorly hidden smile out of Maya. He took the cup from her hands and felt her push down into his ribs. She was literally nudging him to continue.

He drank some tea, then did as his witch told him. "Power. If we have the key, we can get anyone who wants to use it to do anything we want. We'd be unstoppable."

Dumbfounded, Vera asked, "Wouldn't that make you deserving of Hell's Gate too? Especially after letting people out just because their friends did you a favor?"

"I didn't say we'd actually allow anyone out," he responded with a smirk that would irk them dearly.

Hunter noticed Maya roll her eyes from his periphery as he watched Harry lean back against the dresser, folding his arms before his chest. Intrigue lit the man's eyes. "Who do you know that wants it?"

Hunter shrugged. "My uncle is looking for it. For whom," he anticipated the next question, "I don't know, nor do I care. I'm sure there are others, but seeing as I don't have the key, it doesn't necessarily matter to me right now."

"Fine," Vera conceded, leaning against the dresser beside Harry. "Tell us this, Mr. Power Hungry, what do you know about our mother's death?"

Again, Maya stiffened beside him, taking Harry and Camilla along with her. He quirked his brow at Vera. "What makes you think I know anything about it?"

"Do you?" Maya asked in a soft tone he'd never heard from her.

Hunter didn't move his gaze from Vera's as he answered Maya. He would always answer her questions. He wanted to please her, and he didn't know if that was the after effects of being in Hell's Gate together, or if it was coming from his earlier attraction to her. He fought the urge, but somehow knew it was the latter. Every time he had been around this family, he had gravitated to her. "No." He felt Maya relax into him again. "Now answer my question. What makes you think I would know?"

He felt Maya's gaze on him as Vera answered, "Well, because you seem to be a king in your world, and a demon killed her, so I figured you would know."

Hunter couldn't help the laugh that shot out of him. "Oh, sweetheart, how mistaken you are. Not on the first part." Maya shook her head, but he noticed the smile she bit down on. "You're completely accurate on the first part. But a demon did not kill your mother."

Everyone's attention was acutely on him when Camilla spoke up, "Why are you so certain?"

Hunter smirked at her. "My dear sister, your coven is a lot more difficult to kill than you'd think. Any demon, your king," he raised his arm in demonstration to himself, "included, would brag about such a feat."

"Why?" Vera simply asked.

"It would be a show of power. To defeat a powerful witch like your mother. No demon would be able to let that go. There have actually been demons that have tried to take credit for it, but trust me, no demon did this."

Camilla snickered. "Yeah, because putting our faith in you would be smart of us. You just admitted to wanting to kill us."

"Not true. I said I would gladly brag about it. I didn't say I was going to do it."

"Yet," Vera threw beneath her breath.

Hunter's eyes flickered to her, and he smirked. "Exactly."

The questions seemed to end with that, and they sat in silence for a few moments before Hunter broke it. "Is that why you lot have been after the key? You think whoever killed her was after her piece?"

"Well, yes," Maya answered, "that was part of it."

Hunter drank some more tea. "Makes sense. If it were for that, whoever killed her would be after you now. Especially since you have the full key now. But really, I don't think that was the reason. They would have also had to come after us."

Hunter felt an internal laugh bubble at the thought of someone coming after their piece, though realistically, they would have had a chance, considering genius Augustine had thought it fine to leave it in a college room. He still couldn't believe his father's logic sometimes, even if he had only had the piece placed there a couple of months prior.

But it seemed he'd gotten through to them. Their mother's death wasn't because of the key. Or at least, they wouldn't argue with him about it at the moment. He continued to share the cup of tea with Maya even after Camilla offered to grab Maya a new cup—she'd said there was no need, which had made his cock jump with excitement, even at such an innocent comment—and they'd remained in silence for a few more minutes.

When they were on their fourth or fifth cup, he'd lost count, Camilla moved to take the seat on Maya's other side. She took her sister's hand. "I'm sorry."

"For what?" Maya asked.

"This is all my fault. If I hadn't read Lana's thoughts, we wouldn't be here."

Maya squeezed her sister's hand. "It's not your fault. We're witches. Stuff like this is bound to happen."

"She's right. It's not your fault, Little Sister. It's my dumb brother's fault. Now," he took a final gulp from the cup before handing it back to Maya, "if you'll excuse me, I have a delinquent to take care of."

He shadowed out, ready to clean himself free of the dirt that stuck to his body, then take care of Warren. But he had meant what he'd thought earlier. He would do it all again to have that moment with Maya, and he would have Warren to thank for it, so he would not thoroughly hurt his little brother.

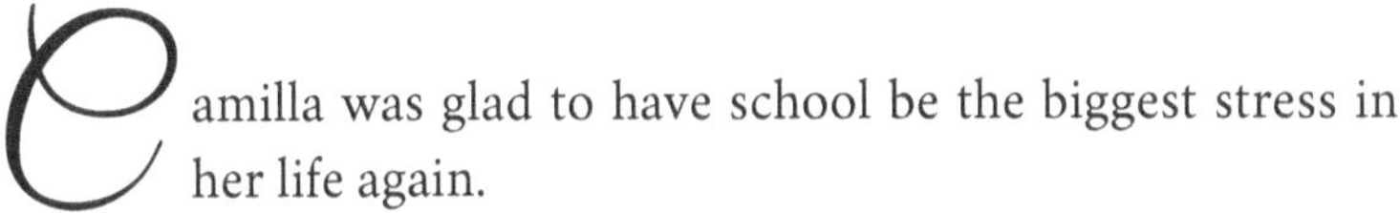

19

Camilla was glad to have school be the biggest stress in her life again.

Almost two weeks since Halloween, and she had missed so much in her classes in her desire to get her sister out of Hell's Gate. She was afraid she'd fail the semester.

Luckily, her professors were understanding enough to allow her to make up all her missed assignments by the end of the week. Especially after learning that her sister had been missing and they'd just gotten her back. It was close enough to the truth that Camilla felt good saying it, considering her superstitious ass didn't like to lie about excuses lest they came true.

She was sitting in a new spot in her literature class: the middle. Mostly because she liked being close to the professor, but at the same time, she loved to people watch. The middle gave her the most exposure to both. And it was farther up the lecture hall than the seats she had shared with Warren before.

She was in the process of people watching as her peers walked into the hall, which was incredibly easy from her position as the doors to the hall were in the front rather than the back. An odd choice, but perfect for Camilla's nosiness.

That was, until a certain someone walked in.

She'd been able to avoid him effectively when she didn't show up at school and blocked his number from her phone, but she knew she'd eventually have to see him again.

He wore a hopeful smile when they locked eyes from across the lecture hall and began to walk toward her. She turned her focus away from him, though her periphery tracked his movements, and she looked to the professor instead. She was talking to a student.

Warren took the seat beside her, and given the hall had now filled up, Camilla had no options to move away from him. And she figured it would be futile since he could just follow her to another seat.

It seemed ignoring his presence was her only tactic.

"Hey, Cam," he whispered to her in a warm tone. Camilla felt her heart flutter at the sound and ignored it.

She wanted to focus on the lecture taking place, couldn't afford to continue missing aspects of this class, but Warren's presence beside her was making that prospect entirely impossible.

He called to her a couple of more times, each time sending Camilla's heart on a marathon, but she kept her resolve—she had no intentions of speaking to him. Ever again.

With Warren's presence beside her, Camilla couldn't help but think of Hunter and what he had told them a few days prior. She didn't know what to make of Hunter's remarks about her mother's death not being from a demon, though Vera, Harry, and Maya believed it. They thought his argument made sense.

Camilla agreed, but she also couldn't bring herself to trust Hunter. She considered what Warren would say about the situation. Not that she trusted him much anymore. She had to continue to remind herself that their past relationship was a lie as she brought her thoughts back to the lecture that had begun.

She was almost successful, more so than she thought she'd be, at keeping Warren out of her head during the lecture. At keeping the entire magical world out of her head.

At the end of class, Camilla ignored the goodbyes Warren called to her. She ignored his presence entirely and watched him walk away from her periphery.

She should catch up with him and find out what he thinks about Hunter's remarks. But she wasn't talking to him. And she did not need his input.

Camilla huffed, and before he was out of eyeshot, gave in and ran to catch up to him. Outside, she pulled his arm to get his attention. He smiled down at her when he realized who was pulling for his attention.

"This isn't me forgiving you," she prefaced. "I just have a question."

Warren's smile dropped, and he nodded for her to continue. Camilla explained what Hunter had told them and noted that she didn't trust Hunter and needed to hear it from him.

He smiled, the prospect that she still trusted him even slightly obviously brightening his mood. Camilla hated the flips her heart made at that small smile.

"It's a good thing, not trusting my brother. He's not trustworthy..."

"You're one to speak," she mumbled the comment under her breath, but noticed when Warren caught it. He sucked in a breath but didn't argue it.

"But I also agree with what he told you. A demon would brag about defeating anyone in your coven, especially your mother. She left her entire coven with only her book to fend for herself here. It's kinda badass. I don't think it was a demon."

Camilla wanted to punch herself for the ease that washed through her, but nodded silently instead. Looking into his eyes, she found them so sincere.

They had always been sincere, and she had never read through them. Camilla hardened her heart and whispered, "Thank you."

She didn't wait for a response as she turned and walked away.

She walked home to find the house filled with music. Following the sounds, she found her family in the kitchen. Maya was standing over the book at the island as she dropped liquids into her caldrons, Harry stood by the stove cooking, and Vera sat at the table in front of her computer. All three swayed to the music as they focused on their tasks, completely unaware of Camilla's presence.

Camilla smiled to herself. Minus Maya's caldron, this was an entirely normal scene.

She watched Maya. Her sister seemed back to normal, the weakness that had lingered after her time under having subsided. Her eyes showed exhaustion, but Camilla hadn't heard anything at night, and Maya had been acting normal during the days, so she'd tried to move past it.

But Maya had been a little too normal. It scared Camilla that her sister didn't want to talk about her time in Hell's Gate, that she didn't show any evidence that she'd been there in the first place. But something in Camilla told her that Maya was struggling from whatever happened. Trouble with Maya was she would never admit to it.

Camilla wasn't sure what to do about that. Maya never wanted to talk about what happened. And Camilla understood that. It had only been a few days, but she wanted to do something to help her sister. Maya could show face all she wanted, but her eyes didn't shine quite as bright as they had before.

Shaking her thoughts free, Camilla made her presence known to everyone. "Fine!" They all jumped, shooting their gazes at her. "I believe him. It wasn't demons. But then we now have to consider all the magical creatures that witches protect. Why would they want to kill one?"

"Well hello, Camilla," Harry greeted her. "Hungry?"

Camilla's eyes slid to the pot on the stove as she slumped into the chair beside Vera. "Starved."

Vera peeked up from her laptop and asked no one in particular, "Any idea what creatures those would be?"

Camilla shrugged. "I don't know. There's humans. Though I can't see how a human would defeat a witch as powerful as Mom."

"Could be faeries. Some of them look like humans. Some of them, like pixies, look more like characters from a movie," Harry cut in.

"I read about some problems centaurs have had with other magical creatures in a book I found in the attic," Vera said.

"Gargoyles," Harry threw in.

"Banshees," Vera added.

"Dwarfs."

"Elves."

"Ghosts."

"Werewolves."

"And let's not forget the animal species," Harry added as he and Vera caught each other's stare and smiled.

"Okay." Camilla threw up her hands. "I get it."

"Satrys," Vera added, her gaze still locked on Harry's as he threw out, "Wraiths." They both laughed at Camilla's grumble.

"Other witches," Maya casually contributed from her perch at the island, not looking up from the book.

All sets of eyes landed on her, and Camilla muttered, "What?"

Without taking her eyes off the book, Maya answered, "It could just as easily have been a witch." She looked up to meet their eyes. "It likely was. The one species witches will trust over any other is their own."

Harry hadn't voiced his opinions about it, hadn't even allowed his expression to change, but Maya's accusation that another witch could have killed Loretta troubled him.

She had been correct. It made complete sense that a witch could have done it and made it look like a demon attack. He was worried about the implications of such an accusation though, so he kept his troubles to himself for the time being.

While he left the girls to look over his meal as it simmered for the next hour, Harry ported to the southern countryside to meet with an old warlock friend of his. He hadn't heard much word of the goings on in the world of magical creatures, but there was one person Harry knew who would know everything going on.

Harry walked up to the barn and watched Rupert pick up a baby goat and hand it to a squealing child. Rupert gave a throaty laugh as the six children surrounding the one holding the goat jumped in excitement.

"They've turned you into the farmhand, have they, old boy?" Harry called out.

Rupert jumped and spun around to face his old friend standing at the end of the barn. He broke into a grin. "Well, if it isn't Old English. What brought you over to me?"

"Just missed your inviting company."

Rupert grinned and rolled his eyes, causing a laugh out of Harry. He looked to the kids still fawning over the goat, then back to Rupert, motioning with his head to move farther from the barn so they could speak privately. The grin on Rupert's face dropped.

Harry had met Rupert a year into the training that was meant to make him a mentor. Luckily for him, Rupert had been just as reluctant to being anyone's mentor, and they'd caused every trouble they could imagine together. Rupert had been as close to a brother as Harry would get. And twenty six years ago, he'd lost that to a woman who would go to bear him children, then these rascal grandchildren.

Rupert followed Harry a couple of dozen feet away. "So, old man, what's happened?"

"I've a question about the magical creatures." At Rupert's expectant look, Harry continued, "Do you know of any that are currently angry with the witches, specifically with the Whittle family? Or their coven?"

Rupert snorted, crossing his arms before his chest. "Many of the creatures are annoyed with the witches. Witches tend to treat them as lesser because they have less power. I know, witches don't mean to, but it happens. They act as if they are the heroes and it antagonizes the others. But do I know of any that are angry?" Rupert shook his head as he thought about it. "No more than normal."

Harry looked out at the expanse of land before them as he thought about what Rupert had said. The man was married to a witch, so he'd never bash against them—and he was a warlock, the closest male equivalent to a witch—but he seemed positive that witches victimized the other creatures. Harry hated to admit that he could see a bit of that in witches—luckily, the Whittle girls were too unprepared and unknowledgeable to play into that.

He finally responded, "I thought so. I figured I would have heard of it if there were."

Rupert shrugged, knowing better than to scrooge for more information. "There is word that the gargoyles have become resentful."

Harry's attention snapped to his friend. "Are you aware of why?"

Rupert shrugged again. "The same old, I believe."

"Then why have their feelings escalated?"

"I hear they've had some attacks that they were unable to fend off because," he motioned in air quotes, "the witches have taken all the power. It's a long way to gargoyle town. I don't know what's going on, but that's the word around here."

Harry nodded, attempting to sort out the possibilities.

He stayed only a few minutes longer to share and receive personal updates from his friend, then thanked him and ported out.

***

Vera hated the library.

The quietude throughout the building caused an unease within her. She had gone to the Theology library at Camilla's school, with the use of her sister's I.D., to check out some books on magic and magical beliefs. She had enjoyed the two books she'd checked out, but they did not tell her anything new.

Dissatisfied with the information, she was returning them.

Vera had just dropped the books in the return bin and was on her way out when her fingers tingled and the feeling shot up to the back of her neck. She gave an abrupt pause and turned in her spot to check if anything was around.

She didn't see anything, but a demon was there, that much she was certain of.

Narrowing her eyes, she continued her trek, feeling the sensation grow stronger as she neared the middle of the library. Vera glanced around for any sign of life around her. On a second glance, her gaze fell on the librarian who was currently doing a horrible job at putting books back onto the shelves.

The librarian paid no mind to the task at hand as she randomly shoved books onto the already full shelf. With her full focus now on the woman, Vera felt the sense awaken the same way it had at seeing Hunter.

Feeling her gaze, the librarian looked to Vera and gave an ugly smile. It stopped the pretense of putting books away, pushed the cart aside, and began walking toward Vera.

Vera stepped back, hitting the bookcase behind her and tripping, before catching herself on one of the shelves and giving the librarian the opportunity to show its true nature—the creature emerging from the woman's skin had an enlarged mouth to hold tentacles, each one whipping out to Vera.

Vera stumbled back and shot her arm out to throw the demon aside as one of the tentacles touched her. The tentacle ripped off as the creature flew back and crashed into a table in the middle of the room, but its tentacle had latched onto Vera's neck and shocked her.

The demon picked itself up and began running at her as Vera turned and ran away. She ran to the back of the library, shooting her hand out behind her to throw bookshelves down to block the demon's path as she checked around the library to make sure no one else was around. No one had walked in at completely the wrong time.

Slowing to check the final row, another tentacle caught her, on the calf this time. With better purchase, the shock felt like six individual holes being pulled out of her skin. She gasped in pain as she turned and once again sent the slimy thing flying.

Vera called out to Harry just before she began to recite the spell for vanquishing slimy demons. She hoped it would work since she hadn't memorized the one for tentacled demons yet. These vanquishing spells came in such a variety of niches, it felt impossible to learn them all. Something Maya would have done by now in her obsession with the book.

Just as Harry showed up, the demon began to combust, sprinkling them with powdered ashes. Harry looked to Vera, astonishment marking his features. He smiled at the scene around them as if complimenting her, then grabbed her hand and ported them home. Fortunately for them, the older buildings at Camilla's school still didn't have camera systems.

That'd likely be something they'd invest in now.

2 0

"*E*ither more demons want that book," Vera stormed into the kitchen, effectively halting the conversation between Maya and Camilla, "or they want the glory of killing a witch from our coven and the power that can come from that."

Camilla and Maya had been cooking, Maya taking Camilla's distraction to add more paprika to the chicken. Ignoring her, Camilla looked her eldest sister over, then looked to Harry who stood beside her. Vera looked like she'd fallen down a set of stairs, a pink wound already reddening around her neck. "What happened?"

Vera pulled a seat out from the table and dumped herself into it, a breath of relief escaping her lips. "Another demon attack."

Harry followed Vera to the chair and kneed before her, his palms already reaching for the wound around her neck. As he healed her, Vera relayed a basic breakdown of all that had happened while she was at the library, about the shock that felt like holes digging into her skin.

"It sounds like a Goolalimb." Maya guessed from her spot by the sizzling chicken as Harry moved to stand and Vera reached out to grab his sleeve, pulling him back down and casting out her leg. She pulled the bootleg jean up to show the wound on her calf. It looked worse off than the one around her neck, like a deep gush of red ready to burst.

Maya continued, recalling the countless hours of hovering over the book. "The good thing is, the tentacles are just supposed to paralyze you, not actually hurt you. It obviously takes some time since you're still fine."

Harry finished healing Vera's leg, his hand skimming her leg a few seconds more than required, then moved to take the seat beside her. He hovered over his knees, looking at the ground for a moment, before facing them. "I went to see an old friend of mine earlier today."

"Old old or old like you?" Maya asked.

Camilla gasped and bit the inside of her cheek to keep from smiling. Harry was family, but it was still a rude question. He didn't seem to mind at all though as a smile grew on his face. "Old like me. Although he continued the aging process again, so now he looks to be in his later fifties."

"You can do that? Continue aging again?" Vera sounded extra intrigued with this bit of information.

Harry nodded. "Warlocks aren't forever immortal. Whenever we choose to, usually when we have a significant other and a family, we can begin the aging process once more. It does have its benefits, since we could wait decades before finding our other halves."

Camilla couldn't help the intrigue wash over her and the warm smile at how romantic that sounded. They still knew so little about the magical world, and essentially nothing about warlocks, other than their powers were always porting, basic memory wiping, and healing. And that Bishop Whittle, Vera's father—and possibly her's and Maya's as well—was one.

"How does the aging process work? How's it decided when you stop aging?" Camilla asked.

"Essentially when your training is done. Not everyone starts training at the same time, so we won't finish at the same time. Plus, some pick it up easier than others. I didn't begin my training until I was about twenty six years old. Quite late."

"Why?" Maya jumped in.

Harry looked solely into his hands, clasped together on the table. Camilla felt her heart ache for him, unaware why, but knowing he likely did not enjoy telling this story, and they were essentially making him. He could refuse, of course, but as their so-called-although-he-refuses-to-call-himself-so  mentor,  it would make more sense to give them more information rather than less.

Harry shrugged. "I was young. I didn't care for the responsibility. Plus, I had a family." Camilla noticed Vera's breath hitch at the mention. "Parents and siblings I didn't want to leave behind when turning immortal."

Vera's breathing seemed to go back to normal as she shifted in her seat to face him. "What changed?"

Harry stared into his hands, his gaze washing away as he focused on the ground once more. "My circumstances. My family was killed. It was a peaceful death, I suppose. Our house was gassed in the night. They breathed in the gas until their lungs gave out. Died in their sleep."

Camilla couldn't imagine the pain of losing them all at once. Losing her mother had been hard, but she had still had Maya. She softly asked, "What about you?"

"I guess the warlock healing power kicked in. My lungs were fine, so I didn't notice anything until the next morning. I found them all *gone*."

Vera pushed closer to him. It looked like she wanted to throw her arms around him and hug him until he transferred all his pain away, though she remained still. "Did you find out who did it?"

Harry still looked to be off in a memory as he nodded. "Yes.

A bit like a group of serial killers. They gassed multiple houses, killing about a hundred people. Almost thirty families." He pulled himself out of his memory and looked them all over. "But that is the past. Now, I went to see an old friend. Rupert. He's a lot better connected to the inner goings on of other magical creatures. I asked about any problems against witches or your family he may have heard of."

"And?" Camilla didn't stop the question from jumping out of her mouth, even knowing full well he was about to tell them. She had completely stopped dinner preparations the moment Vera and Harry had walked into the kitchen, though she still had a cutting board of vegetables sitting before her. She lightly put the knife down.

Maya did not seem to be disturbed by the news as she checked the rice and placed a cover over the finished chicken, but Camilla knew Maya processed emotional information better if she kept herself busy.

"He did not know of anyone with problems against your family in particular, but said he thinks the gargoyles may have problems with witches. He said he cannot be too sure of the information, but I think it is something to look into."

Vera slowly nodded. "Gargoyles. It's a start."

Vera knew it was probably not the best idea for all four of them to have their focus on the gargoyles for days rather than diversifying their research, but they didn't know what else to do. Harry, for his part, was used to a more peaceful life as a warlock. Given he had never finished training, he'd never become a mentor and was learning alongside them of the problems beginning to plague them.

Most of what they could find had to do with witches and gargoyles being friendly with one another. And the little bit they did find of the problems with the gargoyles and witches had come from love affairs gone poorly. Overall, they had come up with nothing in their research.

And with no reason to visit the gargoyles, they could not head to the manor. The gargoyles were known for only allowing people into the manor if they had an official reason for visiting, not allowing just anyone to access their property. And the Whittles didn't want to go in attacking, it was still more likely than not that they were innocent. The little game of telephone that had given Rupert the information could have over-dramatized their frustration.

Vera and her sisters agreed that limiting visitors made sense given they did not hold much power other than their heightened strength. It worked greatly in their favor to watch who they allowed in. Especially if there was a rumor going around that they might go against the other creatures.

With nowhere to go with their research, Vera was ready to give up and just go knocking on the gargoyle doors. That is, until Harry got a call from Rupert about some 'things' taking place at the gargoyle manor. When asked what he meant, Rupert had answered he didn't know, but he'd heard from the nymphs that there was a disturbance on the lands.

Technically, not much to go on.

But Maya seemed to think otherwise.

To her, this was the perfect opportunity to check out the situation. If asked of their presence, they could say they heard something had happened and wanted to check in, not to play hero, but to help. Maya hated heroes, which was a fact about her first sister that Vera had been shocked to find out.

And she had convinced the rest of them.

Harry ported them into the clearing in front of the woods that stood before the entrance gate to the gargoyle manor. It was an enormous place, made entirely out of nature and dark in atmosphere, perfectly blending into its surroundings. The landscape was perfectly upkept, showing the amount of work and love that the gargoyles placed on their small piece of land.

And it was eerily quiet.

Vera wasn't sure if that was a common occurrence for the gargoyles. She also was unaware about the activities of gargoyles. There was no one out, which could be normal for this time of day for them for all Vera knew. But she had imagined at least some outside keeping watch.

"Is it meant to be this quiet?" Vera asked through the silence.

"I guess we found the problem," Harry answered as he pushed the gate open then walked onto the property.

They were not greeted by anyone, nor were they stopped as they walked right up to the front door. Vera and her sisters followed closely behind as they walked into the house that was equally as quiet as the outside.

Vera felt shivers chase across her skin. No powers at work, just pure instinct.

Harry stopped in the middle of the foyer, his features set and analyzing. "This isn't right. The gargoyles are known for being rambunctious and loud."

Vera let her gaze travel around the foyer before walking into the living room off to the left—likely the formal meeting room when they had guests. The furniture was upturned, books and trinkets thrown about the room, food sitting on the furniture.

"Is it normally a mess in a gargoyle household?" Vera asked.

"Rambunctious as they are, it can get messy, but not like this. They are known for their organized messes. This looks like someone took their time in throwing everything in disarray. Even left food lying about."

The quartet continued their perusal around the ground floor of the manor before heading out the back French doors. It was a complete disaster, nothing like the impeccable cut of the front of the property.

The fields were completely ripped apart, trees thrown around and patches broken. A complete catastrophe.

But still, it was unnervingly quiet. Vera especially didn't like the silence that hovered over her in the backyard.

Just as her family turned to walk back inside, Vera spotted something from the corner of her eye. It was the slightest twitch. So slight, she was almost sure she had imagined it. As she slowly turned to follow her family, she saw the twitch come from beneath a fallen tree.

"Wait!" she called to her family as she hurried over to the tree, concentrating her power to lift the tree up. Given she had never moved anything so large, it took more energy out of her than she had been expecting. Beneath it, she found an injured gargoyle.

He coughed with relief and spoke almost inaudibly, "Thank you."

Her family ran over to the injured man and helped him up, Vera still holding the tree in the air as she used her concentration to move it far back, unaware where to put it to make sure it touched no one. She decided the spot her family had just been standing was the safest bet.

Vera looked out to the other fallen trees littering the field—there were at least a dozen thrown haphazardly around the back of the manor. Vera began with the farthest one, figuring if she could clear the back, she could move the ones closest to her to the back. As she used her power to lift the tree, she listened to the others beside her.

When the man was able to speak, he introduced himself as Uzark, the leader of the North American gargoyles. He resided in the American tribe, though the Canadian tribe had far more gargoyles in it. He felt it the middle ground for the North American group.

He thanked them as Harry bent down to heal him and Vera moved the tree to find no one beneath it. She allowed it to slowly fall back down, then moved to the next one over. Finding two others beneath that one, Camilla and Maya moved to help them up as Vera placed the tree over the previous one. She moved to another.

The third one had no one under it, but the fourth had three fallen beneath and nine stuck in one way or another, unconscious but breathing. Harry was making his way to heal the first two, with Uzark following Maya and Camilla to help the fifteen that had been stuck under the tree. Uzark told them what happened. "We had a visit from the Delvaux family. Apparently, they were unhappy with the rumors that gargoyles are trying to take the Powers for themselves." The girls had learned early on that the 'Powers' referred to the special abilities that only witches and creature demons possessed. "It was ridiculous, of course, so I denied any accusations. Hunter, that bastard, didn't believe us. Said there have been a lot of demons going missing. It wouldn't be too much to assume we had killed them and taken their powers. He let his goons run havoc in order to *show us our place.*"

Vera moved two more, finding twelve more gargoyles. At the seventh, she found the lot. Most hadn't been hit by the tree but just lay unconscious behind it. There had to be at least thirty of them.

"Of course Hunter is involved." Disgust dripped off Camilla's tongue.

Uzark nodded as Harry made his way through the mess. "Of course, we were no match to a load of power-filled demons. They destroyed our property and walked away. I just do not understand why they would think we would want any part of the power wars between your two species."

"Unfortunately, they're not alone. Witches have heard the same news. It's the real reason we came," Maya responded with a blunt remark.

They did not speak again for some time, Vera moving all the

trees and larger chunks of broken property out of the way and falling back to rest on the original tree she had moved. She had no idea where she had found the power to move all of that, but she was ready to sleep for a month straight.

They had found at least two hundred gargoyles—though Vera guessed closer to double that—scattered around, most of which had been unconsciously hidden behind a couple of fallen trees. Harry worked his way around the field, healing one after another.

"Wait." Camilla abruptly stopped and stood ramrod straight. "You said the Delvaux family?"

"Yes, dear." Uzark looked like a patient man. "It's a position play in the demon world. That family needs to show that they are one of the most powerful within the species. Hunter is a smart man. He knew we were planning no such thing. But he can't let his lackeys know that he trusts us not to attack."

Vera looked to Camilla and noticed Maya and Harry doing the same—they knew what she meant.

Camilla shook her head at Uzark. "Was Hunter the only Delvaux brother here?"

Uzark's eyebrows furrowed at the question, but he answered anyway. "No. The little one, what was his name…"

"Warren," Camilla breathed out.

"Yes. Warren. He was here, too. Wouldn't have expected anything less. It is a family matter, after all."

"And that's worth killing you?" Maya sarcastically bit out.

Uzark's smile didn't reach his eyes. "He wasn't trying to kill us. Scare and destroy, yes. But not kill. Though I hardly think he'd actually care if he had. It would cause problems with the other North American tribes. We're powerless, but strong. We can cause other sorts of problems."

Camilla nodded numbly and looked away, but Vera knew her sister was hurting extra hard now. It was one thing to hear the man you loved was a demon and another completely to see the outcome of that.

Harry grabbed Uzark's attention as he continued healing the many unconscious members. "Do you have any idea as to why someone would be targeting the gargoyles?"

Uzark shook his head. He looked around at the carnage of his property, at his companions who either stood healthy or lay unconscious waiting for Harry's assistance. "Thank you for healing them. For coming."

They spent a couple of hours with the gargoyles, waiting for Harry to finish healing the others and for both Harry and Vera to gain a bit more energy back before they left. Maya and Camilla helped the gargoyles tidy up as much as they could in the short time they were around.

On their way out of the front door, Vera noticed Warren standing just beyond the entrance gate. He seemed to be standing alone, and as they walked toward him, Maya shot a bolt of fire directly at him.

Warren shadowed out of the way, just nearly missing it, and landed about fifteen feet away from where they stood at the gate. Maya readied another bolt of fire in her hand but didn't shoot.

"What do you want?" Vera made her vehemence clear.

Warren's gaze fixed on Camilla, a desperate pleading in them. "Camilla. I had nothing to do with this."

Vera scoffed at the same moment her family did.

"I. Promise. You. I was only here to make sure no gargoyles were killed. Hunter gave the demons free rein over the place and left. I had to make sure nothing serious happened."

Vera felt the fire breathing around her heart. The disgust she felt was mirrored on the faces of her family. Warren's attention never wavered from Camilla's.

"You. Disgust. Me," she spit out and gave him no time to respond as she stepped closer to them. Vera looked to Harry and gave him a nod to port them out as Maya allowed the bolt of fire to shoot out just as they ported. Again, he shadowed out of the way, this time much closer to getting hit.

<hr>

W arren shadowed to his original spot beyond the gates and looked to the spot the Whittles had just been standing. He then took in the two areas Maya's fire bolts had hit. The fire magic reminded him of his brother, and as he stood there, his fury with Hunter grew.

He shadowed to Delvaux manor where he was hoping to find his big brother. Lucky for him, all the other residents at Delvaux manor were out when he arrived home, and he didn't have to deal with them. He hated being around everyone his father allowed into the home.

Warren found his brother lounging by the fireplace in the family library. Hunter looked so nonchalant in the large armchair, like he didn't just give a load of demons permission to destroy the gargoyle's manor, essentially giving them permission to kill the creatures.

"Are you going to continue ogling me, brother?" Hunter spoke up, his gaze never leaving the fire before him.

Warren felt the bile and fury grow in his throat. It was a feeling he was very familiar with around his family, but he felt it more powerfully than he ever had before. He moved so that he was standing beside the fireplace and turned to his brother. "They think I had some part in your little adventure today."

Hunter smirked, his gaze flickering to Warren. "But you did."

"I did not!" Warren yelled, rage reaching a peak.

Hunter didn't seem fazed in the slightest by his brother's outburst as he remained relaxed in his seat. "You were there. You didn't stop it, brother. You played your part."

"I couldn't stop it!" Warren spit through gritted teeth.

Hunter laughed under his breath and moved his gaze back to the fire. "You're as much a Delvaux as I am. You could have told them to stop when I left. You could have told them to stop while I was there."

Warren was stunned into silence. His brother truly believed *he* could have stopped the demons. That they would have listened to *him*. Ridiculous.

"They wouldn't have listened to me."

Hunter merely looked at him, quirking a brow in challenge.

"Look. That doesn't matter right now. You've destroyed my chances with Camilla. She hates me!"

Hunter took his time standing in the most graceful and lazy way Warren had ever witnessed—it was a trademark for his brother.

He walked over to Warren and placed a hand to his shoulder. "I did nothing to your relationship. You took care of that on your own."

With a light push, Hunter walked away from Warren. It was in that moment that Warren realized something. "You never meant for something to truly happen to the gargoyles, did you?"

Hunter turned his head to show Warren the smirk on his face, the glint in his eyes, then winked and shadowed away.

## 21

Maya had gone to her room and waited for her family to clean up from the mess that had been the gargoyle manor. She figured she would wait for them to go through their night routines and head to bed before doing so herself. The later she went to bed, the better. The less sleep she got, the better.

Maya had not been able to let go of her dreams from Hell's Gate. She would find out soon enough if the Althea one was true, which she strongly suspected it was, but it was still forever burned in her memory. Worse off, her second dream was forever burned into her memory.

In the week since her family had gotten her and Hunter out of Hell's Gate, her sleeping thoughts were plagued with the dreams, and her waking thoughts were always sending her back to Hunter.

The Hunter ones were almost worse. Especially after the day's events, Maya knew she shouldn't be thinking about him, remembering their time together. She was angry with him for the gargoyles, but still found, like Uzark, she understood. Didn't approve, but understood where he stood. Especially considering caring didn't come naturally to him.

And she continued to think of him knowing her family would disapprove, yet unable to help herself. They would not judge her for her sleeping thoughts—the horrors that were forever plagued in her memory causing sleep to become a distant memory—but these thoughts, they certainly would judge.

But she had been afraid to sleep since her first night back. She'd learned the first week of reading the book how to cloak her room in a silencing spell, and it had been one of the first spells she cast alone. She hadn't known why she was doing it at the time, but was glad that she did. Her family did not need to know what had happened to her. Camilla did not have to feel more guilty than she already did.

She'd been sitting at the edge of her bed, legs scrunched up to meet her chest, for an hour as she waited for the house to quiet. She suspected another ten minutes and she would be safe to quietly clean up and avoid sleep.

In her wait, her waking thoughts found her sleeping ones and brought them to life. Maya squeezed her eyes shut, trying to push away the memory of Vera bludgeoning their mother with a hammer, Camilla taking her life with a knife, and Maya herself beheading her with an axe. She could still feel the blood splatter against her skin. She could still hear her own cruel, rich laugh as her mother's head lolled to her feet.

The memories were more crisp in her mind than had they actually happened.

She shot out of bed, concluding she'd waited long enough, and headed for the bathroom. The walk down the hall confirmed that the house had gone to bed.

Closing the door behind her, Maya cast a temporary silencing spell on the bathroom. She wasn't sure if it would be needed, but caution took hold of her.

Maya started the water for a bath and began to undress as she waited for the bath to fill. She stared into her deep brown eyes in the mirror, finding the exhaustion ringing the edges of her eyes. She'd used a spell to wipe it away, but that was a purely aesthetic spell. It could not hide what was evident in her gaze.

As the steam from the full bath filled the room, Maya made her way into the water, slowly dropping herself in. She let her head fall back as her muscles relaxed in the steaming water. Even with her eyes open, she could not escape the memory of the dreams as they haunted her.

She shook her head, deciding she'd rather think of Hunter, even if her family wholly disapproved, than of the dreams that had been made a vivid memory.

She allowed herself to only think of his looks. His tall form, built to fight, but also to lazily and gracefully stroll into everyone's lives. His bow shaped lips that felt like they were always in a smirk. Sometimes cruel, sometimes wicked, sometimes teasing. His black eyes, which bled into his pupils, but somehow still shined to intrigue Maya more than any set of eyes ever had. She found a deeper sense of wicked teasing in them than in his smirk, inviting her to want him more.

Even the way he dressed, always in boots covered by trousers and a button up or an expensive sweater or nice shirt. His fire power ensuring he never needed a coat in the colder weather.

His fire power, the same as her own.

Had she not felt the need for him the moment she had seen him, she'd have assumed the only reason she wanted him was their shared power. Though she knew it wasn't the case, she found she was intrigued by their shared rare power. Was intrigued by his way of life, his disregard for everything and everyone around him.

And Maya would never admit it to her family, but she understood it. Understood why he could attack the gargoyles and walk away without a care. It was not something she would ever do, but it was his nature. To not care, to remain unfazed. And Maya would not, *could not* blame him for it.

Lying in the water, she felt the effect that thoughts of Hunter always had on her body as every inch of her stood at attention, as her nipples hardened and her core tightened. As her entire body remembered what it had been like to have him pressed against her, to feel his skin under her hands.

She hadn't allowed her hands to go wandering since the day she'd met Hunter, knowing that he would pop into her mind, and she would be biting down on her bottom lip to stop from screaming his name.

She hadn't wanted to come to thoughts of him.

All she wanted was to come to thoughts of him.

His tongue, his touch, his presence. She wanted him in her.

Maya felt her mind give in as her hands found their way down her body, one hand taking a breast as the other slipped between her legs. She felt her entire body jump as she touched her most sensitive spot, and Hunter's wicked grin invaded her thoughts. Even with eyes open, she could clearly see him.

Letting her head fall back, eyes fall closed, and the montage of memories of Hunter in her thoughts, her hands brought her closer and closer to her peak.

It did not take long. She'd wanted this for too long for it to take any time at all. Within minutes, she was screaming his name, calling it out over and over again as her body convulsed.

When she came down from her high, she was more thankful than ever before that she had silenced the bathroom, preferring her family to hear her terror over this pleasure. And she allowed her hands to do as they pleased, allowed Hunter to plague her, as she relaxed into the tub again.

Camilla walked into the kitchen in the morning to find her entire family already there. No one was surprised to find Maya up. She'd always been an early riser, going for a run and getting ready before anyone else had woken. The rest of them, on the other hand, played a bit of a gamble on who would be last.

Maya sat at the table, a cup of black coffee in hand. Vera and Harry stood by the kettle as Harry readied their cups with tea bags, and Camilla walked straight to the brewed coffee Maya had left in the pot and filled herself a cup. She walked to the fridge in the silence of the room and pulled out creamer, filling her cup. She could not drink like Maya. Black was far too bitter for her.

They all met at the table, taking their seats as usual—Maya with her back against the wall, Harry and Vera next to one another opposite her, and Camilla at the head.

Maya stared into her coffee, her thoughts looking to be far off. Camilla called out to her sister once, twice, a third time. With no response, she made sure her power was controlled so she wouldn't invade her sister's thoughts and gripped Maya's arm, shaking it.

Maya came out of her reverie and looked to her sister, eyebrows up expectantly.

"Are you okay?" Camilla knew not to allow too much worry into her tone. Maya would not like that.

Her sister nodded, evidently shaking her head from the lingering thoughts. "I just had a…dream last night."

"Anything serious?" Vera had not perfected the 'not too much worry' tone.

Camilla could see the slight annoyance at Vera's tone that plagued Maya as she shook her head. "Just something that happened in Hell's Gate."

Camilla came to attention—Maya never spoke of her time

down below. "Does it have to do with how you got those bruises?"

Maya nodded ever so slightly. She obviously still did not want to talk about it.

Camilla knew her sister would not clarify, so she changed the subject, turning to the others at the table. "We need to talk about what happened yesterday."

Harry scoffed under his breath. "Well ,there's an understatement if I've ever heard one."

Maya bit down on a smile at Harry's comment and Camilla rolled her eyes, glad that her sister wasn't lingering on the events in Hell's Gate.

She ignored Harry's statement. "Here's what I don't understand—why the gargoyles? Why try to set them up?"

Harry shrugged as he took a sip of his tea. "Could be because they do not truly possess powers. They'd be easier to take out. Depending on who is behind this, if they took out the least powerful species first, they would have less to deal with at the end."

"Like a trial run on fighting a magical creature." Maya's comment was a joke, but there was a seriousness to it—that was essentially what had happened.

Harry's eyes glinted with thought. "If the goal is to ultimately attack one of the Powers, it would make sense to train, to take down others. Especially if this is a demon or a witch, they'd know just how powerful our two species are. *Especially* if they're also responsible for your mother's death. The confidence in bringing her down could be pushing this person forward."

"I think I'm back to thinking it's a demon," Camilla voiced.

"I think it's a witch," Maya countered.

"I disagree with both of you. I think it's one of the less powerful species," Vera said.

Camilla blew out a breath of frustration. "But we can all agree to put demons back in the running?" To her surprise, everyone nodded. She was definitely expecting some arguments.

In the bit of silence, they all drank from their cups, and Camilla's thoughts rushed back to Maya. Her eyes were still exhausted, but she somehow looked more relaxed than she had since she'd come back from Hell's Gate. Camilla couldn't help but wonder how much sleep her sister had gotten that night. Had the dream kept her up all night?

Harry broke her thoughts. "Last night I did get to thinking about this whole situation, and I remembered your mother telling me she was worried for the coven. I don't know how this had slipped my mind."

"The coven in Europe?" Vera asked.

"Yes. Before she left, they'd been fine, but after a few years, she thought someone was trying to get to them. She was never certain, but she thought someone was after a member of the coven."

"So an attack on our coven, or witches as a whole?" Vera questioned.

"I haven't a clue. Could be both."

Camilla broke in, "Okay. Let's imagine for a moment it's not witches or demons. Who would attack our coven, and why would they want to? Especially if they're attacking cross continentally."

"Could be faeries," Harry began. "They're the most powerful after witches and demons. It could be a power game—attack one of the most powerful covens within the most powerful creatures."

"Making their way to the top? Beat the most powerful witch, and witches become afraid. Go after some powerful demons, and demons may begin to respect you out of fear," Vera thought aloud.

Camilla hated the jump her heart made. "That would mean

Warren's family is just as likely to get hit. His family is feared and respected within demons."

Harry nodded. "Yes. If it were a faerie, I would suspect they would go after a demon or two before revealing themselves."

"Right. And if it's not a faerie? Any ideas? Something that maybe doesn't hold much power. They might try to force their way to more respect," Vera asked.

Harry thought about it for a moment. "Dwarfs. They hold some of the least power. Now that I think of it, they also receive some of the least respect."

"So it could be dwarfs," Camilla commented.

Harry shrugged. "Could be. Could be any lot of magical creatures."

"Why are you hesitant?" Vera asked.

"I don't see it being dwarfs. At least not to this coven," he responded. "This coven shows the most respect to them. Your mother was friends with some. I don't see it being them."

"Resentment isn't always seen," Camilla rebutted.

"Okay. Let's say not demons or faeries or dwarfs. What else?" Vera thought aloud.

Maya interrupted them with a simple call, "Harry?"

They all looked to Maya's contemplative expression as she faced the warlock. "Yes?"

"I need to ask you something, and I need you to be honest with me," she said.

Harry looked both worried and curious. Camilla felt both. "Okay."

"I had a dream while I was in Hell's Gate. Kind of like a memory," she began, and Camilla felt her heart drop to her stomach. Maya was finally speaking up about something that happened down below.

Camilla did not break her attention from her sister as Maya told them the story of her dream—of their mother, pregnant with her, and the witch who had tried to exorcize her. Camilla's heart fell deeper into her stomach, bile rising up her throat as Maya continued about Harry's appearance, and the fact that had he not shown up, Althea would have gotten away with it.

Camilla sat motionless at the table with Harry and Vera as they all took in the visions that had been plaguing Maya since they'd brought her out of Hell's Gate, and Camilla had a feeling this wasn't the only one.

Maya didn't remove her gaze from Harry as she waited for his response.

"I do not know how you know that, but yes, that did happen," he finally answered, and the bile in Camilla's throat inched higher.

Maya nodded. She'd been expecting it to be true. "Then I believe it was a witch from Althea's coven."

Camilla wanted to fight that a witch would never, but after that story, she wasn't so sure anymore.

"Althea was part of the Bridgers coven. They have different ideologies than most covens do," Harry vaguely explained.

Vera pulled her gaze from Maya, something Camilla had to force herself to do, and looked to Harry. "What kind of ideologies?"

"We know that there are dark and light powers and that both demons and witches can possess both powers. It just so happens that most demons get dark, and most witches get light."

They all nodded.

He continued, "The Bridgers coven does not believe in that. They think that dark powers are for demons alone and light for witches. They have been in quite the bit of problems with others for accusing witches with dark powers to be evil. The same with demons with light powers—they accuse them of stealing. The biggest problem with their ideologies is that they continue to be passed down to each generation. Althea had been taught that idea her entire life. She truly believed your mother needed her help."

Maya scowled, and Camilla couldn't help but follow her sister. "She can rot, for all I care."

"Did Althea have any family? They could be angry that she died because of our family." It seemed Vera and Harry were the only ones to continue rational conversation.

"Yes." Harry thought back. "Yes, she had a daughter, just a couple of years older than you, Vera. Her name was Lila, an awful girl. She was always causing a mess. A nightmare at events, I heard."

Camilla made herself join the conversation and rinse Maya's dream from her thoughts. "That puts her at about thirty now. Perfect time to get revenge for her fallen mother."

Harry nodded. "I believe they still have their family warlock as well. And he's quite a bit older than me. If we do go to Lila, Tamire will be around to help her."

"And we have a very angry Maya," Vera responded nonchalantly, causing Maya's lips to twitch in a cruel smirk as she sat back in her chair, reminding Camilla that her sister played the demon very well. Possibly also including not caring whether she hurt—or killed—someone.

## 22

For once, Maya was feeling good about the lead they had. Surrounding the book in the attic, they looked for the locator spell that would find them Lila Bridgers.

They needed something of Lila's, something to indicate who they were looking for. Maya felt the twinge of annoyance, unaware how they would get something like that.

Harry perked up. "Hope may not be lost." And he walked right out of the room.

Maya looked to her sisters, at a loss. "Were we meant to follow him?"

Camilla and Vera shrugged, small smiles on their lips. Before the sisters could decide to follow their warlock, he walked back into the attic, framed photo in hand. "Lila had made this for your mother right around the time you were born, Vera."

He handed them a picture of Loretta holding a little girl, the frame homemade with macaroni and stickers. Maya recognized it as one of the photos that had been in the office. Now she knew who that was.

And she didn't care for the sentimentality of it.

Taking the framed photo, she placed it on the table in the

center of three candles. An open map sat beside the candles. With a final sprinkle of salt around the perimeter of the table, Maya joined hands with her sisters—knowing it wasn't necessary, but that Camilla liked to do so—and recited the spell.

They all watched the map as it expanded and shrunk until it landed on two spots; one in Kent, England and the other in Quebec, Canada. After another second's wait, the map moved to Kent and stayed there.

Harry looked confused as he stared down at the location. "That's odd. The Bridgers coven is known for sticking together. They reside outside of the Seattle area. I just didn't know the exact coordinates. But another continent altogether?"

"Maybe she's on vacation," the snarky comment left her mouth before she could stop herself.

Harry rolled his eyes and took Vera's empty hand, the other still clasped around Maya's, and ported them to the exact coordinates the map had given.

Maya had expected to port into a lovely cottage home, not the crumbling building they found. From their expressions, it seemed her family were all on the same page.

The home was burning in different areas, most of it destroyed from something other than fire it seemed. Maya used her power to put out the remaining flames, and they made their way around the debris.

As they entered the cottage, they found more crumbling bits, but no Lila or Tamire. Or anyone.

Maya led her family through the mess as she put out any fires still burning. In the hallway, she heard voices coming from the room at the end and turned to her family. They nodded in acknowledgement, and Maya looked to Vera, mouthing, *Demons?* and received a nod in return.

Maya continued leading her family until they rounded the corner. She stopped in her spot, feeling her family circle around her. Hunter was here. Of course he was.

He stood in the middle of the room, two goons behind him, and bits of fire still lightly burning in bits of the room. In the far corner stood what Maya supposed must be Lila and Tamire.

Tamire was, indeed, playing protector as he stood completely before the witch, blocking her from view.

He stood tall, dark skin and broad shoulders, his brown eyes meeting hers as she walked into the room.

As Tamire's gaze fell on them, Hunter tilted his head to see the newcomers and rolled his eyes. "Of course you're here to ruin the fun."

Maya allowed her power to subconsciously put out the fires in the room as she stood tall before him, felt his gaze take her in through his schooled expression.

Camilla grumbled, "Why are you always around?"

Hunter looked to her, bored. "I could ask you the same thing, Little Sister."

Vera jumped into the conversation before Camilla started the same argument she seemed to always have with the demon. "Hunter, what the hell is going on?"

"You witches seem to make a habit of stealing from demons. We're merely here to take back what's ours," he responded, turning his gaze back to the two in the corner.

Maya noticed her family turn to the two in the corner and followed suit, though her periphery remained fixed on Hunter, taking him in entirely with his impeccable dress and slicked back hair. He almost looked dressed up for the occasion of terrorizing witches.

"You guys stole something from him?" Vera asked Tamire calmly.

He answered with two distinct nods, but said nothing.

Vera turned to Hunter. "What did they take?"

"A vial of unicorn blood." He seemed to be enjoining the way they pressed closer to the wall under the scrutiny of his gaze. Maya couldn't help but feel his effect on every inch of her. It was a ridiculously annoying habit her body was picking up, her bits becoming too vocal.

Camilla turned to Tamire, true curiosity in her voice. "Why?"

Tamire took a moment to take in everyone in the room, likely figuring the demons would not attack again with them there, so he stepped aside to reveal Lila.

Lila, who looked similar to the photo of the child Loretta held—golden brown hair, hazel eyes, and slight figure. Well, her figure would've been slight, because standing before them was a pregnant Lila.

A heavily pregnant Lila.

"She's pregnant." His gaze evaluated everyone, his stance ready to move before her once more. "And the baby isn't doing well. We have a potion that could help, but unicorn blood was required. Demons are the only known species to have unicorn blood, and we needed it."

"And we would have been happy to give it to you," Hunter remarked.

Tamire turned a hateful look to him. "We don't have sufficient funds for your type of business."

Vera lifted a hand to halt Tamire and turned to Hunter. "Do you have any more?"

Hunter gave a singular, matter-of-fact nod. "Plenty."

"Then what does one vial matter?" Camilla asked, her frustration growing.

"One vial I allowed to pass. A month ago. But Lovey and Dovey here thought they'd come by for some more. Gave me a little chase to their little abode." He looked around the room. "Shame what's happened to it."

Maya had been watching the two in the corner as she listened to the conversations, the way Lila cradled her bump, and couldn't help but remember her mother cradling her belly in that dream. She interrupted their conversation. "It's the principle. If they leave it unpunished, it'll spiral."

Hunter turned haughty eyes her way. "My girl understands completely." Maya tried to fight the effect his words had on her. She was glad when his gaze moved to the two in the corner, his tone as bored as ever. Tamire moved quickly to cover Lila as Hunter's hand lit aflame. "Stealing is a no no. If they want it, they must pay for it. Maybe I'll take the child as payment."

"But you let the first pass. Why not a second?" Camilla's voice raised an octave as the stress of his comment settled.

"I let the first pass because I had other things to worry about. A little vial of unicorn blood wasn't going to take that away. *Now*, I don't have anything else to worry about."

As much as Maya had been enjoying the bit of cowering Hunter caused in the two, she had come to the cottage for a reason. She allowed her mind to move toward Hunter's arm, extinguishing the fire. His gaze shot to meet hers. "Give us half an hour. We may have a proposition for you."

Intrigue lit his black eyes as they stared into her chocolate ones. After a moment, he took a step back and nodded to his goons before shadowing out of the room.

All five pairs of eyes shot immediately to Maya once Hunter and his goons were gone. Her family remained silent as they watched her.

Maya turned to the corner Lila and Tamire were still huddled in and mentally cast a ring of fire around them. Her family stiffened beside her, but they allowed her to continue.

She moved an armchair from the edge of the room to the center, facing them, and lounged into it. With her back against one arm and her legs thrown over the other, she was sure she looked every bit a demon.

Tamire's eyes widened as he stepped back, closer to Lila, the fire raging around them. "You're a dark witch."

"Is that what you call it?" Maya mimicked Hunter's nonchalance, though her heart raced with the possibility that these two could be responsible for her mother's death.

Lila was trying to look over Tamire's shoulder, and Maya felt the cruel smirk blossom as she took them in. Lila seemed to be analyzing them all before her eyes fell onto Maya. "You're the dark witch that killed my mother."

Maya snorted at that, a humorless laugh escaping. She definitely had not been expecting that comment, but before she could say anything, Camilla stepped up and grit out, "She hasn't killed anyone."

Lila's hands moved to grip Tamire's arm, moving him to the side. He only slightly budged. "I know, I know. I worded it wrong. I meant..."

"I know what you meant, and I don't care. That's not why we're here." Maya relaxed into the chair.

Tamire's eyes hovered over each of them, remaining a bit longer on Harry, before landing on Maya. "Why *are* you here?"

Maya lounged deeper into the armchair, her legs stretching before falling back over the arm. "Well, Tamire. Our coven has this problem, and we think the two of you are behind it."

"What!" It wasn't a question, simply a shocked statement.

Vera explained anyway. "Members of our coven have been killed in recent years. We hadn't put it together before because they're in Europe, and at home there was only one, but we believe someone is very angry with our coven."

"And you think that someone is *us*?" Tamire asked incredulously.

"Is it?" Maya asked.

"No. No! Why would we even be a consideration?" He was truly flabbergasted, it seemed.

"Because bad old me killed Mommy Dearest." Maya's tone dripped resentment.

Both Lila and Tamire seemed to be waiting for more, their gazes jumping from person to person in the room. When they didn't get it, Lila looked to Maya and spoke up, "I know that came out sounding bad, but I didn't mean it like that. I was happy when my mother was killed. She was a miserable woman with that entire brainwashed coven. When she died, I had nothing holding me there anymore. I left."

Tamire nodded, the arm that Lila gripped hovering cautiously over her bump. "I had only stayed because of Lila. When Althea died, I took Lila to a coven for lost witches. That's where she grew up."

Maya narrowed her eyes at the two. He didn't look like a simple warlock helping his charge. He looked like a father protecting his child. Maya felt the cruel insinuation in her tone. "Completely off topic, but is that child yours, Tamire boy?"

A blush immediately told Maya the answer as his arm tightened across her belly. "It is."

Maya shook her head slowly, an accent awakening in her tone. "Naughty, naughty warlock."

She couldn't help but notice her family from her periphery: Camilla stiffening, Vera's gaze flickering to the ground, and Harry's shooting to Vera before settling on the fire still surrounding Lila and Tamire.

"Maya. Stop it," Camilla condemned her. She had allowed Maya to continue longer than expected. Maya gestured for them to take over, falling deeper into the chair with a smile. Her family turned to the couple in the corner.

"The coven was entirely psychotic," Lila started. "To them, any dark power made you evil, and any demon with a light power was worse than those with dark powers. They were completely deluded. I thought back on it a lot, how my mother was allowed to be friends with yours."

"Why would you think about that?" Harry cut in.

Lila's brow quirked. "Because your coven has had the most dark magic associated to it than any other. Your coven is like the holy grail of what the Bridgers coven hates."

Maya watched the couple and thought about Lila's remark—she was right. How had Loretta and Althea been friends?

As she thought about it in the silence of the room, Hunter shadowed back into it. Alone. He stood just behind her family, a few feet from the arm of Maya's chair. His eyes danced with intrigue at the scene before him, the fire still holding the couple huddled in the corner. His gaze flickered to Maya's. "Are we finally agreeing on something?"

"Yes." Maya's gaze remained on Lila, though her periphery told her that everyone but Hunter stiffened. "But not this one."

She wiped the fire away and turned to Hunter. Still lounging comfortably in her chair, she looked over her legs at him. "Ready for a coven hunt?"

Those black eyes danced.

He smirked greedily.

Maya felt her heart jump, whether from Hunter or the anticipation for the hunt, she wasn't sure. All she knew was that she wanted some sort of retribution for her mother.

## 23

 era was beginning to notice a habit of getting home tired and wanting nothing more than to get to bed.

Harry and Camilla had taken their showers, gotten ready, and headed off to their rooms immediately after arriving home. Maya set up a bath for herself to soak in after one of them had finished, and Vera waited in the kitchen with a cup of tea. When she heard no more shower running, she quickly rinsed her cup and headed up for her turn.

She'd just finished getting ready for bed and was finally closing the door to her room, breathing out her exhaustion as she walked to her bed and fell dramatically into it, immediately feeling the comfort it offered.

Vera laid snuggled into her comforter, thinking about what Lila and Tamire had referred to Maya as. A dark witch.

Vera had never thought about it like that, but 'dark witch' did seem to fit her sister. Not only because of her dark powers, but much more than that. Her ability to make a bargain with Hunter. Her ability to understand Hunter's motives and throw away the lives of witches. Maya spoke of the Bridgers coven with no remorse. On top of all that, her attitude and overall way of being screamed demon.

So, yes, Vera did think that Maya fit 'dark witch' impeccably well.

She moved her thoughts from her sister—knowing there was no use ruminating over her—to the Bridgers coven and their twisted ideologies. And part of her couldn't argue what Maya saw. Especially with the memory that Hell's Gate had given, she couldn't argue that her sister did have some reasons for hating the coven more than any of the rest of them, reasons that constituted death.

But she also couldn't help but focus on Camilla's side. The coven had bread Lila as well. They couldn't all be so bad.

Lila.

Apparently her first friend ever. And she was now married to her warlock. Vera knew, could tell from the way Tamire had blushed when Maya had asked about their particular relationship, that it was looked down upon for a warlock to form a romantic relationship with his charge.

She knew this, yet she couldn't find a problem with it herself. They had fallen in love. He wanted to protect her. What was so wrong about that?

She remembered the way Tamire touched Lila and couldn't help but remember Harry brushing against her in one of their meetings in the piano room. Vera sighed and tossed to the side, switching thoughts once more back to her sister and how she resembled a demon more than a witch. Somehow, this had become the safe train of thought.

In the morning, Vera found her family in the kitchen setting the table for breakfast. As they got everything ready, Camilla told them of the assignments she had due in school and how thankful she was that they were about to head into Thanksgiving break. Even though the Whittles did not celebrate, this gave her the chance to catch up with everyone else in her classes.

As they sat around the table, out of their unassigned-assigned seats and began piling their plates, Hunter shadowed into the edge of the kitchen. He ignored the annoyed expressions that acknowledged his presence and strolled over to the table, taking the seat beside Camilla and throwing his arm around her. "Well, if it isn't my sister-in-law."

Vera scowled at the demon at the same moment Camilla threw his arm off of her and scooted her chair away. Bad day to break her unassigned-assigned-seat it seemed. "Ugh. I am *not* your sister-in-law."

Hunter laughed at her, giving a dramatic act of shock. "No? Shucks, Little Brother will be upset to hear that."

Camilla flipped him off, then turned to her breakfast, completely ignoring him. Hunter laughed harder at her irritation, then turned his gaze around the table. His grin seemed to widen at seeing the annoyance on everyone's features.

He moved to grab toast and dump a load of eggs on top with a couple of cherry tomatoes. He went in for a bite when Maya commented, "Sure, help yourself."

He winked at her as he took a large bit of the egg and toast.

Vera sat motionless and waited. When it seemed Hunter did not deem it necessary to explain his appearance, she asked, "You're here because?"

Hunter glanced at her as he made himself another toast and egg, seeming to gouge them down faster than the rest of them took a single bite. "I'm here for the plan, partner."

"Don't call me that." Vera scowled at the same moment she noticed her sister biting back a laugh.

Camilla turned her irritation to their middle sister. "What?"

Maya looked to both of them with a smile, dumping her attempts at hiding it. "You guys let him get to you too easily. Your response to him makes him continue. It's amusing."

Vera and Camilla now scowled at Maya the same way they had at Hunter. Harry seemed to find this as amusing as Maya had and joined her in laughing at them.

***

At the end of breakfast, they cleared the table, then went back to their seats to begin planning. As Hunter went to take his seat, Camilla shot her hand out. "This seat is taken."

He narrowed amused eyes at her. "By whom?"

"The house ghost," she bit out at him.

"You do realize ghosts are a real magical creature right, Little Sister?"

She harrumphed but did not relinquish the seat. Hunter rolled his eyes at her and walked around the table to take the seat beside Maya.

Maya made sure to keep her attention glued to the others around the table as he pulled the chair out and sat beside her. Her entire body came to attention at the proximity, shivers racing across her skin when his knee brushed hers. She gave him no mind, knocking his knee away as Harry began to speak. "Essentially, we don't *know* anything right now. We are moving on the hunch that the Bridgers coven is behind this, the same way we were moving on the hunch that Lila and Tamire were behind it."

Hunter used the time Harry spoke to move his knee to touch Maya's again, locking it in place so she couldn't push it away. She glared at him, and he smirked back before they both moved their attention back to Harry.

"Basically, we need to do the same thing. Go over there and find out," Vera stated.

"Yes. But it won't be as easy. This won't be two people, but dozens. We can't walk in, especially with a dark-powered witch and a demon, and ask them about our coven. I'm not even sure we *can* ask them about our coven. How honest they would be."

"Yes," Hunter elongated the word. "Witches do have a tendency, don't they?"

The lot of them ignored his remark as Vera spoke, "I think, at the very least, we need a layout of the coven house. We need to know what we're going into. I got Lila's number yesterday. I could call her."

Hunter took this moment to move his hand beneath the table and graze Maya's thigh. She made a small jump and tried to inconspicuously glare at him as his hand continued to move into her inner thigh.

Harry responded, "Yes. You do that, and we'll port over when they have it ready!"

"Until then," Camilla began as Vera got up from the table to call Lila. Hunter's hand hitched up on Maya's inner thigh, and her hand shot out to grab his, holding it in place as she growled lightly so only he could hear it. He laughed as Camilla continued, ignoring him entirely. "We need to think about how we would go in. I think we should split up. I don't know the layout yet, but more people in different areas I feel like would help out the situation."

"Agreed," Harry said. "Which means you girls need to split up between me and Hunter."

Maya had just pushed Hunter's hand down so it lay just above her knee, grazing the bottom of her inner thigh, when Camilla grimaced. "Why him?"

"We're the only two that can port, or shadow, in and out. We need a quick way out in case anything happens," he answered matter-of-factly.

Camilla did not try to hide her disdain, which caused a teasing smile on Maya's features. "It's fine, Cam. I'll go with Hunter. You and Vera can stick with Harry."

Camilla smiled a thanks to her as Hunter's touch grew

stronger, grabbing a hold of her thigh and moving higher once again. With her hand still on his, Maya stopped him and let her elbow fall to hit him as she hissed, "Stop!"

Hunter laughed quietly at her side as Harry and Camilla turned their way. With twinkling amusement in his black eyes, he allowed his hand to relax at her lower thigh, lightly grazing her with his fingertips. Her family narrowed their gazes at him but didn't make any remarks. Maya wondered if they noticed anything, or if their hatred for Hunter had them overlooking the obvious. She, for instance, felt him everywhere, and she hated that he could smell how badly he affected her.

Vera came back to the table and took her seat. "Lila said they'll have the layout ready in an hour."

They all nodded, finding there was not much else they could do without the layout.

Hunter stood, removing his touch from Maya—and causing an absence that was felt in every cell in her body—then looked to the group. "I have to go home, need something."

"You could just not come back." Camilla smiled sweetly.

"But I'm just getting to know you, Little Sister." He smiled sweetly back and shadowed out.

Camilla turned to her family. "I don't trust him."

"That's not obvious." Maya smiled as she stood for a cup of coffee.

Camilla rolled her eyes as they all began to stand, following Maya to crowd around the island in the center of the kitchen. She moved to the fridge and took out the cookie dough she had left inside the day before. "I just think he has an ulterior motive to being here, and I want to know what it is."

"Yeah, well, it's not like we could read his mind. We just have to trust he won't betray us," Vera commented offhandedly.

Camilla froze at the remark, then looked to her family. "But I *can* read his mind."

Maya scoffed. "Like he'd ever allow you to touch him long

enough to get an accurate reading. He knows about all of our powers."

She stopped to think about it, then threw out a remark that stopped them all in their tracks. "I could kiss him." Even she looked shocked by it.

"What?" came everyone's response.

The disgust was evident, but Camilla seemed to be coming around to the idea right before Maya's eyes. "I could kiss him. He would be distracted, and I'd have the time required to read his mind, without him manipulating them. I could even try making my way around his thoughts to find what we need. I've kissed a demon before, a Delvaux even. It shouldn't be too different."

Maya couldn't believe what she was hearing. And she couldn't help the bark of laughter that slipped past her lips. She could already imagine Hunter's reaction to Camilla's advances.

Camilla drooped in her spot, moving the cookie dough into small chunks on a baking sheet as the oven preheated, then grew tall. "You don't think I can do it?"

Maya didn't hide the shit-eating grin. "Oh, no, please. Do it." She knew her eyes danced with anticipation for the scene she was about to witness.

She didn't know what it was, but standing at the island, Maya knew Hunter would reject her sister. Immediately. She didn't like how sure of that she was, but she ignored it. There was a scene she had to prepare to witness; this would only come once in her lifetime.

Camilla turned to the others. "Ridiculous?"

"Yes," Harry simply said.

"Ridiculous? Yes. Necessary? I think also yes. If we can get a read on his mind when he's not ready to manipulate it, we could know if we have a problem to look out for there too." Vera's support seemed to give Camilla the confidence boost she needed. Camilla took the sheet to the oven and placed it in, setting the bowl in the sink and moving around the island again.

Maya didn't have to wait long for the show because only a few minutes passed before Hunter shadowed back into the kitchen. He stood by the table behind Camilla, putting him directly in her line of fire.

Maya watched Camilla's face as she realized it was time. It would've probably made sense to wait until they were alone, but Camilla would likely back out before choosing to be alone with him.

She turned seductively and quickly walked over to Hunter, grabbing onto his shoulders and lifting herself so she was level with his lips before he could follow what was happening. She needed to wrap her arms around his neck, the only bit of exposed skin that would allow her to read his mind. Just as she leaned in, her arms moving to touch skin, Hunter stepped back, throwing her arms off of him. "What the *hell* are you doing?"

Maya bit down on her lip to hide the smile. She'd felt the pang of fear that Camilla would get a kiss in before he realized what was happening and was more relieved than she cared to admit that he'd caught on.

*He's mine,* she heard a possessive growl in the back of her mind.

Camilla brushed the rejection off and leaned in once more, letting her hand trace down his arm. "I just want a little kiss. Effectively erase me as a little sister in your mind."

Maya almost broke at hearing that come out of Camilla's mouth, but kept her composure. She was sure it took everything in Camilla to play this role, and she didn't want to be the reason her sister broke character.

Hunter threw Camilla's hand off of him and walked past her. He'd gotten about two steps from Camilla when Vera used her power to push him softly against the wall and hold him there.

Maya eyebrows rose, not having expected Vera to join in the fun, this was getting better and better.

"She just wants a kiss. You sure you don't want one?" Vera cooed softly, almost seductively herself. Maya was impressed with her sisters.

"Absolutely not! What is going on with you two?" He grimaced as he looked around the room to each of them in turn. When his eyes landed on Maya and the joy in her eyes, understanding that they were playing at something and not just completely losing their minds clicked.

Maya knew her eyes said she would allow this to play out and read the response that he would make her pay for this in his black ones, causing her to break into a smile. She liked the idea of him making her pay for it.

Before Camilla could come any closer, Hunter shadowed himself across the kitchen, behind Maya. "What the hell are you up to?"

Vera and Camilla leaned against the island on the other side. "Just don't want you to see me as a sister any longer."

Maya tilted her head back to watch Hunter's reaction and saw his face scrunch in disgust and utter disbelief—if nothing else, he knew the entire family wouldn't be fine with it, even if Camilla's desires were true—finally breaking Maya's resolve. She laughed and held up her hands to her sisters' wide eyed features. "I'm sorry. I'm sorry. I couldn't hold it anymore." Annoyed glances were thrown her way. "I'm sorry. You guys did quite well, though. Far better than I was expecting. Be proud."

"They did well with what?" Hunter's breath tickled Maya's hair as he grit through his irritation.

Maya ignored him, focusing on her family. Harry had been quiet throughout the entire encounter, seemingly enjoying the scene as much as Maya had. "You guys, he doesn't have any ulterior motives. He's here because we made a deal. That simple."

Hunter looked from Maya to the two sisters across the

island, and understanding began to dawn on him. Then he laughed. "That's it? You were trying to read my mind?"

Camilla scowled at him.

"Clever in theory. Unfortunately, you're not the sister I want." Maya heard the dark tint in his voice. He moved slightly out from behind Maya so that he was standing just to the side of her, although if she fell back, she'd still fall into him.

They ignored his comments, which Maya was thankful for, Camilla turning to her. "What are the terms of this deal, exactly? He gets to track down a coven, that's it? I don't buy it."

"You shouldn't," Maya began. "That's not it. I promised him he could take the head witch's power."

Her entire family stood erect at the revelation, eyes popping wide.

"Stealing powers! Are you insane?" Harry argued.

Maya shrugged. "We get his help, he gets a new power. It's a win-win."

"We can't let him kill a witch, Maya," Harry rebuffed her comment.

"Well, Mr. Mentor Man, she's not any witch. It's a witch killing other witches. I have no problem with getting rid of her."

Hunter smirked at that comment, moving his hand to the top of Maya's head and letting it slide down. "That's my girl."

Maya rolled her eyes back, slowly tilting her head to face Hunter. She looked at him, quite annoyed. "Pet me like a bitch again, and the deal is off."

Hunter seemed to read more into the comment because his lips twitched into an ecstatic grin as his gaze challenged her. He moved his hand to the top of her head and began to pet down. Instead of finishing the movement, however, he took a fistful of her hair and pulled her head back so her neck was open to him. "I love when you speak to me like that, love." With his final words, he took a large inhale of breath and laughed darkly.

Maya pulled away from him, walking to stand on another

side of the island, between her family, who looked annoyed with Hunter's antics, and Hunter, who looked very pleased with himself. If nothing else, their annoyance at him clouded their judgment, likely believing she was disgusted with his attempts, which worked in Maya's favor.

Hunter took another deep breath, inhaling exuberantly. "Mmh. It smells amazing in here." Maya refused to meet his twinkling gaze. "Almost orgasmic."

She clenched her teeth together and walked away before she allowed her desire to show in front of her family. Before she left the room, she heard Camilla respond to Hunter, "I'm baking cookies. Behave and I might let you have one."

## 24

They had moved the meeting to the living room after Harry and Vera came back with the Bridgers coven's layout.

Maya sat cross legged on the ottoman by the fireplace, Vera and Harry on the couch to her left, and Hunter on the couch to her right, the second closest spot to the fire. He sat legs spread wide, taking up almost half the couch by himself.

Camilla walked in holding a tray of freshly made cookies and glasses of milk. She had even poured one for Hunter this time, knowing they didn't have time for petty arguments. She set the tray down and grimaced at the only remaining seat beside Hunter, taking the far edge of the couch.

They each took a treat and got lost in the gooey after falls of chocolate, Camilla's special recipe. She smiled to herself until she heard the moan come from beside her. She grimaced at him as both Vera and Maya choked on their glasses of milk. Hunter grinned in Maya's direction, and Camilla narrowed her eyes at the two of them. They had secrets that only they shared, the family knew that much. A fact Camilla didn't like, but in moments when Maya could put Hunter in his place, worked in their favor. This was one of them.

Maya looked away, her eyes still narrowed in admonishment when they collided with Camilla's. She blushed lightly—Maya never blushed—and looked away entirely. Camilla frowned with a glance at the demon beside her, then back to her sister.

It seemed she was alone in noticing this interaction because Harry and Vera looked preoccupied with their treats and the debate of whether to dip, then eat, or eat, then drink. Maya moved the conversation away from treats and back to the problem at hand. The map lay outstretched on the coffee table, the cookies pushed off to the edge to accommodate it.

The five looked over the layout, pointing out spots that would be a good spot to land: the front of the property—obvious spot to begin if they only wanted to speak to the coven, but also a dangerous spot for Maya and Hunter given they would not be welcomed; the back of the property—unlikely to have anyone about, but also less likely to show them what they would be dealing with; either side of the property—least likely to be detected and a small show of the one side of the property, and again, no way of truly seeing the coven.

Lila had let them know that the house was normally left unprotected unless they felt an attack. Apparently protecting it with the spells they liked—impenetrable—took a lot of energy, and given they never actually got attacked, they wouldn't do it unless they had to.

With that knowledge in hand, Hunter wanted to shadow into the house. Any room could prove dangerous, given they could shadow directly into a room with witches, but he figured it useful. The basement would be a perfect way to get into the house with no detection, as witches preferred attics, so there shouldn't be witches down there. Plus, it made for a great way to sneak up to the rest of the house. Or a room on the upper floors. Because witches loved attics, a top floor would get them close enough to hear, but less likely to get caught. Or the dining room—considering the time they planned on shadowing in, he doubted the dining room would be in use, and it would get them a favorable spot in the center of the house.

Camilla couldn't argue with the fact that Hunter did seem to know what he was talking about. Plus, having him work the more dangerous spots meant her family would be safe. The only problem was Maya would be joining him. But she had to admit it, out of everyone in her family, Maya would likely be the one ready to try these more dangerous spots about the house.

Hunter let Maya choose which spot to shadow into, and she chose the dining room, seeing that they would be well balanced in the middle of the house.

Harry and Vera looked to Camilla and decided on the back of the property, at least to begin with.

Relaxing back into their spots now that they had a tentative plan on where to land and check out the coven, Camilla looked over her family, unable to stop the pang of fear that something might happen to them.

With the night dying down, Maya moved to the kitchen to make a pot of tea, and Camilla took the opportunity to talk to her sister alone.

As Maya filled the kettle with water and set it on the stove, Camilla bluntly asked, "About your time in Hell's Gate, what happened between you and Hunter?"

Maya's entire body froze, and she slowly turned to face Camilla. "What?"

"You and Hunter. Did something happen?"

Maya's eyebrows scrunched together as she shook her head. "Nothing. Why?"

Camilla felt the relief wash around her heart and shrugged, shaking her head. "I don't know. It just looks like you guys have some insiders. Like you look at each other and remember something...not bad."

Maya blushed again—twice in one night—and shook her head. "Nothing. Maybe it's the dark magic in us."

That blush had brushed the relief away from Camilla, and part of her, a large part, didn't believe Maya. But she let it go. If Maya didn't want to talk about it, she could understand. She had to. For now. Plus, the small part of her that did believe Maya considered the alternative—that it truly was because of their shared dark magic, the exact same dark magic. "Okay."

The doorbell rang, pulling them out of their conversation and Camilla yelled to the rest of the household as she walked out of the kitchen. "I'll get it."

She opened the door to find Warren on the other side. Before she could get a word out, he blurted accusatorially, "You're working with my brother."

"Not by choice," Camilla answered as Warren let himself into the foyer. She took a slow breath, closed the door, and turned to face him.

"How did he force that to happen?" Warren questioned.

"Not by *my* choice," Camilla clarified. "Maya's decision."

Warren looked her in the eyes. "I want to help too." Before Camilla could rebut his offer, he added, "If my brother can help you, I don't see why I can't. I'm more trustworthy than he is. Plus, the more help, the better, right? I want to do it. No strings attached."

Camilla looked at him a moment, then gave in. "Fine!" She walked past him into the living room, where she saw Harry and Vera heading into the kitchen.

---

Maya had taken the moment to relax after her sister's interrogation. Had Hunter and she been acting differently with one another? She certainly knew what looks Camilla was talking about, but to make it so noticeable?

She didn't have time to think about it as Hunter walked into the kitchen right as the kettle whistled. Maya acknowledged his presence with a look, then turned to begin pouring tea into two cups. Surprisingly, she and Hunter were the only two who had wanted any.

As Maya turned back to see what Hunter wanted, she collided into his chest. She hadn't heard him move right up behind her. Looking up at him, she plastered annoyance she definitely did not feel onto her features. "Do you mind?"

Hunter looked completely unconcerned. "Nope."

Maya rolled her eyes and put both hands onto his chest, pushing him away. As he took the two steps the push had garnered, Maya took the couple of seconds to feel his chest though his shirt, to remember what it had felt like under her fingernails.

She quickly pulled her hands away. "Can I help you?"

"No." Hunter looked down at her. "But I can help you."

Maya was not expecting that. "With?"

He pulled a vial from his trouser pocket, holding it up for Maya to see. "It's a potion that works like a pain reliever, except it relieves," he paused to think of the right words to use, "tough memories. It won't wipe your memories, but it will wipe any feelings that come with it, essentially wiping the constant torture, so you won't have to re-experience it."

Maya looked him in the eyes, unsure why be brought this to her. Hunter answered her unasked question. "Love, you're quite transparent with me. You've been reliving the dreams you had down below, and it's taking its toll on you."

Maya wasn't sure if she was shocked he had noticed. She moved her gaze to the vial he still held up. She was unsure how she felt about Hunter's ability to read her, and she was equally unsure if she should trust a potion from a demon with no strings attached.

As her hesitant eyes moved back to meet his, he read her

thoughts once more. With a smirk, he eased her worry. "I wouldn't drug you, love. I still have plenty of things I'd like to do to you."

She knew her eyes dilated instantly and felt her thighs tighten in response as her gaze moved to his lips before slowly making their way back up to his eyes.

Hunter stepped toward her, back to his original position, a few inches from touching. "You'll remember everything we did, all the feelings connected to what we did." He bent forward a fraction of an inch, his voice dropping the more he spoke until it hit a final seductive whisper. "You'll be able to re-experience it again and again and again in that little head of yours. That wasn't torture." He smirked at the last bit. "At least not the type of torture you'd want to get rid of."

Maya hated that he could read the true reasoning behind her hesitation, hated that it had *been* the true reasoning behind her hesitation.

She took her time savoring that moment between them before backing away and hitting the counter behind her. With a renewed breath of fresh air, though she still picked up his scent all around her, she looked back to the vial and took it from him. Staring him in the eyes, she uncorked the vial and downed the potion.

He gave her a genuine smile and reached behind her for a cup of tea, stepping back just as her family began to fill the room. Maya pulled herself out of the moment and grabbed the second cup, turning to find a new member to their group.

Hunter noticed his brother following Camilla into the kitchen and smiled darkly. "Finally decided to give in to that demon side, brother?"

Warren narrowed his eyes at his brother, but gave no response. Instead, he stood there and allowed for the family to fill him in on the plan. "A coven hunt? No. You guys can't take Hunter's suggestions in this."

Hunter laughed from beside Maya. "Little Brother, it was entirely their idea."

Warren looked to the rest of them for confirmation and found the truth there. He didn't like the sound of it, that much was obvious, but given his current standing with the family, he didn't have space to argue. They now had two demons on their side. Hopefully that would prove to be helpful.

The six spent the following days preparing, whether that be their plans or their abilities, and waiting. Tamire had informed them the Bridgers coven used to be the most preoccupied on Wednesdays and Thursdays. Although aware that twenty-plus years could have changed that, they waited nonetheless.

On Wednesday morning, they all met at the Whittle house and broke up into their little teams. Camilla would be shadowing in with Warren. Vera had offered to go with him instead, but Camilla had shook her head. They would be shadowing into a top room of the house.

This change meant Maya and Hunter would be shadowing into the basement instead, giving them a view from the bottom and top now.

Vera and Harry would be sticking to their original plan of the backyard.

Everyone met in the kitchen for a light breakfast early in the morning before breaking up. Everyone but Hunter held somber looks; *he* looked excited.

With each couple ready, they headed to the Bridgers coven.

Harry ported into the back of the property. He dropped Vera's hand almost instantly, feeling a tingling that would be all too distracting at the moment.

From the edge of the woods, they got a perfect view of the entire coven property, including the vast amount of land the coven owned and the mammoth size of their house. It was still much smaller than a demon's manor, but far bigger than anything Harry had been expecting.

They'd been anticipating to see a clean lawn leading up to the fortress of a home, but instead, they saw members from the coven. Approximately fifteen women dressed like it was the 1600s were parted into a wide circle, reciting what sounded to Harry like morning witch salutations.

Unfortunately for them, they had decided to stop and watch the women rather than find a way to introduce themselves or get out. And just as Harry realized as much, the coven noticed them.

With all fifteen eyes on them, they both took a step back as a whisper left Harry's mouth, "Bloody hell."

---

Warren shadowed Camilla into a top bedroom he'd chosen at random from the blueprints. It seemed to be quite a big room, and from Lila's memory, these rooms were never used. Hopefully, the memory still held.

After the moment it took to adjust from shadowing, Camilla found that Lila's memories were no longer the case. And part of her wondered, seeing what was surrounding her, if it ever had been.

All around them, Warren and Camilla found witches littering the floors. They looked drugged and weak, shackled to the walls with heavyweight industrial chains, no doubt charmed for precaution.

The witches around them that seemed to be aware jumped with their presence, pleading out, "Please! Please, get us out of here!"

Camilla stood motionless, paralyzed by what she was seeing as her eyes flickered around the room, taking it all in. She turned to the witch who had begged to her. "What is this?"

"We were each taken by the coven because we either have," she coughed as she tried to explain, "or are thought to have dark powers. They drugged us with a potion that paralyses your powers. They force it down our throats every few hours. Please! You have to help us!"

Camilla broke from her paralysis and moved instantly to the woman. She pulled at the chains, and when she couldn't get any leeway, Warren walked up and pushed her hand aside. He grabbed the metal and melted it open. His power worked almost instantly, like it took absolutely no energy out of him.

Camilla stared at him, realizing in that moment that she never knew what Warren's power was. Melting. She could see how that could be powerful. Especially if it could get past any charm they may have placed.

Warren melted the chains off of the woman, then moved to the others around the room, never speaking, though he looked deep in thought as he worked. There were at least two dozen women in the room.

As Warren freed the witches from their chains, Camilla bent to her knees before the witch, one of the only who seemed aware of her surroundings. "What's your name?"

"Genevieve." She coughed in response. She looked old and frail, at least in her sixties. Camilla couldn't fathom how this coven could throw these women in here with no care.

"Genevieve, we're going to get you guys out. Is there anywhere specific we can take you?"

Genevieve looked into Camilla's eyes, hope blistering in her crinkled face. "My coven. It's in the outskirts of Salem.

Everyone here will be welcome. We can find the other covens later."

Camilla gave her a small reassuring smile and nodded as she looked around the room. Warren was about halfway through the melting process.

"Most of us don't have it, you know." Genevieve brought Camilla's attention back to her. "Dark magic. And those that do have low levels."

Camilla smiled to her. "It wouldn't bother me." She thrust her head back to point out Warren. "I'm here with a demon. Plus," she said warmly, "my sister has a high-level dark power. That doesn't define who you are."

Thoughts of Warren plagued her mind the moment the words left her mouth. Thoughts of how she had based all her judgements of him around the fact that his father was a demon. She let that fact define him and ignored his human side.

Camilla thought of her sister and how she had never considered Maya's dark power a definition of who she was as a person, and Maya's power was more powerful than Warren's. Her heart ached at the bias she had held for her sister that Warren had not received. She looked to him now, only two girls from finishing, and her gaze warmed.

Before she could say anything, Warren turned. "That's all of them."

Camilla shook herself from her thoughts, knowing there would be time for her feelings at a later date. "Great! Now I need you to start shadowing them. Take Genevieve first. They're all going to her coven in Salem. She'll get her coven ready for the rest of them."

Warren nodded and walked over to Genevieve, picking her up as she explained exactly where to shadow into.

With them gone, Camilla moved to the other witches. She found the youngest ones, who looked to only be about fifteen, and got them ready. When Warren shadowed back, she pointed to them without a word. He picked one up and shadowed out.

They continued this routine, only taking one at a time since Warren had to carry each one out, until the room was empty of anyone but them.

***

Maya and Hunter stuck with the plan and shadowed into the basement. Lila had told them this was mainly left empty. Any time she'd been down there, it had been spotless.

As the two adjusted to their landing, they found that was no longer the case, and wondered whether it ever was, or if the basement had always been cleared out before Lila had come down. Because the basement was not spotless.

It was packed full.

Littering the ground all around them were dead bodies. The space was quite large, possibly fifty feet each way, maybe more, and almost all of it was covered in dead bodies. Of both witches and demons.

Maya caught Hunter's gaze, and they stared at one another, at a loss of how to react. Breaking, they each chose a different direction and began walking, finding empty spots on the ground to step around the bodies as they examined them.

From what could be seen, most of the bodies looked to be demons.

But not all.

And even had it been all, Maya knew that most of them did not deserve this. Being a demon didn't instantly warrant other species a death on your head. Animal demon, maybe. But creature demon—which all of these were—no. She felt more sick now than when she merely thought this coven was after her family.

Taking a few minutes to process, Maya turned to Hunter. "How? How are the demons still here? Wouldn't they vanquish?"

Hunter looked to her, his face stoic, but his gaze angry. "Only animal demons. Creature demons are just like you witches. Only those that haven't come into their powers yet would vanquish, which could still be the case here. There must be a spell surrounding the room, something not allowing it to happen."

"What makes you think that may still be the case?"

Hunter didn't look like he wanted to answer, like he knew how the next words would affect her, but he did so anyway. "There are some too young in here. It may be the case that they came about it young, like Warren and me, but I doubt it."

Maya tried to control her features, to hold back the vomit she felt inching up her throat. "I'm going to delight in letting you have your fun with that bitch."

Hunter smiled at Maya, nothing seductive or delighted in it. "We have to get them out. I'm going to shadow home and get some reinforcement."

Maya nodded and watched him depart, leaving her alone in the room. She could already imagine her family yelling at her for staying behind with no way of escape.

With no more Hunter, her gaze had no choice but to glance around the room. And land on the kids Hunter must have been speaking of.

She picked her way over and crouched down to look at them. They were each likely only ten years old, and both shared the same frozen stares. A witch and a demon, hands clenched together in a death grip. The same tight grip that Maya had clutched to Hunter with when in Hell's Gate.

Her eyes began to water as she moved her fingers to each of them, closing their eyes to rest. She blinked away the watering as Hunter shadowed back with his goons.

The four he'd brought began working immediately, shadowing demon bodies away. Maya turned to watch them and caught Hunter's gaze.

"Where do you want the witches?" he asked, ignoring the water that still lined her eyes. She was grateful for that.

"My house. Take them to the basement there. We'll find their families later."

He gave a small nod and began shadowing the witches out. Maya stood glued to her spot, guarding the demon and witch children as she watched the five demons shadow in and out, taking bodies with them. She heard familiar names of demons that had been missing as the goons worked, but couldn't get herself to concentrate on their conversations.

When all but the children were left, Hunter told his goons to leave and walked up to Maya. "Let's put them to rest."

Maya's watery eyes gave out, and she let one tear drop and slide down her cheek. Hunter's eyes softened as he reached a hand out to catch it on her cheek, holding it there with his thumb as his hand cradled her head. He said nothing else as he wiped it and stepped closer, taking her hand.

Maya took another moment to breathe out, and they each bent to grab onto a child before he shadowed them all to the Whittle house.

***

Before Harry and Vera could move to grab for one another and port out, the witches threw spells at them. One to knock Harry back into a tree, and another to knock Vera down to her knees.

Then she was moving, and when she looked up, she was in the center of the circle, a protective spell keeping her in. When she tried to use her power to throw the witches back, she found the spell that surrounded her also left her powerless. From

Harry's attempt beyond the circle, it looked like it also kept him out.

Vera got to her feet and turned in her spot, trying once more to use her power. When that deemed futile, she ran at one of the witches, attempting to break her connection long enough for Harry to port in and take her.

Before she could make it more than three steps, she was hit with another spell that threw her back into the center. She landed hard on her back, feeling the air knock entirely out of her lungs.

After a few minutes of lying still, she took in a large breath to settle herself and tried turning to all fours. She raised her head to look at the chanting witches surrounding her, then past them to Harry, who still stood beyond the circle.

All of a sudden, the witches around her stopped chanting and looked to her, now whispering their spell. From behind one of the girls came a woman, who looked to be a few years younger than what Vera's mother would have been. She stood before Vera, just outside of the circle, with a load of confidence. Her black locks held up with two pieces of plants falling just past her shoulders, and her eyebrows arched in a beautiful counterbalance. Her eyes were hazel mixed with green and lit with intrigue.

Vera locked eyes with the woman. This was the leader.

"Who are you?" the woman asked, eyeing Vera like a child with a new pet.

"I could ask you the same thing." Vera scowled.

The woman's lips twitched into an unpleasant smile. "You broke into our coven." She began walking around the circle of witches, causing Vera to constantly turn in spot to keep her in sight. "Now, would you like to tell me who you are, or should I force it out of you?"

Vera narrowed her eyes at the woman. She was confident it wasn't a blank threat, and with Harry still just outside their barriers, she couldn't risk anything stupid. "My name is Vera. Who are you?"

She seemed pleased with the direction Vera had chosen to go, smiling darkly in her direction. "You may call me Melusine. Now, Vera, would you like to tell me what you and your warlock are doing here?"

"I made a bet with him that he wouldn't have the energy to port us to every edge of this forest. This was edge thirty seven."

Melusine's eyebrows rose in amusement. "That's adorable, child. But you truly are a terrible liar. Has anyone ever told you that?"

"Plenty," she grit, keeping Melusine in her line of sight.

Melusine gave a slow sardonic laugh as she continued her rounds about the circle, not paying attention to her. The heels the woman wore ground into the dried leaves underfoot, but Melusine didn't seem bothered. Vera couldn't imagine the amount of practice it would take to walk on grass in heels with so much ease.

Vera took the moment without Melusine's attention to move her gaze to see what Harry was doing. It seemed the time was giving him no luck in trying to get through.

Melusine's gaze snapped to the side and boar into Vera's. "Should I suspect that you and your warlock came here alone?"

Vera knew if she denied anyone else's involvement, she would seem too eager to keep them safe, giving away instantly that they were not alone. She was not like Maya, who could easily brush past any involvement with a demon's nonchalance. So, Vera said nothing.

And that was answer enough.

Melusine sent four witches into the manor to check for anyone else. Three more girls broke out of the circle to make sure Harry could not get to any of them. Eight remained standing around Vera. They seemed very practiced with this little dance of theirs.

Vera hoped she had kept Melusine busy long enough for Warren and Hunter to be able to get her sisters out before any of the witches found them.

It was quiet in the yard, and Vera did not like silent moments. "What's wrong with your coven? Who was it that made your lot so deluded?"

Melusine laughed at Vera's audacity, but did not answer.

Vera herself was shocked with her audacity, but continued anyway, "I thought your coven only hurt people with dark powers. I don't have dark powers, and I'd think even your coven would be aware that warlocks can only have light powers."

Melusine tilted her head to the side to watch Vera. "Where, dear child, did you hear anything about our coven?"

Vera laughed sardonically. "Wouldn't you like to know."

Melusine's smile turned genuine, but she said nothing else. Like she was toying with Vera the same way Maya had been toying with Lila and Tamire.

A couple of minutes later, the four witches came running out. One informed Melusine of their findings, though she looked reluctant to do so. "There's no one else, but there definitely was."

Vera felt her sigh of relief that the boys had gotten her sisters out in time, but felt intrigue rock her on how these witches would know they had been there. It seemed Melusine was just as intrigued.

The witch continued, "All the bodies are gone. The captives as well."

Vera didn't know what she was talking about, but from the look on Melusine's face, it wasn't a good thing, and that made Vera very happy.

Melusine turned back to her. "So you did have some friends with you."

Vera gave a smile as Melusine threw a spell at her.

The spell knocked Vera unconscious immediately, but she looked fine from the view point beyond the witches' circle. Harry watched Melusine turn on him, ready to cast a spell that would knock him out as well. Or worse, kill him. Unwilling, but seeing no other choice at the moment, Harry ported out just as Melusine's spell came for him.

**26**

Hunter shadowed Maya and the kids into the basement of the Whittle house, settling the kids on the ground off to the side of where he'd rested every other witch he'd brought back.

He and Maya stood above them, and to no surprise to Hunter, it took almost no time for the demon child to begin to evaporate, his body turning to smoke and drifting away. The witch lay gripping air.

That final goodbye between the children broke Maya's composure, she turned and shoved her face into Hunter's chest, letting silent tears fall down her face.

Hunter froze, unaccustomed to the act of comforting, astonished that he may want to do it. Relaxing, he allowed his body to do what it wanted. His arms circled her, one hand resting on her back and pushing her in closer, and the other hand messing into her hair.

He'd never admit it aloud, but this was a comfort to him as well. He hadn't been affected by the loss of the children; he truly couldn't care less. But the memory it triggered: a witch and a demon clutching to one another for fear of what was to come next. He understood that.

And he deeply understood the fear of losing grip of her hand. He didn't like this new feeling, but he held Maya anyway.

Her tears fell freely as she clutched onto his sweater. It took three minutes before the tears subsided, and Maya pushed back, one hand still clutching his sweater as the other went to wipe the tears streaking her face. Three minutes too short. That simple thought made him want to bang his head into an axe.

He kept his hold around her as she whispered, "Thank you."

There was more to it than just holding her. It was for the children too. She thanked him for getting them out, for getting all the witches out. She thanked him for gripping her hand in Hell's Gate, and after when they lay in her bed. She thanked him for being everything her family hated, and Hunter didn't know how to understand that. From a demon, he'd have no problem with the gratitude, but from a witch, it was too foreign to comprehend.

Hunter smirked, but there was no conviction behind it. "Don't get used to it, my bleeding heart."

She broke into a smile, her eyes shining. She knew as well as he did that he did not mean it. He would hold her again when her witch heart brought her to tears. As long as she'd like.

They broke apart completely when movement cast from above, and they took the stairs two at a time to meet the others. Coming through the basement door, they found only Warren and Camilla standing in the foyer. Hunter remained by the door under the staircase and felt Maya stop beside him.

"You will not believe what we found!" his dramatic new little sister began.

Hunter gave a sarcastic grin in response. "Wanna bet?"

Camilla ignored him completely and focused on Maya. "The room we shadowed into had captive witches." She began to pace back and forth across the hallway. "Witches drugged and chained because they were *believed* to have dark powers."

Warren jumped in. "I got them loose and shadowed them to a coven in Salem. We checked some other rooms too, but couldn't find anyone else before coven members came running in."

"That's because the rest were in the basement," Hunter said, catching Camilla's attention immediately. She stopped pacing and stared at him. "Though our lot weren't so lucky."

Hunter rolled his eyes when both Camilla and Warren looked to Maya for confirmation. She nodded. "At least a hundred dead. Mostly demons, but some witches too. Hunter got his goons to help shadow the demons out. He shadowed the witches here."

"Here?" Camilla jumped. "In the house?"

Maya nodded and pointed to the basement with her head. "Downstairs. We need to figure out which covens to contact."

Camilla and Warren moved toward the basement when Harry ported in between the two couples. His face was ashen, catching the girls' attention immediately. That, and the fact that their sister was not with him.

"Where's Vera?" Maya questioned.

"We ported into the morning salutations," Harry spit out. He stared into nothing, his gaze frozen in a memory. "They got Vera before I could do anything." He gave them a detailed summary of what had happened, including the fact that the bodies were missing from the house. At that remark, he looked curiously to the four.

As Hunter would have assumed, neither sister took the time to think the situation through before racing to Harry.

"We need to port back. Get her!" Camilla insisted.

Hunter stuck his arm out, catching Maya and holding her back before she could reach Harry. He slid his arm around her waist, pulling her until she hit his chest. She fought, but he didn't break his hold. "You two need to stop. You can't go in there with no information. Calm down and think this through. They won't kill your sister. At the very least, we've found they like to take their time."

It took a few more seconds, but Maya relaxed into his arms, recognizing he was right. Camilla looked to her sister with longing, but gave in; it was obvious the youngest Whittle didn't like the idea of leaving Vera with the coven, but it made more sense than getting the entire family stuck in their grasps.

Harry looked to be on Hunter's side. "What happened? What bodies did you find in the house?"

Camilla told Harry what she and Warren had found, then relayed what they'd found in the basement. Harry turned to Maya, still held against Hunter's chest, then to the basement opening behind them.

Maya pulled herself free and Hunter really hated the loss of her warmth as she stepped into the basement. "Come see."

Hunter followed as they led the group down to the basement, stopping right before the nineteen dead witches.

"Oh my god," Camilla whispered as her hand flew to her mouth.

Warren placed a hand between her shoulder blades as comfort as he took in the sight around them.

Harry looked to each of the dead until his eyes landed on one in particular—an older woman, likely in her seventies—and he walked over to crouch down before her, lightly brushing her hair back.

It still astonished Hunter how much they all cared for people they did not know. Every dead being in that room was a stranger, yet the devastation was evident on all of their features.

Maya was standing an inch before him when she spoke, so he felt the light vibrations. "Did you know her?"

Harry never peeled his eyes off the woman as he nodded and brushed another hair back. He took a final look at her, then stood and turned to face them. "Her name is Elsie. She was a lovely witch, a loving grandmother to all the children of her coven. I visit at least once a year, every year. I was meant to see her in a couple of weeks."

Well, maybe not all strangers.

He didn't allow room for anyone to speak as he kept his eyes forward and walked out of the basement. Hunter looked down to find Maya's eyes on him, and he jerked his head back so that they'd follow. She began walking up, Hunter following close behind, leaving Camilla and Warren to follow minutes later.

Vera felt her eyes flutter open, everything a bit blurry as she laid there. She blinked hard a few times before her eyes were able to focus. Head dropping to the side, she noticed stone—she was lying on the ground.

As she began to pull herself up, she looked around and saw the same thing on all sides but one. She was in a cellar. The one side of the room that wasn't a complete stone wall had a hole carved out in the center large enough to fit a sumo wrestler.

Vera looked around to the candles surrounding her in a circle. She got up on unsteady legs and tried to walk out of the circle, expecting not to be able to but finding no harm in trying.

With a push back, she tried again. She put her hand to the air above the circle and felt it resist her attempts. As expected, she couldn't get through.

She tried her magic. Tried to move a candle. Nothing.

Vera looked around the room and found nothing and no one, so she sat back down in the center and stared at the empty opening, waiting for someone to come down.

She didn't have to wait long before Melusine came through the hole, a grin breaking along her face at the sight of Vera. "You're awake!"

"Unfortunately, so are you," Vera barked out, unsure where she was getting the courage to talk back so abruptly.

Melusine laughed, unperturbed. "Oh, dear child, why so bitter?"

Vera quirked a brow but didn't say a word.

The witch that had told Melusine about the missing bodies walked into the room with a chair—more like a throne—and placed it in the corner beside the hole in the wall. Another witch stood behind her with a glass of wine. They stoically waited for Melusine to take her seat.

When she finally did, it wasn't a lazy lounge like Hunter's. It was straight backed and regal. And somehow, as Melusine looked down at her from such a regal stance on a throne, Hunter's lazy sprawl on a foldable chair was more formidable, more condescending, more powerful. Melusine was trying too hard for her control; Hunter didn't try at all. Vera didn't like Hunter, but she couldn't help the smile that came to her. She was beginning to see Maya's side of the bargain.

The witch handed Melusine the wine, and Vera watched her drink it with all the grace of a queen. The two witches stood off to the side, heads bowed, awaiting their next assignment.

"You've even got your coven afraid of you. Glorious job," Vera filled the silence.

"Thank you." Melusine grinned, a look of greed in her eyes. Again, Vera couldn't help but compare her to Hunter. Hunter, who's greed never radiated off of him, which made him all the more dangerous. Hunter, who had their permission to kill Melusine. And again, Vera was beginning to see Maya's side of the bargain.

Vera sat straight backed in her cross-legged position, not because she wanted to look regal, but because this way she would be on attention.

"Tell me," Melusine began, "why take the bodies?"

Vera felt her brows furrow and didn't bother to hide it. "I still don't know what that means."

"Oh?" Melusine feigned shock. "You didn't know of the bodies we had in the house?"

"No," Vera answered. "But now that you bring it up, why?"

Melusine smirked. "We're cleansing this would of evil, child. Dark powers are for evil beings. They must be rid of."

"Except the entire ideology is complete bullshit!" Vera professed, feeling her blood boil. "Dark powers don't make you a bad person!"

Melusine's brows quirked. "And how would you know that?"

Vera didn't answer, staring back at Melusine with all the hate that she felt. Melusine took her time staring back before something clicked in her mind, her eyes lightening with the realization. "I thought you reminded me of someone. Another witch who was a terrible liar. You are Loretta's daughter? A Whittle."

Vera didn't answer, but the astonishment of being compared to her mother was written all over her face. Camilla was the one who looked like their mother. Vera had taken after her father, and Maya truly did seem like a mix of the two, which fueled Vera's hope that Bishop was also Camilla and Maya's father.

"It's all beginning to make sense now. Your sister," she elongated the word, "she had dark powers. Yes, yes. I remember another witch whispering about it." She sat back in her throne, wine dangling in her fingertips as she rested it over the arm of the chair. "Althea. Yes, the poor girl was frantic talking to herself when I happened to pass by. *Surprisingly*, that was the last I saw of her." Melusine's eyes twinkled. "Your sister killed her."

Vera jumped to her knees. "She did not! She wasn't even alive yet!"

Melusine took a sip of her wine as she looked Vera over. "But she is the reason my coven sister was killed. That is the power of dark magic holders. They don't care for others. She killed poor Althea."

"Having dark magic as a witch makes her rare, not evil," Vera argued.

Melusine's smile turned sweet, and that caused Vera's stomach to swirl more than the smirks had. "Oh, dear child, how she's brainwashed you. From what I heard from Althea's whispers that day, she has the highest levels of dark magic. I assume that's true, and that just means her brainwashing is even more powerful."

Vera didn't think as she spit at Melusine's feet. The action got no response. Instead, Melusine stood, her hand whipping the glass of wine to the side and carelessly letting go. The witch closest to her caught it immediately as Melusine walked to the edge of the circle holding Vera in. "Dear child, once we rid that sister of yours, you will be clean once more. You'll be fine soon."

Vera threw herself at Melusine—at the invisible barrier—and felt her body lunge back from the force. She watched Melusine turn and walk out, the two witches remaining behind and standing to either side of the opening like guards.

---

Warren sat with Camilla, Maya, and Hunter around the table in the kitchen while Harry hung out against the island. He looked lost in thought. They hadn't bothered with drinks, trying to hash out a plan as quickly as possible to get back to Vera.

"Normally it would be safe to assume they won't be in the same spot, but seeing as they saw you today and they know there are more of us, it's likely they're waiting," Warren started the conversation.

"Which is why we'll be landing on tree tops," Hunter added.

"We'll get a better view of the property, and they'll have less of a chance of noticing us right away."

"Right," Warren agreed. "And we'll take the side of the property this time. Again, they'll likely be expecting us to change locations, so they'll have witches in all areas, but I'd harbor they'd focus most of their attention to the front and back, given they have the most expanse to cover."

"That works for us. We want them separated. It'll be easier to infiltrate," Hunter spoke.

Camilla and Maya looked between the two of them, Camilla's features holding slight astonishment.

"What?" Warren asked.

She shook her head. "I see it."

"What?" Warren asked hesitantly.

"You guys are brothers. I see it. I didn't before, but now I do."

Warren sucked in a breath, frozen in spot. Hunter smirked, his arm thrown around Maya's chair. "Funny. I still don't see how you and Maya are sisters."

Camilla rolled her eyes and looked back to him, changing the conversation back to the situation at hand. "What will we do when we get there? If there are witches guarding the entire property, how do we find Vera?"

"Easy," Hunter simply commented.

"Locator spell," Warren clarified. "The same one you did to find Lila. It'll give you exact coordinates. I would guess they're keeping her underground on that spot, but we can always check all levels if it's within the house."

Maya looked between him and his brother. "Getting past the witches?"

Hunter tilted his head with slight consideration. An act. Hunter knew the answer as well as Warren, better even. "That depends what they're doing, but the probability will be you and I taking over."

Exactly as Warren had thought—Hunter and Maya's fire would be the strongest weapon.

"What about shadowing straight into the house again?" Camilla suggested, clearly not happy with the thought of Maya helping Hunter with their powers.

Warren shook his head. "Knowing there are others with Vera means they know we're coming. Half the witches standing guard will be there just to keep the protective charms around the property."

A look of defeat crossed Camilla's features, and Warren hated that he couldn't wipe it for her. She looked to Harry, who didn't seem to be paying too much attention to the conversation.

She walked up to him and lightly grabbed his arm, giving it a light shake. "Harry? Are you okay?"

He pulled out of his thoughts and looked to Camilla as if just noticing her standing so close. "I should never have let go of her hand. The only reason they got a hold of her is because I was no longer holding her when we landed. If I had, we could've ported out."

Camilla's voice softened, and her hand tightened on his arm. Warren was glad to find he wasn't jealous; there was quite literally no romance between the two. "Harry. It's not your fault. They're savages!"

Harry didn't seem to believe it.

"You didn't see what we did," Warren cut in, trying to convince him that what Camilla said was true. "They've been doing this a long time. They've mastered it. You can't blame yourself for that."

Harry didn't respond.

Maya looked to him. "The best thing you can do now is get her back, Harry."

Camilla remained by his side as they finished their discussion.

Vera didn't know how much time had passed, but she was sure it hadn't been much. The boredom was making it seem longer. This must have been what Maya felt when she was in Hell's Gate.

Sitting cross legged at the edge of the circle, she banged her head against the invisible barrier. "You know." In true Vera nature, she broke the silence and began to speak to the witches sitting guard at the entrance to her cell. "I agree with you now. There are evil witches." She stopped banging her head and looked up at them. "But I also know it has nothing to do with what kind of magic they have. It's just the type of person they are. For instance, this coven, it's just about the most vile thing I've ever seen."

The two witches ignored her, keeping their eyes locked on one another, but Vera could see by the straightening of their spines that her comments had affected them.

Vera gave an ironic smile as she glued her attention to the witch who's jaw had tightened. "No, I get it. I've only been in the witch thing a few weeks. I haven't seen it all. I agree. But, I did see a demon burn a child with no remorse, and I still think you're worse."

They stood ramrod straight now, and Vera continued, "Have you ever seen a child get burned alive, screaming in pain? No, I suppose not. You guys kill your captives differently, I'd bet. Well, actually, this child didn't die. No injuries either. It turns out the demon knew exactly how to control his power to play with us." The other witch let her eyes hover to where she sat, and Vera had to bite back the smirk that she had garnered both of their attentions. "That demon held an entire school of children hostage. He killed a priest. Went to Hell's Gate and came back! And you're still far worse."

That seemed to trigger a reaction. Vera didn't have time to

move before the second witch threw a spell at her, causing her to fly back. She hit the barrier on the other side and crumpled to the ground. Vera looked up and caught the witch's eyes with a smile. "That was cute."

It was exhilarating, getting them worked up like this. No wonder Maya fell into moments like this so simply.

The first witch turned and threw another spell her way. "Shut up!"

This spell hit Vera on the side of the head, dropping her to her stomach. She lifted herself to all fours and looked up through hooded eyes. "You've just proved my point."

Both witches turned in her direction this time, preparing to throw another when Melusine walked in. They both froze and went back to their guard positions immediately. "What is going on in here?" When no one spoke, Melusine barked out. "Answer me."

The witch that had hit her in the head spoke to her master. "She was comparing us to a demon. That a demon doing vile things was better than us."

Melusine looked over to Vera, and Vera didn't even try to hide her sardonic smile. Melusine tilted her head to the witch who had spoken and back handed her. She turned to the other and delivered the same. "She was goading you, and you fell for it? Pathetic. You'll each be sent to solitary for a week."

The witches' eyes bled fear and pleading, but they gave a nod and held their positions. Vera laughed at them as Melusine rolled her eyes and moved to her throne in the corner.

***

They had decided to break up into small teams again even though they were all going to the same spot. This time, when they met in the living room, Warren would be going in alone, Camilla having volunteered to port in with Harry, knowing he needed the company. Hunter and Maya gravitated toward one another without a word, as if it were obvious that they would be together. Camilla's logical side told her it was because they may have to use their powers to get them through.

She took the few moments before they left to watch her sister and *that* demon. She wasn't sure why, but she got a feeling that something was going on between the two of them even though everything seemed normal. And yet, Camilla couldn't shake the feeling that they had some secret between them, something, Camilla assumed, that happened in Hell's Gate and they could really only talk to one another about. That, she thought, but also the sense that they seemed to always naturally gravitate toward one another, even the slightest bit, and even before Hell's Gate.

She allowed her thoughts to hover over her sister's relationship with Hunter for only another second before shaking them away completely. She had another sister to focus on. Maya was a sister she knew deeply, a sister who was too good to be in any sort of favorable pairing with a demon willing to burn children. They just had an agreement, and Maya was carrying it out.

With herself mostly convinced, Camilla focused on Vera.

She moved to Harry's side and watched him. He looked fine, but Camilla could see in his eyes that he was battling with the guilt of leaving Vera with the coven. Worried about him, but knowing there was nothing to do but get her sister back to make him feel better, she grabbed his hand. The group looked to one another, and they all ported—or shadowed—to the treetops surrounding the east side of the Bridgers coven property.

Hunter and Maya landed in a tree to the right, Harry and Camilla in the middle, and Warren to the left. Where Maya and Hunter shared the branch they stood on, Harry and Camilla stood on separate ones, though he kept his hold on her hand.

They looked out at the property and didn't see what they had expected.

"Well, it seems we were wrong," Hunter commented.

Maya stood behind him, one hand stabilizing herself on the bark of the tree and the other in a death grip to the back of his black, luxurious looking sweater. He held onto a thin branch above his head as he let his body lean forward so he was more hovering than standing. It was astonishing the strength he had to hold himself up with the one arm. Maya's hand fell from its grip on his shirt to grab the top of his trousers, her fingers looping into a belt loop.

Poor Maya was afraid of heights.

Instead of the dispersed witches, Harry pointed out that they were in the exact same location and stood in the exact same shape as they had that morning. Except this time, there seemed to be fewer of them. With a count, it looked about five members were missing.

Maya's hand tightened around Hunter's trousers as she turned her body away from the bark to get a better view of the star shape—so slight a shape it would look like a circle from ground level—the witches were standing in. "It looks like a spell from the Book. It's like a combination of a protective spell, but also of reflexes and abilities. That's how they were able to detect and attack so quickly. It basically puts you into slow motion without you realizing it."

Hunter released the bark above him and came back upright, colliding his back into Maya's chest. The hand that had been on the bark moved to grab onto his shirt, her fingers digging into his side. Camilla narrowed her eyes at the demon, hoping Maya left scars—he had no care whether Maya had protection so high off the ground. If he fell, he could shadow to safety; if she fell, she *fell*.

"Okay, Ms. Know-It-All, how do we get past it?" he spoke to Maya, though he didn't take his eyes off of the Bridgers witches.

Maya inhaled. "We need to get them out of it. Break the circle, break the spell."

"How do we do that?" Camilla asked as the wind blew harder, and her hand tightened around Harry's. Knowing that the boys could easily escape if they fell and the girls couldn't sucked.

Maya shook her head in response. "We should be able to travel within the circle. The protective spell I would assume would be for the property. These spells only work on magical infiltrations, so a mundane task like walking or running wouldn't be detected. If we walk onto the property, then shadow into the circle, it should work."

"And do what?" Warren broke his silence from Camilla's other side. His branch was closer to her than she had realized before. Almost as close as Harry's. And he stood with his body angled toward her as if ready to catch her if she fell and Harry lost his hold.

"How much fire do you think they'd suffer before breaking?" Maya countered.

Hunter smirked and turned in his spot, Maya's hands tightening their grip as he moved on the thin branch that held them. He seemed to enjoy the hold she had on him and made no moves to hold her in turn. For once, Camilla wanted him to touch her, and he wouldn't.

Their faces were so close—too close for Camilla's liking—as Hunter tilted his head down to her. "What did you have in mind, love?"

## 27

*H*unter shadowed Maya down so that they were standing on the ground, right below the trees they had just been atop and right outside of the protective circle. They were still too far out for the witches to notice, especially in their concentrated state, so she smacked him.

Hunter still hadn't moved to touch her, allowing her grip around him to be the thing that shadowed her alongside him. She narrowed her eyes at him.

"What, love?"

"Did you have any intentions of holding me up there? I could have fallen!" she whisper-yelled.

He had the audacity to crack a smile. "You wouldn't have fallen."

"Because I was holding on!"

He moved to grab her jaw, holding her immobile. It was a rough, domineering hold. "You could have been on a tree across the property. If you so much as lost your footing, I would've caught you."

His black orbs told her just how serious he was. He wouldn't allow her any harm. Breathing in to calm herself, she stepped back and nodded to the property—they had a reason for being there.

They remained quiet as they took a single step into the barrier, Hunter's hand in Maya's. If the reflex thing was active, he would have to shadow them out immediately.

The witches didn't seem to notice them as they crossed past the invisible barrier. Maya would have thought they hadn't crossed it had she not felt the slight change in the air in the spot the barrier lay.

Hunter looked to Maya and tried shadowing them a few feet to make sure that the power was still working within the protective barriers. Finding that they had their escape route, they kept their hands interlocked and lifted the ones not in use. Each of them got a fire bolt ready and aimed to either end of the circle of witches.

Their bolts hit, and flames erupted, creating a ring around the witches, entrapping them. This got the witches' attention as they jumped in spot and turned to the source. Before they could see them, Hunter shadowed them to the opposite end of the property. Not seeing the source, the witches turned back to face the center of the circle, apprehension in their stances as their chants grew louder.

Maya caught herself staring Hunter in the eyes, their smiles wide as the fire raged around the witches. They turned their gazes back, and Hunter shadowed them again, this time landing in the center of the circle.

They stood back to back and ready with a bolt of fire in hand each. Hands still interlocked, they each threw their fire bolts to create a ring around themselves. The witches were now boarded up from both ends with the only escape being that they break their stances. Without the position they stood in, their chants would be useless, and they knew it.

Hunter and Maya began playing with the fire around them as they made the rings move closer to the witches, beginning to lick their feet. In the fun they were having, they didn't notice another witch come out and throw a spell at them. Luckily missing, Hunter shadowed them out of the circle to another end of the property where they could watch the chaos around the coven. Harry, Camilla, and Warren met them and watched the witches around the circle.

As they watched the one new witch try to put the fire out, Maya increased the flames, knowing Hunter was doing the same by the flick of heat that crossed in their still joined hands.

"Let's hope they're not as stubborn as some other witches I know." Hunter looked blatantly at them.

Melusine strolled into the cell as Vera played a game of pushing the barrier with each leg. She'd lain flat on her back and pushed against the barrier with one foot and watched it get thrown back just as the other leg began to push, continuing the motions out of boredom.

"Why haven't you done anything with me?" Vera asked before Melusine could get a word out.

Melusine smiled sweetly, her tone matching and making Vera sick. "Well, dear. You haven't done a thing wrong. Your sister is at fault, and we will take care of that. I only care for your well-being."

Vera grimaced at her. "You're disgusting, and I hope my sister uses that dark power of hers to end you slowly."

Melusine kept that smile on her face, but was interrupted from speaking when a witch came running to the hole in the wall. She merely nodded and took a step back, awaiting her leader. Melusine's smile turned dark as she turned back to look at Vera. "It looks like your friends are back."

Vera's heart jumped in both anticipation and fear as she flew to a sitting position. Maya had to get out of there.

S tanding at the edge of the property, out of sight from the coven, the fivesome watched. The witches did, in fact, fall under the stubborn card and held their positions as the flames grew closer.

Camilla had watched Maya and Hunter work together from the top of the tree and couldn't deny that they did so perfectly. They were able to match their powers and their magic to create hell without having to speak to one another. She recognized a bond between them that made her shudder, and although she didn't like the idea of her beloved sister working well with a cold-blooded demon, at the moment, it was working wonders for them.

Camilla watched in horror as the witches held their ground, and she began officially freaking out when a flame on one end grew until it caught on the cloth of the dress of one of the witches. With a sharp inhale, Camilla turned to the fire controllers within the group. "Extinguish it!"

Neither Hunter nor Maya paid her any mind as they watched the witch's leg begin to twitch, though her concentration continued to hold. Camilla yelled again at them, not caring if she drew attention to their location.

Hunter's gaze didn't hover for a moment. "No."

Camilla turned her full attention to her sister, pleading for her to stop the fires from burning the witches alive. "We're already within the protective barriers. This isn't needed!"

"They knew we were within the barriers when we sent the first ring. This chant isn't to protect the property," Warren explained coolly. "If we want to get inside, we need them to break."

Camilla hated that Warren was defending this, that her sister was actively participating in it. She turned to Maya, begging through her gaze, but Maya did not break. She turned to look

Camilla in the eyes. "They made their decisions. If they would rather burn to death than be decent witches, let them burn."

Camilla couldn't believe the words as Maya turned her gaze back, her hand still in Hunter's. They looked to be equally gripping one another, his thumb trailing lazy circles.

*Let them burn.*

Camilla grimaced, though she understood the need to keep the hold in case they needed the escape—she still held Harry's hand—she didn't like that he was drawing circles. It was intimate. And she was focusing on the wrong thing.

Standing alone in her thoughts, since neither Harry nor Warren wanted to join her side, Camilla turned to watch the witches in horror. She watched as a second witch's dress caught flames. Then a third, a fourth. And finally, there was a witch fully engulfed in flames. She couldn't bear to watch any longer as she turned to Harry, hiding her face in his shoulder.

The other four stood and watched as the witches burned in silence for as long as they could. Eventually, one witch broke and let out a scream. Camilla couldn't see it, but her imagination was active enough. Then another, and finally, all of them were screaming.

Listening to those screams was a torture Camilla didn't know how to block. She lifted her head from Harry's shoulder and looked to Maya, making sure to keep her back to the burning witches. The sounds would torture her forever. There was no need to add the sight to that nightmare.

Maya stood in between Hunter and Harry, completely unfazed. Unaffected by the sight of the witches burning, their screams filling the woods, or the scent that was beginning to fill the air. She stood uncaring, and that fact, above all else, scared Camilla the most. That the sister she had grown up with, that Camilla knew loved and cared for people, didn't care now.

Camilla's gaze moved to Hunter for a moment, then back to her sister, finding them holding the same unfazed expressions.

The same straight postures that said they were in control of the situation and they were allowing this to happen. Seeing the similarities so blatantly drawn between her sister and the man she loathed made Camilla's stomach quiver.

---

Vera came to a sitting position, back straight as the first scream broke through the walls. As the screams picked up, she turned to Melusine. "Aren't you going to send help?"

Melusine wore a bored expression as she lounged in her seat in the corner of the room, still attempting to look regal, though she looked less terrifying than the lazy lounges she had seen Hunter and Maya dawn. Melusine didn't budge at the sound of the screams, as if it were merely the sound of the wind whistling.

Vera watched in disgust, imagining how often she had hurt people and heard those exact sounds to become so immune to them now, because unlike demons, she was not born with the ability to just not care. That was bred into her.

Vera's disgust only deepened when Melusine answered her question. "They're replaceable."

---

With the screams ebbing away as the witches' hearts stopped beating, Hunter and Maya pulled the fire away so the land didn't burn. Together, the five moved to the burned corpses. Camilla stayed back, remaining half turned so she could watch them from her periphery only, as the four of them walked around the corpses, making sure they were all gone.

Maya was looking down at the charred skin of the women

and oddly not feeling a twinge of guilt—there was no mercy for what these women did—as they danced around the bodies.

"Get down!" Camilla screamed just as a blast of three spells came at them.

All five of them dropped to the ground, narrowly missing the hits, as seven more witches came running out. With no more protective barrier to stop them, the witches were now at a disadvantage. Jumping to her feet, Maya turned to her sister as her arm lit aflame. "Take Harry, go find Vera. We'll take care of this."

It was obvious from Camilla's reaction that she didn't like the sound of them 'taking care of this,' but she didn't argue as another spell came her way. Warren pulled her out of the way, and Camilla turned to look to Maya with a nod before moving to Harry.

With the two of them gone, Maya could focus now, no longer worrying about keeping them safe, keeping Camilla safe.

She took her stance between the brothers, feeling the dark magic they each held lick the air, enticing.

Warren was the first to take action, shadowing toward two of the witches and racing out of the way of their shots as he pulled a knife out. Shadowing behind one, he easily held her head back and sliced a gush of blood from her neck. An instant death.

Maya let her neck dance as she readied herself, feeling Hunter's eyes on her. She wasn't feeling as forgiving as the younger Delvaux and knew Hunter would follow her lead, would love the opportunity to be merciless.

He proved her right in the next moment. "Let me take their powers."

Although it wasn't part of their arrangement, Maya tilted her head to look at him as Warren moved to another witch and nodded. She threw her fire, capturing three of the witches and holding them back as Hunter went to work on the last two remaining. He mentally captured both of the witches' arms with his fire, no longer allowing them to make a move, as he moved his arms up. He aimed a hand at each of the witches' chests and began to breathe in, as if he were inhaling their powers. And instantly, Maya could see a glimmer of movement from the chests of the witches to Hunter's palms.

He looked almost ethereal as he did it, his black eyes illuminating as they took in the power, hungered for more. His brown hair, though gelled back, flickered in the wind, catching Maya's attention. She raked her eyes down to his arms, strong and powerful, the veins bleeding through as they captured more magic.

A flick to the side showed Warren hadn't had such quick luck with the second witch, only now getting the upper hand as he ran his knife through her chest and watched her crumple to the ground. Turning, he found his brother stealing powers, and from the looks of it, he didn't like the sight.

With the power of those two taken, Hunter increased his fire around them and incinerated them instantly. He then turned to the remaining three that Maya still held with her flames. She had been using her arms, as mentally doing it would have required far more concentration, and she was too busy watching Hunter to concentrate on them.

Warren shadowed behind one of the three in the fire-hold and stabbed her through the chest, saving her from having her power stolen as Hunter raised his hands to the other two. What difference it made to the witch whether her power was taken, Maya didn't know. Maybe Warren just didn't want his brother to carry more power, no matter how much weaker the power would be in him than in the original carrier.

Warren's gaze turned on her, astonishment written all over his features. He couldn't believe she was helping his brother, that she was okay with the outcome.

Maya had dropped her arms, no longer holding the witches,

when Hunter got to work. And when he finished, he let his arms fall as the flames engulfed these two as well. Warren looked between them, and Maya knew he would find the same uncaring reactions on both of their features.

***

Camilla and Harry ported to the exact coordinates that they had detected Vera to be in and found no one. They did, however, find a circle of candles half burned, concluding that she had likely been held there. They looked to one another as Harry tightened his hold on Camilla's hand and ported them upstairs.

Landing in an empty hallway on the ground floor, they remained silent and listened. Camilla heard bits of shuffling, from what exactly, she couldn't be sure, so they took caution and slowly creeped up to the entrance of the hallway. Poking their heads to the edge and giving a single-eyed glance of the room, they saw a group of four witches holding a protective circle with Vera sat cross legged within. Fear spiked in Camilla at seeing Vera in the hands of the coven, but she relaxed when she saw that Vera looked fine.

Vera's eyes flickered all about the room, eventually landing on them. She stiffened at the sight, her eyes shooting to each of the witches around her. They were each half lidded and concentrated on what they were doing.

Vera looked back to them and mouthed, *I'm okay.* Camilla felt herself and Harry relax even deeper with that. Vera looked back up to make sure they weren't caught by the coven witches, then looked back at them and mouthed, *They want Maya.*

Camilla froze.

Vera had exaggerated every syllable so Camilla knew she understood correctly. Breathing in to remain calm, she looked to Harry, who gave Vera a nod before porting them out of the house and landing them in the same spot they had been in before the second round of witches. The scene looked the same though, except with more witches lying about.

Sickened by the scene, Camilla kept her eyes up and tried not to look in Hunter's direction. Deep down, Camilla knew this was half Maya's responsibility too, but she convinced herself that had Hunter not been there, she could have convinced her sister to stop.

"They've moved Vera. She's come upstairs now, ground floor," Harry told them.

"She's okay. It doesn't look like they've hurt her at all," Camilla added.

Maya's brows furrowed. "That doesn't make any sense for their M.O."

"I think that's because they don't want Vera. They're holding her safe to attack someone else," Harry continued.

"Hunter and me?" Warren guessed.

Harry considered the assumption. "Well, yes, that would be a benefit to them. But, no, not you." His eyes drifted to Maya.

Hunter stiffened from her side, his body drifting closer, standing right behind her. His black eyes danced like they were full, swirling with energy. That was odd. If Camilla didn't already know how much the man didn't care for others, she would have been convinced that he cared for Maya's safety.

Maya quirked a brow. "Why am I not surprised?"

Hunter's lips twitched to a small smirk. "This is perfect. We'll send you in as bait."

Nope. He definitely did not care.

"And put *both* of my sisters at risk? Absolutely not!" She truly did loathe him.

Hunter's smirk grew dark as he looked to her. "She won't be alone. She'll just look like she's alone." His body drifted ever closer to her as he spoke, like the idea of sending her in alone was such a ludicrous thought, it was ridiculous Camilla would even think it.

Everyone's attention was now on Hunter. "The invisibility serum you used to break into our rooms in the Theology building." Maya smiled at the memory, and Camilla tried to bite back on her smile. "The rest of us will take some. I'm assuming you have more."

Harry nodded, and a smile finally erupted on his face. "Yes. I'm sure Maya has a whole truck load."

Maya smiled proudly. "Make fun, Mr. Mentor Man, but see how useful it's coming out to be?"

They decided Harry would port back to the house to pick up the vials, since Maya would require assistance in the travel aspect and it would be safer to lose one from their group rather than two. Especially the two more powerful ones.

Warren shadowed Camilla to the edge of the property as Hunter took Maya. Waiting there, the foursome heard a bit of movement from the edge of the house, the part closest to them. Turning their full attention to the spot, two little pairs of eyes stared back in fear. Realizing they had been caught, two little girls jumped up and began to run toward the woods. Seeing them answered Camilla's question of why she had only seen teenagers or adults—the few kids they likely had were in hiding.

As Maya, Camilla, and Warren allowed the kids to run off, Hunter's hand lit aflame. Camilla jumped in protest against hurting the kids alongside Warren and Maya, but Hunter was deaf to them. He let the bolts fly, hitting the kids straight in the back where their hearts would have been.

Hunter turned back to the others in time to see Camilla's horrified expression. She was sure her gaze told him how much she hated him, but it didn't seem to affect him in the slightest.

His eyes fell to Maya, who had her hands clenched at her sides, her mouth grinding as she stared at him. He hadn't taken her hand to shadow, rather looping his arm around her waist, and it remained there as he stared back. Camilla couldn't understand how Maya could bare to be so close to him.

"It was an effective, easy kill. It had to be done, love," he defended himself, his gaze never leaving Maya's. Camilla guessed the defense was for her alone, as he didn't seem to care what they thought.

Oh, how she couldn't wait to be done with this so she never had to see him again.

Melusine walked into the room about ten minutes after Harry and Camilla ported out. With the information of the coven's current interests, Vera was hoping her family would come up with a plan that would keep Maya far from this bitch.

Melusine strolled to the chaise ottoman at the far back of the room. It was a formal living area that looked like it was never used, with all of the furniture looking to belong to a Parisian castle from the 1800s. Melusine threw herself against the one back support, throwing her legs across the ottoman. "Well, this is boring. You would think they would do more than burn some witches." Melusine gave a puff before focusing her attention on Vera. "Maybe we should give them some encouragement, hm?"

Before Vera could tell Melusine to kiss her ass, they heard the front door open and footsteps moving toward them. Melusine's attention snapped to the entrance to the room as she shot out of her seat, anticipation dripping off her. Vera, too, turned to look at the entrance, wondering what her family had planned.

To her horror, and Melusine's excitement, Maya walked in. Alone.

Then she felt a tingle in her hand that shot its way to her neck. Hunter was here, somewhere. So maybe Maya wasn't alone, but Vera didn't trust Hunter to be of much help.

"I heard you're looking for me," Maya said nonchalantly, showing the room that she was in charge and she had no other care in the world. Something that put her right up there with Hunter's confidence.

As Vera watched her sister play this role once again, she wondered if, in fact, it was a role to fit the dark magic superstition that this coven had, or if this truly was Maya in unpredictable situations.

Melusine smiled wickedly. "Smart child. Or arrogant. Either way, doesn't matter to me."

Melusine's hungry expression made Vera sick in a way she hadn't realized possible. She turned to her sister and banged on the barrier and yelled. Yelled for Maya to leave. Her sister paid her no mind, instead reciting a spell under her breath and sending it Vera's way. A silencing spell.

The witches that had been surrounding Vera turned so that they were all facing the new entrant. Now fully aware of the dark witch before them, they grew their power, whispering a constant chant under their breaths to grow the protective barrier so that Melusine and all of them were held within.

As they held the barrier, a child of maybe nine years old walked out and used her power to lift Vera and hold her before Melusine's body as a second form of protection for their leader.

Maya's gaze didn't waver from Melusine's.

Melusine raised a hand, creating an icicle, and shot it toward Maya. Maya didn't move out of the way, allowing for the icicle to hit her in the shoulder and blood to immediately trickle from the wound. Her fire power erupted and melted it away, but the injury was still there.

To the shock of the room, Maya began to heal. Her shoulder going back to normal in seconds. Vera's breath caught; Harry must be there too.

"Oh, sweetheart," Maya's sickly sweet tone was a perfect mock of Melusine's earlier one. "That was adorable."

Maya took their moment of shock to mentally shoot a blaze of fire before the barrier. That, or Hunter sent it; Vera couldn't be sure.

Vera watched from her place in the air as the flames licked the barrier, looking as if they were going to break through. She shot her eyes to her sister, then looked about the room. She couldn't see anyone else, but there had to be others around. At the very least, she felt Hunter's presence, and Harry had to have been there to heal Maya.

Watching the fire, Vera wondered if it was controlled by Maya or Hunter. And if it were Hunter, would she be safe?

"Keep that up, and you'll hurt your sister," Melusine goaded.

Maya's eyes blazed with cruel intent, and she smiled more wickedly than Melusine could ever dream of doing. "She's not my problem."

Vera knew this was an act. She knew, and yet, she believed her sister when those words left her lips. Vera knew it was because Maya played a great demon, but she also knew it was her insecurity at being the odd sister out coming to play with her emotions. Now was definitely not the time for that. But she couldn't fight away the pain that pierced through her heart when she heard those words.

Pushing aside her insecurities to deal with at a later time, Vera paid attention to those around her and began to notice bits around Maya. A bit of color was beginning to bleed through, and Vera realized their invisibility was wearing out. Maya had done well with the potions, but she needed to learn a way to elongate how long it lasted.

As the others came fully into view and the coven realized

Maya wasn't, in fact, alone, the witches tightened their hold on the barrier and the little girl holding Vera up began to tighten the air around her. Adding to the smoke that was coming from the fire, the tightening of the air around Vera made it almost impossible to take in sustainable air.

Melusine looked over all the members standing before her—Hunter beside Maya, Harry at the edge of the barrier to their right, and Camilla and Warren to the left—before her gaze landed on Maya. "Working with demons too? You truly are a dark witch. And these poor souls," she indicated Vera, Camilla, and Harry, "are trapped under your spell."

Maya's expression revealed nothing. "Kind of like your coven is trapped under your psychological mindfuck?"

Melusine narrowed her eyes at Maya, then looked down to the little girl standing beside her and spoke with no remorse, "Kill her."

The little girl tightened the air around Vera, completely cutting off her oxygen as she remained stuck in the air, powerless. As the girl crushed Vera's lungs, Melusine created more icicles in her hands and shot them flying at the group.

Vera noticed Maya's attention on her, then on the girl holding her up. "Stop!" The girl ignored her and the pounding of the barrier from Harry, Warren, and Camilla, the flames having been released so the three of them could stand against the barrier. The girl was playing with Vera, tightening slowly so Vera felt the burn of losing all her air.

Melusine threw an icicle, which Vera assumed Hunter's fire blocked since Maya was focused on the Bridgers witches.

"Stop!" Maya shouted. Vera's gaze was beginning to fill with stars as she noticed her sister's eyes darken and fill with a fire she'd never seen before. But nothing could be done with the witches barrier up around them.

Melusine continued throwing icicles all about the room,

though she either missed or the pieces were caught by the flames. Until they weren't.

Vera's wavering gaze caught Hunter getting hit in the heart, the sharp end of the icicle slicing into his chest. She noticed it melt away almost instantly, but he'd fallen back hard with the impact.

Maya's eyes were red with lava as she shouted a final cry. "Stop!" And impossibly so, a portal opened under each of the five witches Maya threw all her anger toward—the four holding the barrier and the little girl holding Vera.

Everyone in the room looked down, and the girl lost some of her concentration, giving Vera the chance to cough through her sore throat, getting oxygen in again. The shock written across everyone's faces was exactly alike, whether Bridgers or Whittle or Delvaux—there was a portal to Hell's Gate open under the witches, and there was no ornament, like the staff, around to have done it. No ornament, but Maya's flame-filled eyes.

All eyes shot to her, and the five witches standing above the portal looked on in fear as they immediately dropped Vera and the barrier, backing away from the opening in the ground. Unfortunately for them, the portals were there and ready to take their prey, so each of the five got sucked in with the portals closing behind them.

Now released and the protective barrier gone, Harry and Camilla ran for her. Vera's gaze instantly shot to Maya, who was still staring at the spot the five had stood, the flames still alive in her eyes. Maya turned to Hunter, finding him uninjured and on one knee—he'd barely been able to lift himself from the shock of the moment—and the flames danced away. Her eyebrows furrowed in and she pursed her lips, but her gaze never left Hunter's as he stood to both feet and looked at her with fascination.

Harry helped Vera stand and they all stared at Maya until,

finally, she looked away and caught Warren's gaze as he spoke in awe. "Your fire control is a high-level dark power, one of the highest actually, that witches and demons can have." He moved his attention back to where the witches had previously been standing and Melusine remained cowering. "Opening a portal," his gaze met hers again, "is *the* highest level. A level reserved only for our species. No witch has ever had the power. Even demons have been few and far between. It hasn't been around for millennia."

It was information for them all because Vera had also been wondering what had just happened, but Maya looked to register the news for only a moment before turning to Melusine, who had backed up to the corner of the room with nowhere left to run or hide. She looked almost ready to wet herself as Maya's attention settled on her.

"Why did you kill our mother?" Maya asked, back to business.

Melusine's features radiated fear, but the confusion bled its way through. She gave a little laugh, though there was no amusement there. "Is that why you lot came here? I had nothing to do with your mother or your coven."

"Why should we believe anything from you?" Camilla questioned from beside Vera, helping Harry hold her up.

"You don't have to. But I can guarantee you that you will have something else to deal with. My coven was far too smart to target a coven as powerful as yours. Any powerful witch or demon families were left out."

With nothing left to say, Maya walked to where Vera stood between Harry and Camilla, then turned her attention to Hunter. They didn't speak aloud, but they must have had a conversation through their looks because he gave a nod.

Maya looked once more to Melusine. "She's all yours."

Vera stood with her family and watched Hunter step up and raise his hand. Melusine's power was being stolen right in front of them. And surprisingly, Vera did not care, though she knew it likely wasn't smart to give Hunter more power.

With her primary power gone, Melusine crumpled back as she glanced up at them.

As Maya held Camilla's arm, linking them all so Harry could port them out, Hunter turned to look at her. "I may be a while." He acknowledged Maya's nod, then turned back to Melusine. "Demons may not care for each other the way you witches claim to, but I did know a couple of those bodies in the basement."

Melusine's face drained as she realized she wasn't getting out of this with a mere powerless existence. She looked to the others for help, but got nothing in return. Vera couldn't help the smirk that came to her lips. Melusine's fear-filled gaze fell back to Hunter as Harry ported them out.

# 29

Harry ported them into the kitchen of the Whittle house and instantly helped Vera take a seat at the table. He got to one knee before her and lightly took her face in his hands so he could look her directly in the eyes. Finding her eyes clearly staring back and her breath flowing okay, he relaxed slightly and began to heal her. He was being extra gentle, extra attentive.

Warren had shadowed behind them and took a seat at the table, and Camilla followed beside him. They watched in silence as Harry healed Vera.

When he finished his third check of her and Vera pulled him up, insisting she was all right, he took the seat beside her, remaining close. Harry faced the others around the table, and it was like they all remembered what had happened at the same moment, and turned to Maya.

Vera and Harry turned completely in their seats to find Maya by the stove waiting for the kettle to whistle. She had her back to them, paying close attention to the steam escaping the kettle.

As the kettle whistled and Maya pulled it off the stove, she looked to come out of her thoughts and realize how quiet it was, and her body stiffened. She didn't turn to look at them as she poured the water and finished making her tea.

She picked up her cup in both hands and turned to face them, placing it on the island and leaning over to lightly blow into the warm liquid. Maya allowed the steam from the cup to wash over her features for a moment before breathing out, "What?"

No one spoke for some time, even Vera at a loss of how to start. They all just sat and watched Maya, letting their eyes drift around the room before eventually landing back on her.

Eventually, Camilla plucked the courage. "Do you want to acknowledge your new power or…?"

Maya began drinking her tea without waiting for it to cool and allowed the hot liquid to flow down her throat. She didn't respond for a couple of minutes before she shook her head. "I don't want to consider what it means right now."

"Maya," Camilla scolded.

"It's a solely demon power, Camilla. Not dark, but demon. What does that mean for me?"

"Nothing," Vera spoke gruffly, then cleared her throat and continued, "No matter what powers you get or what others say, you're not evil. I may not have grown up with you, but I believe it."

Maya smirked at her. "I never said evil. I said demon. Those aren't synonymous."

"Regardless," Harry jumped in, "you aren't a demon. Trust me, you're full witch."

No one spoke after that, but they all looked in their own directions. Camilla sat in the silence and felt her mind return to the Bridgers coven and to the woman, Melusine. "What kind of power did she have? The one Hunter stole?" She spoke about both Melusine and Hunter with a grimace.

Harry acknowledged the reaction with a breath of a laugh.

"It's a high-level light power. The exact opposite of Hunter and Maya's fire control. Water."

"So now he has both?" Vera asked.

"Yes," Warren chipped in unenthusiastically. "The only positive is that he won't have full control of the water power. When you steal powers, you can't control it like the primary owner could."

"Meaning he'll barely be able to use it, or just less than Melusine had?" Camilla felt her adrenaline spike, not liking that Hunter had any more power.

Warren shrugged. "Could be either one. That's the difficult part. We won't know until he tests them out."

"It won't matter too much anyway," Harry cut it. "You steal powers to have more. Whether those powers are extremely powerful or not doesn't change the fact that you have more."

Camilla scoffed. "Just what we need. For *him* to be more powerful."

Maya remained quiet as the rest of them continued their conversation for another couple of hours. They all got tea, Maya refilling her cup a few times as they moved on from talking about the Bridgers coven to discussing what they were going to do with the bodies downstairs.

Harry mentioned that he would begin looking around immediately for covens with missing witches, starting with Elsie's coven, and trying to find leads from there. Camilla still hated the thought of all those in her basement. She even hated the thought of the dozens of demons that Hunter and his goons had taken.

As the hour reached nine in the evening, Warren got a message telling him to get home. He stood and thanked them for letting him stay a while, and Camilla bit her lip as she looked him over, her thoughts running over the fact that she should be the one thanking him as she stood to follow him to the foyer.

They walked together to the front door and stopped in the middle of the foyer, Camilla smiling to herself at the ridiculousness of walking to the door when they were both well aware he would be shadowing out.

Warren turned to face her. "I'm sorry. Hunter returned and my father decided he wants a late family dinner tonight."

Camilla's lips twitched into a warm smile. "It's okay." They stood there just looking at each other almost awkwardly before Camilla added a shuffled, "Thank you. For helping us. You didn't have to."

Warren shrugged. "I did. For you."

Camilla's smile grew as she looked him in the eyes and remembered her conversation with Genevieve in the top room at the Bridgers coven. "I think," she began, then hesitated a moment. "I think we should try again." Warren's eyes instantly brightened at her comment, but he kept his features controlled. "This time, we'll be our full selves in the relationship, two magical creatures."

His control broke, and a wide grin erupted across his face, but he remained hesitant. "I'll still be half demon. I can't change that."

Camilla took his hand in hers. "I know. But you've proven your human side. You're not your brother, and I understand that now."

Warren's smile grew to cover his face as he leaned in, his lips pressing to hers. Camilla sighed against his lips. She'd forgotten how much she enjoyed his lips. He moved his hands to cradle her face a moment as he deepened the kiss, and Camilla's bits erupted into a chorus. Maya would be proud.

He broke away and winked at her, and Camilla couldn't believe the giggle that resulted from it. She remained staring at the spot he had been standing and felt herself turn into a blushing, giggling schoolgirl.

Maya hadn't had much to say to her family after they returned from the Bridgers coven. Seeing the portals open had reminded her of her time in Hell's Gate. Although she no longer felt the terror she once did of her time down below thanks to Hunter's potion, she remembered what she had experienced in only a few days. Knowing others would remain down there longer, for decades or centuries, she could not imagine the psychosis they would be enduring. And she could not find it in herself to care.

That's what scared her the most.

Unable to contribute to her family, Maya excused herself after Warren left and spent the night soaking in the burning bath, allowing her body to light flames any time the water began to cool down, her power making sure the water was always scolding her as she listened to Evanescence and felt her muscles loosen.

With a clear mind, she was able to relax and let her mind go to places it desired. Places specifically like her reoccurring dream of having Hunter against her, their bodies tangled and skin pressed together. The thought of Hunter brought another memory, one from that night.

The only thing she had been able to focus on while her family spoke that night was the icicle flying past her and landing in Hunter's chest, throwing him back. She'd seen it only from her periphery, yet the image plagued her. It had played on loop in her memory, and the bath had been doing its job of allowing her to forget it.

And she needed to keep that memory away, that feeling that lodged into her soul when her periphery caught the icicle fly past her, the liquid fire that had erupted within her.

She pushed those thoughts aside and thought of Hunter in

the woods the first official time they'd met. His golden slicked back hair, his impeccably expensive and simple style, his black eyes that showed Maya more emotion than she'd ever witnessed in anyone before. Those eyes did it for her.

She remembered him in the gym when he'd held those children hostage, his lazy lounge on the chair, his careless flip of the dagger, those eyes that told her everything she wanted. Those eyes did it for her.

Those eyes, black and depthless, but liquid and full all the same.

Maya felt her body burn at the thought of him, of his eyes roaming over her body, drinking her in, and tried to bite away a smile but couldn't. She was alone, and she would allow for her thoughts to go wherever they'd like to. She hadn't silenced the bathroom, but her music was loud enough to cover any noises she might make and she could bite down to keep from screaming.

After spending hours in the bath, Maya got dressed and headed downstairs. Being the middle of the night at that point, the others were fast asleep, and Maya made sure not to make any noise as she headed out the front door.

After tipping the cab she had drop her in front of Delvaux Manor and watching him drive off, Maya looked back to the gates then walked up to them. It was so dark out and the path to the manor so long that she could not see the actual manor. She tried opening the gate, but wasn't surprised when it wouldn't budge. She stepped back and looked up at the height. She'd never jumped a fence before, better yet a gate. Camilla was the girl for that.

Before she could contemplate whether or not to jump it, a figure walked out of the darkness toward her from beyond. As it got closer, Maya recognized him.

Hunter had a wickedly charming smirk on his face as he

strolled up and stopped a few feet away. They stared at one another a moment before Hunter raised his brows and gestured toward the gates. "Please, give it a try."

Maya narrowed her eyes at him, trying to keep from laughing as she crossed her arms before her chest. She was sure he could smell what the sight of him was doing to her. She looked at him expectantly, but he didn't move. "Let me in, Hunter."

Before she could process his disappearance, she felt him behind her, his arms working their way around her waist to latch together at her belly button. "Your wish," he whispered in her ear and shadowed them into the foyer of the manor, "is my command."

With his arms still around her, Maya's eyes roamed the extravagance of the room. Hunter let his arms fall from her waist and walked around so he was facing her. "You're here because?"

Maya's gaze moved to meet his. "To see you."

Hunter gave a small laugh, his gaze never wavering. "Well, then you're lucky I was here. This isn't my house."

Maya's brows flew up. "You don't live here?"

Hunter allowed himself to fully laugh now as he shook his head. "It's my father's manor. I own another Delvaux Manor."

"Where's your manor?"

"It's a secret," he replied, obviously having fun with their conversation.

Maya quirked a brow. "Really?"

"Yes, ma'am. My family doesn't even know. No one but my resident cleaners have been."

"Why?" Maya couldn't fathom the loneliness.

"I like the privacy. Plus, someone in my position must take care to keep things hidden."

Maya watched him with a slight tilt to her head, then gave in. "Fine. Take me there."

Hunter's brows rose in astonishment. He wore an 'excuse me' expression as he stared at her. He *had* just told her he allowed no one to his manor.

"You just said," Maya teased, "that my wish was your command."

30

The shock left his features, immediately getting replaced with wicked delight as he laughed. He stepped up to her, taking only her hand in his, and shadowed them into a bedroom.

"I said your manor, not your bedroom," Maya remarked, though she was far from annoyed.

Hunter smirked as he walked to stand about ten feet from her. "We are in my manor, love. You didn't specify a room." Maya bit back a smile and rolled her eyes as he continued, "It's actually a good thing we came here. My father's house is crawling with demons. Not sure how well they'd take a witch." He let his eyes roam her from head to toe—those liquid black eyes—and back up until they met hers. "Even a witch with more powerful demonic powers than anyone else in the house."

Maya's gaze dropped to the ground, her good mood washing out as she grimaced. "Ugh. Don't remind me."

"Why? I think what you did was sexy."

The eye roll was real this time as she looked up to find the wickedness that never failed to get her bits into motion staring back at her. "Of course you do. Don't act like you're not itching to take it from me."

He grew serious. "I'm not. Plus, it's not your primary power. I couldn't even if I wanted to."

Maya tilted her head. "So it's not that you don't want to, it's that you can't."

Hunter grinned at her. "No, love. I wouldn't take it from you even if I could." Maya didn't believe that for a moment, narrowing her eyes at him. He laughed at that. "We're allies. The power is still on my side."

"We could always go back to being enemies. Would you want to then?" She played along.

He stepped up a single step, though the space between them remained vast, allowing his dark eyes to capture hers in a wicked way. "Absolutely not. It wouldn't have the same effect as watching you use it. Plus, last time I tried to take more power, we ended up down below."

Maya didn't even consider his remark, instantly replying, "Not true. You took those four witches' powers on top of Melusine's only a few hours ago."

Hunter scoffed. "That wasn't *true* power."

She shook her head. "Whatever. I just came to thank you. For helping us."

*Liar. He could smell damn well why you came.*

He played along. "A deal's a deal. And you gave me far more than we bargained. Those are the types of allies I like to keep happy."

"Yes, well, as a show of good faith, I brought you this." She held up a vial of liquid and watched his brows raise in question. "It's a vanquishing potion made specially for you. I found a recipe in the book I thought would work. I can't be sure how well it'll work, but still," she handed it out, "a thank you."

Hunter's gaze narrowed instantly to the vial. "Won't your sisters be upset of your handing it over?"

"They don't know about it."

He stepped up slowly and took it from her fingers, their skin touching only briefly, and raised it to eye level before looking back at her. "How do I know you don't have more?"

Maya smirked at him this time. "That's your show of good faith."

Hunter scoffed a laugh, then turned and headed for the fireplace. He extinguished the fire with his mind and grabbed for the dagger he kept at the back of his trousers. He placed the vial on the trim of the fireplace as he cut his hand and allowed some blood to fall into the fireplace. He replaced the dagger with the vial and stepped back, throwing the vial into the hearth and watching the instantaneous fire break loose. His brow quirked as he turned his head to Maya. "Looks like it works."

Maya smirked with delight to match any of his. "Good to know."

Hunter's arm jut out against the trimming of the fireplace as he leaned into it, staring into the fire. His form leaning over the fireplace, firelight flickering against his front, sent wicked thoughts through Maya's head. Without breaking his gaze from the fire, he asked, "Why only the one vial?"

Being as he wasn't paying attention, she allowed her gaze to settle on different aspects of his form. Her eyes lingered on his forearm, supporting his leaning weight against the mantle. His hand fisted atop the mantle. Her thoughts raced to the feeling of those fingers against her hair as he petted her a few days ago, against her throat as he held her in Hell's Gate. She brought her thoughts back to the present as she answered, "The main ingredient is difficult to come by."

He turned curious eyes to her. "Which is?"

Her smirk turned to a teasing smile. "Your sperm," she answered matter-of-factly.

His eyes widened as he pushed off the mantle and turned to face her entirely. "Excuse me?" Her smile grew, having expected this reaction. As she dipped her head in two nods, he asked, "And how did you get any for this vial?"

"I found this transfiguration spell in the book," she began, "I turned myself into you…"

"And that worked?" he asked, bewildered.

She laughed. "You didn't let me finish." He waved his hand for her to continue. "I turned myself into you," she repeated, then continued, "then went to one of your lackeys. I told him that I, being you, wanted him to follow me the next time I was to please myself and collect the towel I used to clean up." His eyes narrowed at her in disbelieving shock. "I told him," she continued, "that this was to stay between the two of us. He was to not make it known, even to you at the moment. When he brought me the towel, I gave him a potion that drained his memory of the past night. Honestly, it was far simpler than it should have been. Probably because the request didn't seem dangerous in the least. And lucky for me, you did the deed at your father's manor as well."

"I always do the deed after seeing you. No matter where I am." He was completely unashamed. Good.

"I'm guessing your lackey's have picked up on that habit," Maya teased.

Hunter shook his head in disbelief as he folded his arms across his chest. "I'll have to make sure to train these lackeys of mine better."

Maya bit her bottom lip as a smile broke out on her face, her fingers tangling together behind her. "Don't worry, the spell is unique for our Book alone." Her eyes drifted over him once before meeting his eyes.

"Already thinking about making another, aren't you?" he asked.

Her shoulders shrugged playfully. "You can never be too sure."

Hunter dropped his hands to his sides and began to walk

toward her. More of a prowl than a walk, Maya thought, and her insides tightened at the suggestion.

He stopped a foot away from her, stared her in the eyes mischievously, then took another step closer. He leaned into her ear, never fully reaching it, as he whispered against her cheek, "As a show of good faith." He moved so his lips lightly brushed hers before moving to the other cheek, over to her ear. Pressing lightly against her ear so that shivers ran through every inch of her body, he whispered, "I'll donate."

He moved so he could look her in the eyes, putting a few inches between their faces. Her eyes shimmered as they met his, her tongue darting out to lick her lips, stealing his gaze to focus there instead. His eyes jumped back to hers for only a moment before his hand shot out, grabbing her by the side of the neck and holding her jaw in place as his thumb brushed against her chin, moving up to her parted lips.

She took an infinitesimally small step forward, giving him all the encouragement he needed as he crashed his lips against hers. She took a half second's hesitation before kissing him back, their lips moving together in desire. One hand still holding her jaw in place, the other shot into her hair, massaging her scalp as his tongue shot out, licking her lips in anticipation. Her hands skimmed his chest, grabbing two handfuls of his shirt as she opened her mouth and allowed his tongue to explore.

Pressing against him, she loosened her hold on his shirt and skimmed around his body, grabbing for the edges of his trousers. With no space left between their bodies, they pressed every inch together and moaned in unison.

Moving the hand in her hair to mirror the one holding her jaw in place, Hunter walked her backward as her hands skimmed up the inside of his shirt, pulling it up. They broke apart only long enough for him to pull the shirt off and tug hers up as well. He had only a second to appreciate that she wore no bra, her tightened nipples inviting him in, before Maya kissed him once more. He continued backing her up, his hands skimming her waist and hips before stopping at the button of her jeans.

They hit the bed, only then breaking their clash of tongues as Maya fell. Standing over her, Hunter felt an overwhelming sense of joy as he leaned over her, and gripping the edges of her jeans, simultaneously locking his fingers into the edges of her underwear, he pulled down. Skimming the two articles of clothing down her legs, he pulled them off until she was completely bare to him, lying at the edge of the bed, hair splayed out.

Hunter growled in appreciation at the sight of her, naked on his bed. He dropped to his knees before her, his hands moving up her calves, watching her twitch at his touch.

Brushing the insides of her thighs and spreading them wider, his gaze narrowed to her center. Flicking his eyes up to hers, he watched her watching him. His cock twitched at the sight as he smirked at her, moving to kiss the inside of her left knee. He watched her bite her lip lightly at the contact.

He moved up slightly, pressing another kiss to the inside of her thigh before moving to the other leg. He worked his way up, pressing two kisses to one leg then moving to the other and back again, until he reached the highest point of her inner thigh, centimeters from her dripping folds.

He pulled away slightly and looked back up at her, she was still watching him, holding herself up on her elbows. With a smile, he dipped his head back down, keeping his eyes on her, and darted out his tongue, running it through her sweet lips and flicking the tip to her clit. He watched as she moaned out, falling to the bed, her back arching ever-so-slightly. He moved his hands up the insides of her thighs, reaching for her folds before pulling them open, and beginning to feast.

His tongue moved over her wet flesh before dipping into her opening and tasting her fully. He felt her arch and writhe at his ministrations, bucking her hips to his lips. His hands moved to hold her hips down, immobilizing her enough for him to enjoy her taste.

The rest of her remained mobile as her hands shot out to grab fistfuls of the bedsheets and his hair, as her thighs shook, her back arching completely off the bed as she screamed her pleasures.

Hunter felt his cock pulsing at her screams, her touch, her taste. His senses were overloading and his cock was enjoying every moment of it. "Come into my mouth, love. Let me taste you. It's all I've been dreaming of."

As his tongue dipped inside her one more time, his thumb rubbing her clit, she climaxed loud and hoarse.

Enjoying the taste of her climax, Hunter remained between her legs, sapping up every drop as she spasmed above him.

As she came down from her high, body relaxing, Hunter began to kiss and lick his way up her body, stopping at the tip of one breast and flicking his tongue out her nipple. She arced up to his mouth as he flicked out again before moving to the other breast. Her moans begged for more.

Holding himself above her with both hands, he lowered his trouser-clad hips against hers as his mouth descended on her nipple. Her entire body bucked, her hips rolling against his, as her head fell back. His tongue devoured the taste of her nipple before licking his way between her breasts to the other, giving it the same attention its sister had received.

Maya's legs tightened around his waist, her fingers scratching down his back. Giving her nipple a final suckle, Hunter pushed off the bed completely, removing himself from Maya.

He heard her whimper in protest and laughed. He began to unbutton his trousers as Maya crawled back on the bed on her elbows. She stopped when she reached the middle and watched his trousers fall with hungry eyes.

He was sure his eyes gleamed as he fell to the bed on all fours and prowled over her, dipping his head to lick his way up her leg and over her belly to the opposite breast. He circled the nipple with his tongue, then moved upward still. He laid kisses up her neck, biting the spot between her neck and shoulder to hear her moan deepen.

He moved over her jaw to one ear, biting down lightly, as his hands roamed her body, touching every inch. "The moment I take you, witch, you belong to me," he spoke with the same possessive growl that had come out of him in Hell's Gate when they'd kissed.

"I'm already yours," she sighed as her hands held nothing back, taking their pleasures touching his chest and back, his thighs, his ass.

He kissed her hard as her touch grazed his cock before sliding up his chest. With a final flick of his tongue against hers, he pulled away and rolled off her, lying beside her on the bed.

Stunned, Maya turned to face him, confusion written all over her features. He moved both his hands behind his head to refrain from reaching out to her, although to anyone watching, he would have looked as if he were lounging lazily, his trademark.

Raising to her elbows and watching him in question, he turned to her with a smirk. "I'm not going to give you the excuse that I seduced you into this. If you want it," he nodded toward his cock, "take it."

He expected to watch her fight with herself mentally before giving in, but to his shock, she took no hesitation before rolling over him. She straddled a single thigh as she kissed his chest, enjoying her turn of tasting him. He watched in bewilderment, his cock twitching violently as she licked her way up his chest, moving to straddle his hips.

His hands still behind his head, he gripped fistfuls of his hair to keep himself still. She took his bottom lip between her teeth as she reached his lips, moving her hands down his chest to grip his cock. His entire body twitched at that.

She smiled, dropping his lip, as she positioned him against her wet folds. They moaned in unison, their breaths mixing. She flicked her tongue against his lips. "I've been fantasizing about this for weeks."

Hunter almost ripped out his hair in anticipation, but finally felt her lower onto his cock, taking him in inch by inch. Fuck, she felt amazing. So fucking tight for him.

"I think this means I'm taking you," she teased against his lips as her cunt took him in completely.

As she began to lift back up, emptying herself to the tip, her tongue darted out to lick his parted lips as she rode down to the hilt.

Hunter moaned in ecstasy, moving his hands to grip her thighs, her hips. As she propped her hands onto his chest, her nails digging in and leaving marks, he helped her get a rhythm as her hips drew circles above him.

At the sight of her riding his cock and her breasts bouncing for him, Hunter growled and flipped them around.

On his knees, he moved her legs to his shoulders and a hand to hold her by the neck, hard enough to leave a bruise. He growled at the possessiveness of marking her as he pumped into her. Watched her arch in another climax, then dropped her legs to the bed, spreading her wide once more. He moved both hands to cup her ass, lifting her off the bed.

"You're mine, love."

"No," she shot back, defiant and wicked eyes staring back at him. "*You're* mine."

With a few final pumps, he felt his climax take over. He came inside her harder than he'd ever come before. More than he'd ever come before.

He felt the waves of his pleasure shoot into her, no end in sight. Until finally, his body relaxed.

He dropped his hold of her body and pulled out of her, watching his come spill out with her pulses as he fell against her. His forehead an inch from hers, he held himself above her.

Her fingers moved to roam over his face as she said, "You came a lot."

He snort-laughed as he responded, "It's been a while." He moved in closer so that his lips were touching hers as he said, "How many vials do you think you can get out of this?"

Maya gave a small, sinful laugh as her tongue darted out to taste him again.

31

The morning after their time with the Bridgers coven, Camilla and Vera sat in the kitchen with their breakfast of hard boiled eggs with toast, tomatoes, and cucumbers. Harry had just grabbed a piece of toast as he ported away to immediately begin finding the covens of the witches in their basement.

Vera looked to her sister as she placed her orange juice back on the table. "I'm surprised we beat Maya. She's usually up first."

Camilla nodded. "Don't get used to it. She's probably taking in what happened yesterday. She'll be back to waking up at the ass crack of dawn tomorrow."

Vera nodded in acknowledgement, unable to ignore the giddy nature of her youngest sister that morning. She narrowed her eyes at Camilla as she sat there eating her breakfast, too happy. "What's up with you?"

Camilla's attention jumped to Vera's. "What do you mean?"

"You look like a fourteen-year-old schoolgirl who just talked to her crush." Vera quirked her brow. "You weren't like this yesterday. What happened?"

"Yesterday, we were saving you and the other witches from the Bridgers coven. That was no moment to be happy."

Vera kicked her sister under the table. "You know what I mean."

Camilla broke faster than a child promised candy and told her about the conversation she'd had with Warren in the foyer before he'd left the night before. Her eyes lit up with every word. "I think I freaked out at first because it was such a big revelation, and I had one idea of how demons should be. I don't know, I just know he's good. His human half is strong. I think we both deserve to try."

Vera smiled. "You do. I'm happy for you. He is good, and he's trying. That's what's most important."

Now that it was out, Camilla jumped into talks about Warren, and Vera sat quietly and listened to her sister, trying to hold in a laugh. Eventually, she couldn't hold it in any longer and burst out, blocking away from Camilla's smacks from across the table.

Vera looked to her sister with the widest grin she'd possibly ever worn and got up from the table, walking her plate over to the sink. She left the room singing, "Camilla and Warren sitting in a tree." Vera heard Camilla scoff as she dropped her dishes into the sink and followed Vera out of the kitchen, "K.I.S.S.I.N.G."

Camilla pushed her, but her face showed pure joy. "You'll get it once you start to like someone."

Vera froze at her sister's innocent comment, her memory instantly showing her an image of a warlock before she pushed it aside. "Yeah." She hoped the tentativeness in her tone couldn't be heard.

In the giddiness of her state, Camilla didn't seem to notice. "C'mon. Let's go get Maya. I don't know what's taking her so…"

They found Maya coming down the stairs as they reached the bottom. She looked slightly disheveled and had a light blush, which deepened when she saw her sisters standing at the bottom of the staircase looking at her.

Vera had never seen Maya blush.

Camilla seemed too giddy to notice Maya's out of place behavior. "Speak of the devil. What took you so long this morning?"

Maya shook her head as she reached the bottom. "I was practicing some magic. Lost track."

A tinge of doubt knocked into Vera's subconscious, but she pushed it aside. Vera looked to her sisters and smiled. She'd only been around a short while—not even two months—so she knew it would take a while before they had with her what they had with each other, but she also knew that she was thankful to have found them. To have sisters in this crazy life of theirs.

Vera watched them as Camilla explained to Maya why she was so happy so early in the morning—completely against normal Camilla behavior—and Maya laughed at her.

"Do you guys wanna go for a walk?" Vera asked, finding she wanted to take a simple walk with her sisters.

They looked to her and smiled. "Let's go."

The girls grabbed their jackets and headed for the front door as Harry popped back in. Vera turned and looked at him with a small smile, her heart jumping at the sight. "We're going for a walk."

He smiled back with a single nod as Vera closed the door behind her.

They began their walk in the direction Maya liked to take her runs and ended up in the woods. She said she liked the solitude and tranquility she felt here, and Vera agreed. Especially in their now hectic life, some tranquility was nice.

They spoke about how lucky Camilla was that she was on Thanksgiving break at the moment, and now with this mess over, she could focus on the end of the semester and actually pass her courses, even though the case of finding out who killed their mother wasn't over. They still had time for that.

They walked for a bit, Maya leading them in different routes she liked to explore, until they stumbled upon a large object on the ground ahead of them. Unsure what it was, they got their powers ready and stuck together as they walked up to check it out.

Standing above it, Vera felt the gasp escape her body at the same moment she heard her sisters. Lying before them was the mangled body of a witch.

It was surprising that they could tell she was a witch even through the wreckage that had been done to the girl—her skin was shred apart and bruises lined her entire body—but Vera felt it in her.

She swallowed, unable to take her eyes off the girl. They would still be looking for the person responsible for their mother, and now Vera was sure of only one thing. The killings would not stop there.

# DON'T FORGET TO REVIEW!

Thank you so much for finishing your read! Don't forget to leave a review or rating on all platforms as it helps me as an author more than you can ever imagine!

The platform where you read it and Goodreads ratings help the most but feel free to talk about it everywhere else too—including social medias, blogs, Youtube reviews, and most importantly—word of mouth, and more.

# JOIN MY AUTHOR NEWSLETTER

Sign up for Nelly Alikyan's newsletter to be the first to know about new releases and cover reveals, receive exclusive content —like a special scene or two—and be up to date about any other exciting news, i.e. events, signed copies, etc.

www.nellyalikyan.com

# ABOUT THE AUTHOR

Nelly Alikyan is a girl from the Los Angeles Valley who moved to Boston for school and found she prefers the East Coast. But really, London is where she'd like to be since it's her favorite city ever. She's the only reader in her family—not her only cause as the black sheep—and has dreamt of being a writer for as long as she can remember.

When she's not working on her books or in the real world, she's on Youtube at Nelly Alikyan!

For more books and updates:
www.nellyalikyan.com

instagram.com/authornellyalikyan

tiktok.com/@authornalikyan

youtube.com/NellyAlikyan

amazon.com/author/nellyalikyan

goodreads.com/nellyalikyan

facebook.com/authornellyalikyan

pinterest.com/insinpublishing

ACKNOWLEDGMENTS

Honestly, I never thought this would happen. Mostly because I never really knew anything about indie publishing. But thanks to 2020—yeah, the one time I'll actually be thankful for that year—I found it. And I cannot imagine publishing any other way. Maybe that's the control freak in me coming out, but I love that I'll have control of all aspects of my career!

First off though, I have to thank my mom. Maderjan Baderjan, thanks for smiling when I finally told you I would be publishing, for always looking so proud and astonished when I tell you I'm writing yet another book, and for always putting your faith in the fact that I could do it. Thanks for being a kickass single mom and for always giving us the best life you could afford. Thanks for the opportunities you've afforded me and for all around making me the person I am today. My books wouldn't be here without that.

To my siblings: Mariam, Mher, and Andranik—even though you hate being called Andranik. To being close and kicking each other's asses growing up to supporting each other through our endeavors. You guys were immediately supportive when you finally heard of my publishing goals—probably not shocking considering how much I read and daydream—but you made the whole thing easier on me.

To my friends for always being supportive. There aren't many of you, but you mean it all to me. Thank you to Vanessa,

Jessica, Hector, and Erika especially, for always being my number ones.

To my ninth grade English teacher, Richard Nino, who continued to tell me all throughout high school that I could be a writer. I still think about it all the time.

To Katie Wismer, for being my copyeditor, but also my inspiration. Sometimes those productive vlogs really get my ass into gear.

To Maria Spada, for being my awesome cover designer. Love that you didn't complain once, just kept making the changes I needed. It's been so much fun working with you, can't wait to work on the rest.

To Bettina Luna and my other beta readers. Thank you for the feedback, trust me, it made a difference.

And to anyone who picked up this book and gave me a chance. Thank you for jumping into this world with me, it's been awesome sharing it with you.

www.ingramcontent.com/pod-product-compliance
Lightning Source LLC
Chambersburg PA
CBHW061057190726
48286CB00006B/1782